BEAST-LAID PLANS

A BEAUFORT SCALES MYSTERY - BOOK 7

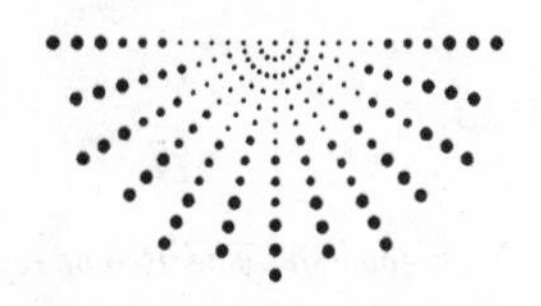

KIM M. WATT

For further information contact: www.kmwatt.com

Cover design: Monika McFarland, www.ampersandbookcovers.com

Editor: Lynda Dietz, www.easyreaderediting.com

Logo design by www.imaginarybeast.com

ISBN (ebook): 978-0-473-64873-2

ISBN (PB): 978-0-473-64872-5

ISBN (Ingrams PB): 978-0-473-64871-8

First Edition: September 2022

10 9 8 7 6 5 4 3 2 1

CONTENTS

To Dad.
One last one for the road.

1
MORTIMER

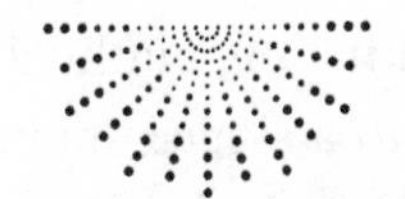

Mortimer hesitated on the small ledge outside the workshop cavern, the sun hot on his wings. He had been planning to tinker with the new dragon scale phone cases, in the hope that he could tweak the anti-loss charms and make them usable. Currently there was no chance of losing the cases, as the instant anyone touched them, they turned into highly determined limpets. He was still missing scales from his chest where one had attached itself.

However, he wasn't sure it was going to be a day for phone cases. Despite the fact that the workshop was at the opposite end of a tunnel that dog-legged back into the mount, he could clearly hear the crashes of someone being very *enthusiastic* with their tools. He considered coming back later, but he'd already tried that twice today, so he padded warily down the tunnel and paused on the threshold of the little cavern. The floor was as scrupulously clean-swept as always, and the light from the hole bored into the rocky roof refracted through a prism just as it should, glittering on the piles of unused dragon scales and dulling the light of the fires in their braziers. The baskets of toys and baubles were neatly stacked on one bench, and at another, surrounded by shattered scales and softly luminous dust, a red-toned dragon was hammering away at something, her wings trembling with every strike.

"Ridiculous"— *tap tap*— "imbecilic"—*tap TAP tap*—"disgrace to the word dragon"—*TAP*—"sheep-loving"—*CRASH*—"oh, ghasts *take you!*" Amelia hurled a broken scale at the discards basket in the corner, where it skidded off the edge and clattered to the floor, already losing its sheen. "Useless!"

Mortimer wasn't sure if she was talking about the scale, her tools, or the design she was working on, but he didn't fancy surprising her. That seemed a sure route to a singed snout or a pair of pliers to the head, possibly both. So he coughed delicately, poised to flee back up the tunnel if it seemed prudent.

"*What?*" Amelia demanded, spinning to face him with a hammer in one paw and her snout flushed an unsettling maroon. "Oh. Morning, Mortimer."

"Afternoon." He eyed the hammer. "Everything alright?"

"Of course." Her voice went up an octave. "Just a tricky design, is all."

"Right." He scratched his chin with a forepaw, looking at the broken and charred scales cluttering up the discard basket. They were smouldering slightly. "Perhaps a small break ...?"

"A break? We need baubles. I'm making baubles." She picked up a scale and glared at it, as if daring it to be uncooperative. "Not that anyone else is helping."

"Ye-es. But we don't need them right now. We're already ahead."

"We want to be ahead. Christmas shopping starts early, and we completely sell out every year."

"That's good, though. We don't want a surplus. Best to keep them wanting more, right?"

She squinted at him. "Don't humour me."

"Right. Of course. Only ..." He glanced at the discard basket again. The trail of smoke rising from it was intensifying. "You seem to have gone through half a basket of good scales and the workshop's about to catch fire."

For one moment he thought he was going to be the one on fire, then she sighed. "Ugh. I know. *I know.*"

"We don't want to end up having to use Walter's scales or something."

"Ew. No."

All dragons shed, old scales slipping away naturally due to wear and tear, to be replaced by soft new ones. Baby dragons shed like kittens, scattering delicate little scales everywhere as they grew, but they weren't strong enough to be useful. Older dragons' scales, though, were tough and pliable and perfect for working with, and all the Cloverly dragons were encouraged to donate their cast-offs to the workshop. Mortimer donated more than his fair share due to stress-shedding, and was only rivalled by Lord Walter, who was so old that his scales seemed to have forgotten how to stay attached. Every time Mortimer passed him, it seemed, the old dragon would shove a pawful of scales at him, but they had proven impossible to work with. They resisted any attempt to be polished or shaped, remaining stubbornly dull and resolutely inflexible.

Now Mortimer wrinkled his snout and said, "I keep thinking that anything I make with his scales will turn around and bite someone. Me, probably."

Amelia snorted and put the scale down. "It wouldn't surprise me."

They were both silent for a moment, then Mortimer said, "What's wrong?"

"Nothing," Amelia said, brushing dust off her bench without looking at him.

"Are you sure?"

"Yes."

Mortimer considered the wisdom of retreating with his snout unsinged. It was tempting, but Amelia's mood seemed to have been deteriorating steadily over the past few days, and at this rate they'd have no scales for the Christmas baubles at all. So he said carefully, "This isn't your normal ... work standard." She gave him a fierce look and he added quickly, "I just mean you make *really* good baubles. And this ..." He waved at the smoking basket. "Well, isn't usual."

Amelia picked up a different scale, ticking one talon off it. "I s'pose. Are you sure we've not got Walter's scales mixed up with the good ones?"

"No," Mortimer said. "I've got a special basket for his." Baskets, actually. He didn't want to just throw the scales away, in case the old dragon found out, so he had a steadily growing collection of baskets filled with worn, dull, and pocked cast-offs in the back of his personal cavern. At this rate he'd be sleeping on a bed of them within the year. "Maybe take a break," he suggested again.

Amelia shrugged, a stiff little movement, then spoke without looking at him. "Have you seen Gilbert?"

"Gilbert? No. Why?"

"Oh, it's probably nothing. We fell out."

"Oh dear." Mortimer had heard Lydia, one of the older dragons, describe the fights between Amelia and her little brother as the sort of things humans would have written stories about in the old days. "What happened?"

"Oh, nothing really. He was just being Gilbert." She glanced at Mortimer. "You know, complaining that since we couldn't go near the village there was no one to watch over the hedgehogs and so on. Apparently autumn's even worse than summer for them, and he wanted to get ahead of the bonfires or some such rubbish."

"That does sound like Gilbert," Mortimer said. The young dragon had made somewhat of a name for himself among the Cloverlies by being the first dragon to embrace vegetarianism. That, and the fact that he had some issues with flying. "He wasn't going to try and get to the village or something, was he?" The village being Toot Hansell, where the dragons had, over the last few years, broken centuries of isolation by befriending the ladies of the Toot Hansell Women's Institute. It was a friendship characterised by tea, cake, the burgeoning bauble trade, and a surprising number of criminal investigations, which always made Mortimer feel a little queasy. But Toot Hansell was currently not the welcoming place it had been, due to a sudden influx of journalists who were far too interested in the possibility of dragons. Mortimer hadn't even had a scone in *months.* Well, weeks. But weeks without scones *felt* like months.

"I don't think he'd go there," Amelia said. "I mean, he's an idiot, but he's not silly."

Mortimer wasn't quite sure he understood the difference, but he said, "Of course not. He'll be around."

Amelia made an unconvinced sound. "I thought that too, but I haven't seen him."

Mortimer looked at the tight lines of her shoulders and felt a coil of unease in his belly. "For how long?"

"A week."

"*A week?* Amelia, that's *ages!* He's never been away that long, has he?"

"No," she admitted. "But he'll be fine. He *has* to be fine."

"He hasn't been back at all?"

"I'm his sister, not his bloody keeper." She glared at him, then her shoulders slumped and she scratched her chin with the hammer. "He's just got the hump. He's probably off rescuing bloody hamsters somewhere."

Mortimer examined the younger dragon. The maroon had faded, leaving uneasy grey tinges around her snout, and he said quietly, "How bad was the fight?"

She hesitated, then put the hammer back on the bench and looked at her forepaws resting on the hard stone next to it. "I might've told him that I was going to stuff his roast pumpkin with mice unless he started acting like a real dragon."

"Ah," Mortimer said, realising it wasn't a euphemism but rather an insult to the young dragon's vegetarian stance. "Quite a bad fight, then."

"You know how silly he is! Bloody Rockford and his lot were trying to push him off a ledge to make him fly – or to watch him do that silly fall-glide thing he does – and he was getting all upset, of course, because he hates even *trying* to fly, so I stopped them, but … but they're *right,* you know? And they're never going to stop. So I just said he needed to at least *pretend* to be a proper dragon so they'd leave him alone, and he—" She stopped and took a breath. "Anyway. I haven't seen him since."

Mortimer nodded, then said, "Shall I go and ask around? See if the sprites have seen him? The dryads?"

Amelia looked at him, and he braced himself for her to tell him in no uncertain terms that his help was not required when it came to her family. Instead she said, "I've checked all his favourite spots. No one's seen him."

"No one?"

"Is there an echo?" she snapped, then added, "Sorry. I mean, no. No one at all. He's just *gone,* and I can't even find a scent beyond his favourite pond."

Mortimer blinked. "I mean, he *has* flown. In an emergency. That could explain not finding a scent."

"Then where did he fly to?" Her voice was quiet. "There're journalists in the village, Mortimer. Monster hunters, not to put too fine a point on it. And Gilbert's disappeared. Where's my brother?"

And Mortimer, staring back at her, didn't have an answer.

MORTIMER MADE sure nothing was about to catch fire before he left the workshop, and persuaded Amelia that she should at least go and eat a rabbit before she did any more work. She became a little upset over that and admitted that she'd been feeding the unofficial menagerie of orphaned or injured animals Gilbert maintained in his cavern, and that the smallest rabbit had fallen asleep on her shoulder two nights ago and she hadn't been able to eat anything but fish ever since.

"And I don't even *like* fish," she complained. "The scales get stuck in my teeth." She took a deep breath and stared at Mortimer. "I actually thought about having a pumpkin. Am I ... am I becoming a *vegetarian?*"

Mortimer had reassured her as well as he could, which wasn't very, as he'd been having some trouble eating rabbits himself since spending more time with Gilbert. Then he'd left before she could say anything else about pumpkins. He'd eaten two yesterday and was worried he might be starting to get a taste for them. Rockford would love *that,* if he found out about it.

Now he hesitated on the ledge outside, watching the tarn below being rippled by the wind, and the trees shifting colour as a light breeze turned their leaves, like a hand brushing a cat's fur in the wrong direction. There wasn't much wilderness left these days, but pockets of it clung on, and there was plenty of it left for a young dragon determined not to be found. He watched for a moment longer, not sure what he was looking for – Gilbert to surface in the tarn, perhaps, or to come trotting out of the trees.

But he didn't, so Mortimer launched himself off the ledge, catching the air in the curves of his wings and sweeping up the cliff, keeping his body close to the rock and his scales a dull grey, just in case anyone was looking. Not that there should be anyone out here. It wasn't that the land around them was particularly brutal or the vegetation unusually impassable, but the mount was wound about with a mesh of cloaking charms, runes pressed into trees and carved into stone, old magic that encouraged strangers to be *elsewhere.* They were subtle but irresistible, and made any humans rambling through the networks of footpaths and bridleways that spread across the country like spiderwebs find themselves absently turning onto different routes. So no one should be here to see him, especially as the dragons had reinforced their protections since the appearance of the journalists. But Mortimer still wasn't entirely sure how well their defences might work against people like them, humans who so desperately wanted to see *something.* People like that were dangerous.

So he kept close to the mount as he swept up to its crown, landing on one of the craggy, variegated ledges that offered lookout points in every direction. Beyond the woodlands surrounding them, as the land flattened, the fields were patchwork green framed with the crooked stitching of drystone walls, and Toot Hansell was visible as a jumble of buildings lassoed by the glittering thread of the rivers. Mortimer sat there with the sun warm and un-English on his scales, thinking longingly of Miriam and scones, and sighed.

"That doesn't sound good, lad," someone said, and he yelped, looking around the choppy ledges of the mount.

"Hello?" he managed. "Beaufort?"

"Down here, lad."

Mortimer padded across to the edge of the highest crag and peered over dubiously. Beaufort Scales, High Lord of the Cloverly dragons, who had seen his predecessor murdered by that sneaky Saint George while she snoozed in her favourite bramble berry patch, who had ushered his clan through the retreat of magic from the increasingly human world, who had hidden them in far places and protected them from the greedy and the scared, who had watched villages become cities and cities expand to swallow the land, who had witnessed the endless spread of humanity as it crushed the magical and natural worlds in its path, who had survived countless battles and pointless wars and who bore the scars of them all, who had seen the worst of the humans and yet still somehow counted them friends, was clinging to the sheer rock face, wings pressed to the cliff and his talons embedded in the stone like a particularly large and glamorous green gecko.

The High Lord grinned. "Afternoon, lad."

"Afternoon," Mortimer said, then when Beaufort made no move to join him, added, "What are you doing?" He tried to sound mildly curious rather than bewildered, but he wasn't sure it worked.

"Hide'n'seek."

"Hide'n'seek?"

"Yes. Walter is currently seeking me, but I think I'm winning."

Mortimer nodded, thought about it for a moment, then said, "Does he know you're playing hide'n'seek?"

"Probably not. But he's been telling me – repeatedly – about how we need to take the fight to the enemy, which apparently means the journalists. Or the government. Or farmers. Or Rose's current boyfriend. Or whoever took the last gas bottle. It depends on the day, really."

"We're out of gas bottles?"

"Yes. But it's summer. By the time it gets cold enough that we need them, things will be back to normal. Humans don't have long attention spans, really. We just need to wait them out."

Mortimer sighed, wishing he shared Beaufort's optimism, and said, "I hope you're right. It feels like I should never have started the whole gas bottle thing in the first place." The gas bottles were to run the barbecues that the clan had adopted as beds, and which they bought using the proceeds of the bauble sales. Or, rather, that Miriam of the Women's Institute bought for them, as dragons might be very good at passing unnoticed by humans, but Mortimer was still quite sure that wandering into the nearest shop and asking for a gas bottle might give them away somewhat. But the barbecues warmed the bones of old dragons and heated the eggs of the unhatched, and rather than spending all day collecting wood for fires, the Cloverlies were now free to do things like get involved in human investigations, attract the attention of cryptid journalists, and discover vegetarianism and animal rights. Mortimer really wasn't sure free time was good for dragons, and especially not for old High Lords who insisted on being *interested* in everything.

Beaufort watched him, age edging his golden eyes with deeper burnt amber, then he heaved himself up onto the ledge, his claws scraping dust from the stone as he climbed. He sat down next to Mortimer and said, "What's up, lad?"

"*Everything.* The journalists, and us not being able to go to the village, and we were *safe* before, but now ..." Mortimer waved a paw wildly at the woods and the fields in the distance. "Monster hunters!"

Beaufort *hmm*ed. "I rather think monster hunters were inevitable. We couldn't escape them forever."

Mortimer gave him a horrified look. "Then why did you *ever* let me start this? We should've stayed away from humans!"

"And what fun would that have been? There are always risks to moving forward, Mortimer. But one can't remain stuck in one place just because of *what-ifs.* That way lies stagnation, and we've been there before. It's not a good place to linger."

"But look at us now! It's *worse* than it was before, when we didn't even know about the W.I., and markets, and barbecues, and ... and scones."

"It's a hiccough. Progress is never linear."

"I'm not sure it's good, either."

"Some is, some isn't. But one must always move forward. Discard what doesn't work and embrace what does. Do *more* of what does."

"But what's working, really?" Mortimer asked. "We seem to spend all our time hiding from someone, or worrying we'll be discovered, or running from someone who almost discovered us. Surely if it worked it wouldn't be this stressful."

"*Working* isn't the same as *easy.* Often it's entirely the opposite." Beaufort shot him an amused grin. "Besides, I'm not sure it's all quite as stressful as you make out."

"It is for me," Mortimer grumbled.

Beaufort snorted and patted his shoulder. "I wouldn't swap one moment of any of it, no matter how stressful. Imagine never knowing Miriam, or Alice, or any of the ladies. Or never having a mince pie?" He looked at Mortimer expectantly, and the younger dragon sighed.

"That's true. I'd hate not to have met them." Or to have never tried a mince pie, but that seemed less important, really.

"Friendship is worth risking an awful lot for," Beaufort said. "As are excellent baked goods. Now, what's today's particular stress?"

Mortimer swallowed hard, surprised to find a nasty tight feeling in his throat, as if there was some pumpkin there still. He wondered if he were allergic. That would just cap the day off wonderfully. "Umm," he said, then stopped, staring toward Toot Hansell.

"Are you alright? You've gone very grey."

Mortimer checked his paws. He really was exceptionally grey, and he was fairly sure there were a couple of scales on his tail that already looked like they were going to fall off. And he'd been doing so well. "I don't know," he said.

"I'm sure it can't be that bad, lad. No worse than having Walter threaten to burn a farm down two counties over to *shift suspicion,* as he put it."

"Really?"

"Really. Hence the hiding. But whatever you're worried about, it's not going to be as bad as that."

The tight feeling in Mortimer's throat gave way to a little growl, startling him. He wasn't *angry,* was he? Not at Gilbert and Amelia, surely. He didn't think he was. Well, not *really,* anyway, but oh, the *frustration* sometimes! "This could be worse. It could be the very, very worst."

"Well, tell me, then. We can't fix anything if you're sitting there plucking your tail bald again."

Mortimer let go of his tail hastily. He didn't even remember picking it up. "Gilbert," he said. "He's missing."

Beaufort was silent for a moment, then he said, "How long?"

"A week."

"And you're only telling me now?"

Mortimer swallowed. Beaufort didn't sound angry, but he was definitely *displeased.* It was in the flatness of his tone. "He and Amelia had a fight, and she just thought he'd gone off in a bit of a huff. You know how he gets."

"No one was meant to be going off anywhere, in a huff or not. That was the rule. Even I haven't been beyond the borders. Some rules are not to be broken, Mortimer."

"I'm sorry." His throat was horribly dry, and his tail was hurting. He looked down – he'd picked it up again at some point, and as he made himself let go a scale flaked off and drifted to the rocky ground. He sighed. "I should have noticed he was missing sooner. I was distracted by the silly phone cases."

Beaufort watched him for a long moment, then nodded. "Nothing to be done about that," he said, sounding almost normal. "But you're quite right. This *is* terrible. And we must find him at once. One can walk an awfully long way in a week, should one be so inclined."

"He might even have flown," Mortimer said. "Amelia can't find any sign of him. None of the dryads or sprites or anyone at all seem to have seen him. She's had to feed his rabbits," he added, rather pointlessly, but his heart was still trying to decide whether to sink to his belly with worry or jump out of his mouth in fright, and it was making him a bit lightheaded.

Beaufort got up. "Then we need to start a proper search. He may still be in the area. It's entirely possible some of Gilbert's friends might not have wanted to point his angry sister onto his trail."

Mortimer wrinkled his snout. "I didn't think of that."

"Because you were too busy worrying about it to actually think about it," Beaufort patted Mortimer's shoulder again as he spoke. "Never mind, lad. He can't have gone far. We'll find him."

The sun was suddenly a lot warmer than it had been, and Mortimer smoothed the scales on his tail. Of course they'd find him. He'd just be hiding out with a sprite or something, to get back at Amelia. He'd been entirely overreacting.

Hopefully.

2
DI ADAMS

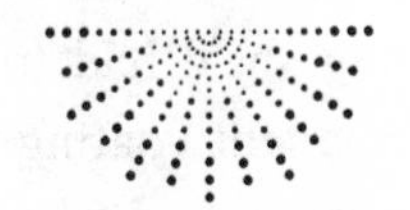

"Drop it," DI Adams said, pointing sternly at Dandy.

Dandy cocked his head slightly, but he didn't relinquish the trainer he had in his mouth. DI Adams didn't even know whose shoe it was. Not hers, which was some small relief.

"*Drop it,*" she insisted.

"Adams, you need to train that dog better," DI Collins said. They were in the small office they shared at Skipton station, and he was leaning back in his chair with both hands wrapped around his mug of tea, watching her with interest. He wasn't watching Dandy, because he couldn't see Dandy. No one could, other than DI Adams and one annoying journalist. Or no one human, at least, which was a fact that didn't sit well with her. Although, neither did the journalist, to be fair.

"I wish everyone would stop thinking I have *any* control over him," she said, and scowled at Dandy. He panted back at her, a Labrador-sized walking mat of grey, dreadlocked hair, his eyes hidden behind the mass of it. "Do you need your hair trimming?" she asked him. "Is that what's bothering you?"

"Are you going to take him to a grooming salon?" Collins asked, raising his eyebrows. "That might be tricky. 'Hi, here's my invisible dog, can you trim him, please?'"

"I thought I could buy some scissors," she said, giving up on Dandy and retreating to her own desk.

"Would his hair be visible after you cut it?" Collins asked.

DI Adams picked up her mug and took a sip of almost decent coffee. She'd bought one of those capsule machines for the station out of her own pocket, because she'd been spending so much on take-aways at the local cafe that it had seemed cheaper. So far she'd had a lecture from one of the tech team about the wastefulness of the capsules themselves, meaning she'd had to buy some reusable ones that resulted in a semi-permanent coating of coffee grounds on the staffroom floor; one of the constables had managed to put a capsule in backward and jam the whole thing up until Collins had jimmied it open, leaving scratches all over the top; one of the sergeants had tried to use it with no water in it and had burnt the element out (at least the warranty had still been current); and Lucas from the lab had brought in some sort of milk frother, which meant everyone took about fifteen minutes just to make a coffee, and every time she tried to get one someone else was using the machine. And when she *did* finally manage to get a cup, like now, she wasn't at all sure it was worth the effort. Even with three capsules worth of coffee in one mug, it still tasted vaguely of disappointment.

Now she said, "How do I know? I can see him all the time anyway."

"Try it," Collins suggested, opening his drawer and taking out a set of scissors. He passed them to her. "In the interests of scientific investigation."

She took the scissors, frowning. They were heavy, decent sorts with a guard that doubled as a sharpener slipped over the blades. She was sure her mum had had the same type in her sewing kit, and DI Adams and her brothers had never been allowed to touch them. Not out of any safety concerns, just because her mum knew that they'd immediately be used to cut sticks, wire, and anything else to hand, and would never be any good as sewing scissors ever again.

"Why do you have fancy scissors in your drawer?" she asked.

"One never knows when one might need decent scissors. And

you've seen this place. PC McLeod would use them to open his cuppa noodle and I'd never see them again."

"Amazing how many things go missing in a police station," DI Adams said, and stood up, drawing the scissors out of the guard. They made a satisfying *shhhick* as they emerged, and Dandy, who'd settled himself on the floor in a patch of sunlight, chewing on the trainer, jerked his head up and stared at her. DI Adams had no idea where he'd got the shoe from. Dandy came and went as he liked, and seemed to have as little regard for doors and walls as he did for her instructions. It was one of the many things about Dandy that DI Adams didn't know, along with where he'd come from in the first place, why he'd adopted her, and why most people couldn't see him. Unless he was in large-and-angry mode, in which case *everyone* could see him, and it wasn't a nice sight. Oh, and why (and how) he changed sizes. She had a lot of questions about her unexpected companion.

"Good boy," she said to him encouragingly, and walked around the desk to crouch next to him. He watched her, unmoving. "This isn't going to hurt," she promised, petting his head.

"Look, he's dropped the shoe," Collins said. "I can see it now."

"I think it's one of Sergeant—" She stopped herself. "One of *Graham's*."

"Well done, Adams. We'll get a first name out of you yet."

"No," she said automatically. Even her brothers didn't use her first name – although at least she wasn't called Colin Collins, unlike her colleague. She plucked up some of Dandy's floppy fringe, revealing an unsettling red eye with an LED glow. She hesitated. Did she really want to see those eyes any more than she had to? Imagine waking up to them staring down at you in the middle of the night. But then again, he really couldn't see, and he'd walked straight through the fence on the castle walk while she'd been running that morning. They'd been on the wall that ran along the moat at the time, and he'd plunged into the water below with a startled yelp. She'd laughed so hard she'd had to take her phone out and pretend someone had sent her a funny video. Even so, she'd had some curious looks from the other morning joggers, although that could have been because Dandy had climbed out and proceeded to shake all over her, proving that invisible dog water was perfectly visible when it was on her clothes. Dandy had been most put out about the whole thing and had whimpered to himself piteously all the way home. "This is for your own good," she told him, and closed the scissors around the hair.

Dandy was very still until the *shhhick* of the blades closing whispered around the office. Then he exploded off the floor with a horrified howl, bowling DI Adams off her feet. She sprawled backward, still gripping the loose hair in one hand and the scissors in the other, and Dandy charged across the tatty laminate floor, heading for the door. DI Adams rolled to her knees just in time to see the door open. She had one horrified moment to wonder whether Dandy could navigate a human the way he could navigate walls, then DCI Maud Taylor walked into the room, apparently without so much as glimpsing the large dreadlocked dog that had just thundered past her. Or *through* her, or however Dandy moved.

DCI Taylor looked at DI Adams, still crouching on the floor with the scissors in one hand, then said, "I don't know how you do things down south, but up here we don't kneel for senior officers."

DI Adams scrambled up, her ears hot. "No. I was just ... I was ..." She looked at the scissors, unable to come up with any reason for why she'd been waving them around on the hard floor. At least she had Dandy's hair tucked tightly in her fist, out of sight. That would've been even harder to explain.

DCI Taylor waited a moment longer, then nodded. "I realise that Skipton may not be up to big city standards, but we do have *some* maintenance budget. You don't have to trim the floor yourself."

"I wasn't—" DI Adams started, then stopped, because she couldn't exactly explain her real reason.

"I suggested some epoxy," Collins said, taking a sip of tea.

"Also an option," the DCI said. "Anyhow, I can see you two have far too much time on your hands if you're taking on floor repairs. Allow me to fix that for you."

"Oh, that sounds good," DI Adams said, dropping gratefully back into her chair, and the DCI frowned.

"Around here we don't usually refer to crime as *good.*"

"Right. No. Of course not. I didn't mean—" She stopped and took a deep breath. DCI Taylor had a round, red-cheeked face and bright blue eyes, and DI Adams always found herself vaguely craving gingerbread around her, as if the DCI should be twinkling out of a Christmas card. And the older woman did little to dispel the image, favouring pretty floral blouses and seasonal headbands to hold her greying hair back. The current one had sunflowers printed on it, and she was wearing little sunflower studs in her ears.

"I'm very glad you're a detective, Adams," she said now. "You'd be a terrible criminal."

"Um, thanks?"

"Yes. I'm far more interested in the scissors – and whatever you've just shoved into your pocket – now than I was when I walked in."

DI Adams nodded carefully. Dandy was at the door, his newly cropped hair meaning she could see his accusing red stare very clearly indeed. "It's wool," she said, taking it out of her pocket and setting it on the desk. She had no idea if Dandy's hair would be visible once it had left him, but she hoped it would be rather like the shoe in the corner.

"I see," DCI Taylor said, giving the wool some serious consideration before looking back at DI Adams. "And you were cutting it because ...?"

"Because, as you rightly observed, we've got no cases right now, and it seemed like something to do."

The DCI regarded DI Adams with those twinkling eyes for a moment longer, then said, "I hope you two do a better job of pretending to work when other officers come in here. I rather like having two DIs. I don't want to have to pack one of you off because you're excess to requirements."

"It'd be a shame to lose you," Collins said to DI Adams, nodding gravely.

"*One of you,* I said," DCI Taylor said. "I can see your phone screen from here, Colin, and you're on a travel site again."

"Sorry," Collins said, flipping the phone over. "But also – I was here first."

"But Adams is more interesting," the DCI said, giving him a broad smile. "Anyhow, you can start earning your keep again now. We've had a report of a missing person out in Eldmere."

"Where's that?" DI Adams asked.

"Northwest of here," Collins said. "Couple of dales over from Toot Hansell."

"That makes a nice change from *in* Toot Hansell."

"Quite," the DCI said. "You two have an unhealthy fixation with that place. I don't even go there as often as you do, and I *come* from there." She tipped her head, then added, "But I'm also not willing to brave the W.I., so I'll just say I'm glad you're on that particular beat."

DI Adams wished there was any choice involved in the matter, but she just said, "So what's happened in Eldmere?"

DCI Taylor pursed her lips, one hand beating a restless rhythm on her leg. Her hands gave her away – they were square and strong-looking, and DI Adams had once seen her changing in the locker rooms. Her shoulders under those pretty blouses made the inspector suddenly want to recommit to some serious time in the weights room.

Now she said, "It's an interesting one. A Jake Cooper has reported his wife Hetty – Henrietta – missing."

"He dodgy?" DI Adams asked, taking her notebook out and flipping to a new page.

"Nothing on record on him, and no previous reports of disturbances."

"Circumstances?" Collins asked.

"Here's where it starts getting interesting. She's been *gone* for three days, but *missing* for one."

"One? She's not just late back from wherever she was?" DI Adams asked.

"No. You see, he'd been saying she was missing for the previous two days, but she was meant to become un-missing yesterday."

DI Adams and Collins looked at each other, and DI Adams carefully moved her cup further from the edge of the desk as Dandy nudged up to her. Then she looked back at the DCI. "Sorry? I think I'm missing something myself."

"Oh, believe me, there's more." The DCI had been standing until now, but she finally sat in one of the seats facing the inspectors' desks. It wobbled, and she peered down at the legs with a frown. "Has something been *chewing* on this?"

"Rats," Collins said. "What was this un-missing thing, then? Why would a couple plan for one of them to go missing? Not exactly an insurance claim if it's three days, is it?"

"Bloody big rats," the DCI said, bending down for a closer look. "If they're that big we'll have to start paying pest control some danger money."

"It was a dog," DI Adams said. "I was dog sitting."

The DCI gave her a thoughtful look. "Is that why one of Graham's trainers is in the corner, too?"

"Um. Yes?"

"I don't feel I should have to point out that police stations aren't for any non-working animals," she said, and Dandy put his chin on the desk to stare at her. DI Adams moved her mug again.

"Understood. Now, this un-missing woman?"

"Oh, she's definitely missing now." The DCI leaned back in her chair. "Or, at least, she's now missing to her husband as well as everyone else."

"Are you sure this isn't Toot Hansell?" DI Adams said. "It sounds like Toot Hansell."

"Yes. Well. Hold that thought. Mr and Mrs Cooper have a farm in Eldmere. Second generation on her side, making a bit of a go of it raising organic-certified sheep, but as with most farms these days, not *enough* of a go of it. They've also invested in llamas, which they do guided treks with, and have recently set up an eco-campsite of sorts. You know, solar showers and composting loos and all that sort of thing."

"I always fancied a llama," Collins said. "I'd need a bigger garden, though."

Both DI Adams and the DCI gave him matching blank looks, then the DCI said, "I'll put it on your birthday list. Now, there's been a bit of a fuss in Eldmere recently, and, more specifically, at the Coopers' farm."

"What sort of fuss?" DI Adams asked. Her stomach was tight, and it was the *hold that thought* that was worrying her. What did that mean? Another W.I. running rampant around the place? More dragons? Probably not the latter, since no one was meant to know about dragons, but ...

"The Beast of Yorkshire," the DCI said.

There was silence for a moment, then DI Adams said, "Is that like the Yorkshire panther? The one that people mostly see around pub closing time?"

"No one's had a close enough look to say, except, apparently, the Coopers. *They've* got evidence."

"What?"

"Footprints – sorry, *paw* prints – plus some dodgy CCTV footage and some other bits and bobs," the DCI said. "Complete bollocks, obviously, but it certainly got the punters in. The village is overrun with monster hunters by all reports, and the Coopers decided that it'd be fun to up the stakes and have Mrs Cooper disappear for a couple of days, then come back all dishevelled saying she'd been hiding from the Beast in the fells."

"And she hasn't come back," DI Adams said.

"No."

"Where was she meant to actually go?" Collins asked.

"She was going to stay in an old hut up by a tarn on their property. When Mr Cooper went to pick her up, there was no sign of her."

The two DIs looked at each other. DI Adams' stomach hadn't eased, but there was nothing to say there was anything unusual in this. Not Toot Hansell unusual, anyway. Maybe Hetty Cooper had simply had enough of llama treks and had taken the opportunity to vanish. It happened more than one realised, people just walking out of their lives.

"We best go and have a chat to Mr Cooper, then," Collins said.

"That you had," the DCI said, but didn't move.

"There's more?" Collins said.

"Well, yes. Shortly after Mr Cooper phoned us to report his wife missing, and just before I came in here, DCI Nathaniel Sykes called me."

"Oh, *bollocks,*" Collins said.

"Who's DCI Sykes?" DI Adams asked.

"Eldmere's Craven district," Collins said, ignoring her. "It's nothing to do with him."

"Well, he is still North Yorkshire Police. And he said that he's been looking into the Beast fuss, as it's causing a public disturbance in the village, and will follow up on Mrs Cooper if needed."

"If needed?" DI Adams frowned. "She's missing."

"Quite. I thanked him for his help and said that the report had already been filed, so my top DIs were on their way. If they can tear themselves away from cutting wool scraps and dog sitting long enough, anyway."

"So that's fine, then," DI Adams said. "Isn't it?"

"There's nothing fine about DCI Sykes," Collins said.

DCI Taylor nodded. "Harsh, but actually quite fair." She looked at DI Adams. "He's in charge of investigations for Harrogate district. Youngest DCI in the north, and he's just ..." She trailed off, waving vaguely.

"Efficient," Collins said, and the DCI pointed at him like he'd won a point in charades.

"*Efficient?*" DI Adams asked.

"Yes. It's horrifying."

There was silence then, other than someone in the hall shouting that the coffee machine was jammed up again, and DI Adams wondered when efficiency had become such a horrifying thing. She was sure it had been rather a desired trait in London, and— "Wait. Is that why PC McLeod always looks terrified of me? Because I'm *efficient?*"

Collins made a non-committal noise. "It doesn't help, I'm sure."

She scowled at him. "Great. I'm glad you told me that so early on in our work relationship."

"What difference would it make? You can't help it."

"No. And I shouldn't have to. Efficiency is a good thing."

"As ever, everything in moderation," the DCI said. "This is not Sykes' case, and I'm not sure why he's trying to muscle in on it, but I'm not having it. You two get over to Eldmere and find out what's going on with the Coopers and this Beast business. If it is turning into a public nuisance, make the call and sort it out. Just don't let Sykes get all DCI on you."

"Right," Collins said. "And just how do we accomplish that last part?"

"Ask Adams. She'll sort him out," the DCI said, and got up.

"I will?" DI Adams asked.

"Of course. I'm sure your London efficiency will be more than a match for him."

"I don't think I've ever engaged in competitive efficiency," she said.

"Sure you have. You're a DI who's a woman of colour. You've done *plenty* of competitive efficiency." DCI Taylor headed for the door. "And put Graham's trainer back before he thinks it's been stolen, would you? We're a *police station*."

DI Adams stared blankly at the door as it swung shut behind the DCI, then looked at Dandy as he made another valiant effort to reach her mug. "The Beast of Yorkshire? Only two dales over from Toot Hansell? With *paw prints?*"

"It might be nothing," Collins said, pushing his chair back from his desk. "I mean, at least *some* of it's faked, right?"

"That's true," she said, grabbing her car keys off the desk and going to pick up Graham's shoe as she headed for the door. "This could be a nice, simple, missing persons case, with no dragons, goblins, or ladies of a certain age involved."

"Just one horribly efficient DCI who's messing about in Maud's backyard," Collins said. "But you can sort that one out."

"Oh, sure. Easy," she said, and led the way out into the unexpected heat of a Yorkshire late summer day. And, really, anything was easy compared to Toot Hansell. Even horrifyingly efficient DCIs.

3
MIRIAM

It had been such a lovely day, Miriam thought mournfully. She'd sat in her garden with a cup of tea as the sun painted long dawn shadows across the grass, her bare feet wet with dew and the birds shouting deliriously in the trees, smelling damp wood and fresh earth and the sweet high scent of the brook that ran along the bottom of her garden, part of the network of waterways that embroidered Toot Hansell onto the landscape of the Yorkshire Dales like a jewel onto some beautiful, multicoloured dress.

She had been thinking that it was a good day for doing laundry, but also far too nice to waste actually doing it, and had been considering making a picnic instead, and seeing if Alice wanted to walk into the woods in the direction of the dragons' mount to find a nice spot to have it. They'd never actually *been* to the dragon's mount, and she would never presume to ask if they could, but that part of the woods always felt more alive with magic than any other, full of half-glimpsed things and the sense that one was being observed by quick, clever eyes, there and gone again in a breath. Plus, it made her feel closer to the dragons, which eased the vague, persistent sense of loss that had settled on her with it being such a terribly long time since they'd seen each other. So yes, maybe she and Alice could find a nice place along the stream, and paddle, or even swim if the day was hot enough. She thought it might be.

Although, if she were honest, she couldn't actually imagine Alice swimming. Not in the splashing in the stream sense. Doing steady lengths of some vast and abandoned pool, perhaps, her arms moving like a metronome, but not splashing. Not that it mattered. *Miriam* could splash, and Alice could be dignified on the bank, perhaps. They could even ask Jasmine if she wanted to come, but not Teresa, who was far too fit and whose legs were far too long for pottering along the river. She'd have walked there and back before Miriam got out of the village.

No, it would be better if it was just her and Alice, and maybe Jasmine, because any more and it'd be a whole Toot Hansell Women's Institute outing, and that felt like a lot. Not that Miriam didn't love every single one of them, but some days were too large and beautiful to be drowned out by voices. Some days had to be allowed to just be, and one enjoyed them best by allowing oneself to drift with them, rather than giving them over to too much talk and socialness.

Of course, all these plans would have been much better with dragons – *everything* was better with dragons – but some things couldn't be helped. Not seeing Mortimer and Beaufort, or even Amelia and Gilbert and grumpy old Walter, made the days seem a little dimmer, the summer sun a little less bright, but the alternative was that the dragons risk being seen by lurking journalists. That was just courting disaster, and not at all worth the risk. One day it would all go back to as it was, and in the meantime there was no point resenting the days without dragons. One had so few days, in the end, so one must just find the magic in the everyday as well as in the truly magical.

So Miriam had sat there on her ageing garden bench with the cracked slat that pinched the back of her legs if she sat in the wrong spot, cradling her tea in her hands and considering picnics, and thinking that it was going to be a most beautiful day.

And, she supposed now, it still *was,* but she was feeling rather less inclined to notice it, even if she was sitting in Alice's very tidy and well-trimmed garden, on a comfortable wooden chair with plump blue cushions, with her bare feet nestled into the soft grass and an umbrella mushrooming out of the table to protect them from the sun. The birds were still singing, the bees rumbling in the heat, and there was cake and tea and neatly folded napkins in front of her. It was all very *nice,* but she was no longer sure she was having a nice day at all. She took a sip of tea and looked from Alice to Rose, who both looked back at her expectantly. She would have liked it if they'd looked a *little* guilty at ruining her beautiful day, but it wasn't in their natures, she supposed.

"Well?" Rose asked. Her hair was dyed orange this week, and the sun lent it neon tones as she tapped the grimy newspaper lying on Alice's garden table between them. "What do you think?"

"I was going to suggest a picnic," Miriam said. "Maybe a paddle in the stream."

"How nice," Alice said, as if a small child had showed her a finger painting. She tucked silver hair behind one ear and turned the paper to face her, examining the photo carefully. "Do you think it could be fake, Rose?"

"It's hard to tell from the photo," Rose said. "But whether it is or not, the fact remains that they're still talking about – *writing* about – dragons in Yorkshire, and Toot Hansell specifically. They just don't give up, do they?"

Miriam peered at the byline on the article. "Katherine Llewelyn," she read aloud. "She really is *very* annoying."

"I'd admire her persistence if she wasn't so fixated on the dragons," Alice said. "It's not even a story about Toot Hansell, and she's still mentioned us."

Persistent wasn't the word Miriam would have used for Katherine. She had some rather choicer ones, although she supposed it wasn't quite fair. The woman was just doing her job. But her job seemed to be very centred around proving dragons existed in general, and in Toot Hansell in particular, and she was the reason that the dragons had been banished from the village. Which meant that Miriam didn't feel much like being fair about her.

"Have you heard of this Beast of Yorkshire?" Alice asked Rose. "Is it some sort of local legend? I thought I'd read up on most of them, but every village seems to have its own ones."

Rose nodded. "Oh, they do. The Beast could be anything, really. It could be another name for the Yorkshire panther, or it could be a black dog of sorts, or it could be complete twaddle."

"I thought the Yorkshire panther was usually only seen after pub closing time," Miriam said, more to herself than others.

"Or in the fevered imagination of cryptid journalists," Alice said. "But the issue is, of course, that it's all drawing more attention our way."

"Here? But this is two valleys over!" Miriam protested. "Katherine never found *any* evidence, and neither did anyone else. Surely they won't bother?"

"They're still mentioning us," Rose said. "The main attention's over there right now, sure, but as long as our name's floating about, there'll be people coming here to look for dragons. Especially if they don't find anything on the Beast. We'll end up turning into a bloody hotspot."

"This is *awful,*" Miriam said. "We're never going to be able to go back to normal! And we haven't seen the dragons in simply *forever.* How long are we going to have to keep this up?"

Alice smiled at her. "It really is most irritating. But we can't risk anyone getting a whiff of them. The whole situation with Katherine was far too close for comfort."

"It was horrifying," Miriam said. Katherine had even *seen* Mortimer once, trapping him on Miriam's own kitchen step while the journalist was snooping about the place with her photographer friend. Trespassing was what it was. The journalists, not the dragons, obviously. The dragons had more right to her garden than she did, when it came down to it. They'd been here longer.

"Well, I've been keeping tabs on this lot," Rose said, tapping the paper again. "On the forums, and chatting to some people, you know. My contacts say Katherine's definitely still stuck on the dragons in

Toot Hansell angle, so I wonder if she's hoping to draw them out with this Beast stuff."

"But they won't know," Miriam said. "If we don't tell them, they can't know, can they?"

Alice tapped her fingers on her cup. "One would hope not, but who knows what networks they have. They might know more than us. Perhaps we should try and get a message to them."

"We *can't,*" Miriam said. "It's too risky. Never mind getting anyone to take a message – if we tell them they have to be even more careful because that same journalist's poking around making up stories about beasts and linking them to Toot Hansell, they'll want to get involved and prove there *is* no beast, in the hope that she goes away. And if she really is trying to draw them out, then they'll be playing right into her hands."

"You're quite right, of course," Alice said. "And the next thing you know they'll be wandering around in dog disguises again, and they were never very good even when people *weren't* looking for dragons."

Miriam shuddered, thinking of the very first Christmas market they'd shared with the dragons. Beaufort had been very proud of the dog costumes he'd come up with, and it was true that in the dark and fire-light, when no one was expecting dragons, they had worked to a point. That point being when Beaufort had had an unfortunate allergic reaction to an actual dog and had set fire to his costume. Miriam had thought that a flaming dragon in the middle of a winter fête would be impossible for people to forget, but it had turned out that photography doesn't really work on magical Folk, and also that people are more inclined to think they've had some dodgy mulled wine than to have actually seen a dragon.

"We can't tell them," she said. "They've been hiding away for weeks and weeks now, and Beaufort will be getting bored. He'll definitely use this as an excuse to get involved, and you know he won't listen to sense once he's decided."

"It's very hard to stop a dragon doing what they want," Rose said. "It took ages to convince Walter to stop coming by all the time to check my garden for lurking men after the whole Dougal debacle."

She considered it. "I think I'm rather done with men, though. Such a hassle."

"Campbell was nice," Alice said, in an encouraging tone that suggested she felt it was something she ought to say rather than anything she particularly agreed with.

"Far too nice," Rose agreed. "He's been unbearable since the body in the freezer. He keeps wanting to be helpful, and to *do* things for me, like I can't do them myself. I had to break it off. I can always call Jean-Claude if I really need some male company."

"Excuse me," Miriam said. "Can we go back to the problem of the journalists and the dragons? What are we going to do?"

There was a moment's silence, then Alice picked up a plate of homemade hobnobs, their tops spackled with chocolate, and offered them to Miriam. "Well. We certainly should do *something*," she said.

Miriam looked at her suspiciously. "Such as call DI Adams, maybe?"

"I'm not sure that would help," Alice said, putting the plate back down untouched. "No one's committed any crimes."

"Crimes against the scientific method," Rose suggested. "Making all this fuss with no real evidence – it's shocking!"

"I don't think you can be arrested for that," Alice said.

"You should be able to. Gives the few people who actually take the field seriously a bad name."

"Perhaps it could be for their own safety," Miriam suggested. "Maybe this Beast might eat them if they get too close to it."

"One can hope," Alice said. "I still don't think the threat of that would be enough to convince DI Adams to arrest them, though."

"Walter said he'd eat a journalist if he spotted one," Rose said helpfully.

There was a thoughtful pause while Miriam wondered if Walter had enough teeth to actually eat anyone, or if dragons, like snakes, could dislocate their jaws and swallow things much larger than seemed possible. She didn't like the thought of it, even if they *were* journalists.

"Walter eating anyone seems unlikely to help maintain our stance regarding the non-existence of dragons," Alice said finally.

"It'd give him something to do," Rose said. "D'you know, I had to chase him out of the garden with a broom not long after we agreed they shouldn't come to the village. He insisted he was keeping men of ill repute at bay."

"I suppose he meant well," Miriam said.

Rose sniffed. "I told him I was rather hoping for a man of ill repute, and he was so put out he stomped right through my pond when he left. I'm sure it upset the goldfish."

Miriam frowned. "You have goldfish in that pond?" Rose's garden was more wilderness than cultivation, and she couldn't imagine goldfish surviving long in there.

"Well, I don't *now*."

"I think we should tell Colin," Miriam said. "About the Beast, I mean. Not Walter."

"That's no different than telling DI Adams," Rose said.

"It is." Colin might be a detective inspector as well, but he never made her feel as if she'd inadvertently stolen something. Whenever Miriam was around DI Adams, she found herself checking her pockets, as if she might find an unexpected murder weapon in there somewhere. Of course, Colin being her nephew helped, but it wasn't *just* that.

"I rather doubt we've got enough information to bother either of the detectives at this point," Alice said. "And they'll only tell us to leave it alone, anyway."

Miriam took a sip of tea to hide the slight twist of her mouth.

"So we just let the journalists carry on?" Rose asked. "It's going to lead right back to us, and the dragons *will* get wind of it at some point. It's no good."

"Quite," Alice said. "Do you know, it occurs to me that one can be discredited, even if one isn't arrested. If one were seen to be making things up for one's own ends ..." She trailed off, looking at the other two women expectantly.

"The journalists?" Miriam asked. "Do you think they would? Isn't that rather unethical?"

Rose snorted and slammed her cup down on the table. "Have you seen this paper? They're selling crystals to cure baldness and serums made from the tears of mermaids. *Ethical* isn't in their style guide."

"It doesn't matter if they're doing it or not," Alice said. "We just have to convince everyone else they are."

Miriam looked at her for a long moment, then reached across the table and took a hobnob after all. She took a bite, trying to concentrate on nothing but the round warm flavour of the spices and the soft chew of the oats, but she couldn't. All she could think of was that awful Katherine and her horrible, *observant* eyes, casting around the garden like she really was some sort of monster hunter of old. "Really? Isn't there any other way we can deal with this? Us chasing after the journalists seems like it might make us look even more as if we're hiding things."

"We could set Walter on them," Rose said.

"Any *sensible* way to do it, I mean."

"We *could* just wait, and hope for it all to die down," Alice said. "But Ms Llewelyn doesn't seem to be the sort of person who would really let go of this. She did actually see Mortimer. She knows there are dragons here. And it's possible that she's thinking up ways to draw them out."

"They stayed hidden for centuries," Miriam said. "They can wait her out."

"I'm sure they could. But that could take a terribly long time. Do we really want to risk never being able to see the dragons again?"

Miriam tried to imagine that, and immediately popped the rest of the biscuit in her mouth. Even the thought of it made the world seem suddenly three shades darker and so terribly, dreadfully *dull* that she could barely stand it. No matter how much one knew there was magic to be found in every day, once one had had *real* magic in their life, it was hard to imagine giving it up forever. It was as if life took on the shades of the worst sort of damp winter days at the very idea, those days when it's not raining, or misty, or *anything*, just cold and grey and flat and lifeless. "If we had to," she managed in a small voice. "You know, if it kept them safe."

"And do you think *they'd* be happy with that?" Alice asked.

"They'd die of scone deprivation," Rose declared. "Or tea withdrawal. They wouldn't stand for it."

Alice nodded. "And there'd be no use telling them they had to. One can't really *tell* Beaufort very much at all."

Miriam looked at her tea, aware that the other women were waiting for her to say something. She wasn't sure why. She might have been the first in the village to befriend the dragons – the first in the world, perhaps, to have befriended a dragon for centuries – but that didn't mean she spoke for them. And she certainly wasn't some sort of authority on dragons, or indeed in the W.I. She was just herself, sitting in the flood of summer sun that suddenly seemed less warm and less bright than it had a moment earlier. She thought of Mortimer, poor dear Mortimer with his patchy tail from the stress-shedding and his beautiful dragon scale creations, and how he loved curling on her hearth on winter days to watch TV, and who adored scones and mince pies in equal measure. And Beaufort, who was so terrifyingly *interested* in everything, but who also believed so firmly that every single one of them were so capable and smart and delightful, far more so than they ever believed of themselves.

She let go of her cup and folded her fingers together on the table. "So. What do we do, then?"

Alice smiled at her. "I think we go to Eldmere to start with. Have a look around and see what we can learn, then we can figure out how to move against the journalists."

Miriam wrinkled her nose. "Really? Straight there? What if we run into them?"

"We have as much right to be there as anyone else," Alice said. "They certainly can't chase us off."

"Besides, we'll have a cover story," Rose said. "I've always taken an interest in the cryptozoology community. It makes perfect sense for me to be there, looking to debunk it all."

"And we shall be your faithful research assistants," Alice said, smiling.

"Yes, perfect! That makes it easier for chatting to everyone there, too. The community's naturally suspicious of anyone who doesn't believe in cryptids. They've been the butt of too many jokes over the years."

"Fancy that," Alice said.

"And you can stop that, too, if you're going to be my assistant."

Alice chuckled, but Miriam gave Rose a dubious look. They were rather too old to be anyone's assistants, she thought, but who knew what the standards were for such things in the world of cryptozoology. "Isn't it going to be really obvious we're not a part of the … cryptozoology community?"

Rose shook her head and tapped her phone. "I've been following all the forums. The village is attracting all sorts of attention already, and it's everyone – serious researchers, weekend warriors, cryptid tourists. You'll pass easily as some friends of mine with enough interest to be supporting me in my research. No one's going to think twice about us asking a few questions." She looked from Miriam to Alice. "We'll have to look the part at least a bit, though."

Miriam looked down at her tie-dyed, sleeveless dress. It was a rather pleasing clash of purples and greens, and she'd chosen some gold flip-flops to go with it. "I'm not sure I have anything that suits monster hunting," she said.

"Not you," Rose said. "You look like just the sort of person who'd go flocking to monster and alien sightings." She nodded at Alice while Miriam tried to decide if she was insulted or not. "You'll have to change, though."

"Me?" Alice asked, raising her eyebrows. "What's wrong with what I'm wearing?"

"You look exactly like the chair of the Women's Institute," Rose said, waving at Alice's white cropped trousers and sleeveless floral blouse. "You'll need to dress down a bit."

Alice nodded and got up from the table. "Then I shall do just that. Do you mind tidying away while I do?"

"Are we going now?" Miriam asked.

"No time like the present," Rose said, stacking their plates as Alice headed up the path to her kitchen door. "We'll swing by mine and pick up my camera and a few bits."

"But we're not actually investigating monsters," Miriam protested. "We're just finding out what's happening over there, aren't we?"

"Well, yes. But what if there *are* monsters? I'd hate to not be prepared." Rose followed Alice up the path with her hands full of plates, leaving Miriam to collect the cups and saucers and milk and sugar. She just stared at it all for a moment, wondering how she'd managed to go from *we shouldn't get involved* to *impersonating a monster hunter* in the space of one conversation, then got up with a sigh.

It really had looked like being a beautiful day.

4
ALICE

It wasn't a long drive to Eldmere – or it wouldn't have been if they hadn't had to go first to Miriam's, who had decided she didn't want to look like just the sort of person who turns up to monster sightings, and so insisted she needed to change into something more practical, and then to Rose's, where they'd been for the last half an hour while she tried to find her cameras and lenses. Miriam had also wanted to make sandwiches in case they needed them, but Alice had pointed out that they were only going two dales over, not crossing the outback, and the remains of their morning tea would be sufficient. They could always get lunch at the pub if need be. Miriam had compromised by bringing a thermos of tea, a large loaf of seeded bread wrapped in a tea towel, an entire block of cheese and a jar of chutney, plus a Tupperware container full of lemon slices, just in case.

Alice wasn't sure what they were *just in case* of, but some things weren't worth arguing about. She crossed her legs at the ankles as she waited outside Rose's, sitting on an old, pink plastic chair under the shade of the pear tree. Miriam was inside helping Rose hunt out her cameras, and knowing Rose's level of organisation, that might take a while. It was going to be well after lunch by the time they got there at this rate. Perhaps Miriam had been right about the lemon slices.

As if hearing her, Miriam and Rose came bustling out of the house, Rose pulling the door to without bothering to lock it.

"Let's go," she said brightly. She'd found an ancient khaki waistcoat adorned with oversized pockets, and matching trousers, and there was a well-worn satchel flung over her shoulder that continued the theme. It looked almost as big as she did. Miriam was carrying two large waterproof boxes and looking at them rather dubiously. One had a peeling biohazard symbol on it.

"Do we really need all that?" Alice asked. "We're not *actually* monster hunting, you know."

"Never hurts to be prepared," Rose said, and Alice couldn't disagree with that. Her own small backpack contained a first aid kit, two head lamps, a torch, rehydration packages, protein bars, foil survival blankets, a compact GPS, a compass, spare socks, thermal gloves, and a multitool, and she'd added an ordnance survey map at the last moment, when she'd taken her summer walking shoes out of the cupboard at home. One just never knew when such things might be useful.

"*I* feel very unprepared," Miriam said. "I'm not quite sure what one needs for monster hunting." She had changed her swirling, tie-dyed dress for a slightly less voluminous, three-quarter length patchwork-style skirt with teal leggings underneath, and some barely used trainers.

"I'm sure we shall be just fine," Alice said. It had taken Miriam long enough to find her trainers as it was. Alice had no intentions of letting her go back to her house for anything else. "Let's go."

"Angelus!" Rose yelled. "We're going!"

Alice managed not to look pained. She'd had dragons in the back of her car. A Great Dane couldn't be that much worse.

❧

A GREAT DANE, as it turned out, was definitely worse. Her small SUV didn't have enough boot space for Angelus to fit into comfortably, so he sat on the backseat, towering over Rose and drooling on the back of Alice's seat. Despite his window being open, he also seemed to like putting his head between the front seats to check where they were going, and every time he did that, he'd try to lunge all the way through, only to be brought up short by his harness, which made him gasp and whine horribly.

At least with dragons she'd only been worried about them singeing the upholstery.

"I've been checking the WhatsApp group," Rose announced, as they wound their way through patchy mobile reception and drystone walls that stitched the fields to the lower slopes of the fells. Stone barns and low-slung grey farms huddled in patches of trees, and sheep puffed across the landscape. The sky was a high, burnt blue, and the cyclists panting in packs down the road were painted with sweat. Walkers in big boots and trousers with the legs zipped off to make shorts strode happily about the place on barely seen tracks, waving maps and phones, and it all seemed most un-monstrous.

"Anything new?" Alice asked, slowing to a crawl while she waited for a chance to get around a straggling group of pink-faced cyclists. Angelus flung himself over Rose, trying to get to her window for a closer look, and left a string of saliva dangling across the seats.

"Lots of speculation on the footprints." Rose hesitated. "D'you know, there's a decent photo here." She reached through the seats, handing her phone to Miriam. "What do you think?"

Miriam was very quiet, and after a moment Alice looked at her. The younger woman had gone a little pale, red spots painting her cheeks. "Well?" Alice asked.

"Well … I mean, it's hard to tell. The shape …" Miriam looked up. "Mortimer helped me plant potatoes once, and his prints were everywhere. It was lovely." She blinked, and handed the phone back. "But then there's size. I can't tell from the photo. They could be anything."

Rose's voice was quiet when she spoke again. "They're saying that from the depth and stride the Beast must be pony-sized."

There was silence for a moment at that. The Cloverly dragons were pony-sized, in a low-slung and barrel-bodied way. But they wouldn't be sneaking about villages. They weren't that silly. Although it wasn't as if they were the only unusual creatures around. Alice had realised over the last few years that the world most humans saw was only a very small sliver of what was actually out there.

"Well, it can't be dragons," Miriam said firmly. "And if it *looks* like dragons, it's probably especially not them."

"What?" Rose asked, while Alice tried to follow the logic.

"You know, like with the goblins the other Christmas. They made it look like dragons to frame them."

Alice's hip gave a stab of pain, as if woken by the memory. "They were working with dragons," she pointed out. "It wasn't entirely a set-up."

"Goblins would be interesting," Rose said. "You two had all the fun last time. I barely even saw them!"

Miriam shuddered. "You don't want to. They were awful. All teeth and wanting to eat people. Ugh."

"Still, from a purely scientific point of view, it'd be interesting. I wonder how you'd classify them?"

"From a distance," Alice said, finally getting around the cyclists on a bit of straight road. "Do see if you can stop Angelus drooling on me, Rose. I just washed my hair."

"I hope it's not goblins," Miriam said, almost to herself, and opened her window to let the breeze in and the dog scent out. "They had so many teeth."

❧

ELDMERE WAS BARELY A VILLAGE, just a nondescript jumble of two-storey grey stone houses lining the main road. It was the sort of place that had grown up to serve the local farms, one where visitors only really stopped on the way through, walkers or cyclists or perhaps those on a road trip. The road as they drove in was crowded with cars parked on the green verge, but that was hardly unexpected. Any place with good walking tracks was the same in the summer. Alice had an idea that once they got into the centre they'd find the National Parks car park half empty. One couldn't begrudge anyone free parking, but it always seemed rather ungracious to her, considering all the work the National Park did, maintaining the footpaths and so on.

"It's awfully busy, isn't it?" Miriam said. "And it's not even school holidays!"

"Told you," Rose said from the back. "Monster hunters everywhere!"

"Are there really so many?" Alice asked. How so many adults could be running around chasing imaginary creatures astonished her. Even if they weren't *actually* imaginary, she amended to herself. But most people didn't know that.

"It's just the start," Rose said. "It's Saturday tomorrow. The weekend'll be *heaving.*"

"How unpleasant."

"Well, if we didn't know dragons, I suppose we'd be quite keen to try and catch a glimpse, too," Miriam said.

Alice gave her a disapproving look. "I certainly would not. And I'm sure Rose wouldn't either. She's a scientist."

"Well, I would," Miriam said. "I'd be very keen to see any sort of magical creature, if I hadn't already. And it seems much more fun than ghost trails. I find them very unnerving."

"I've been on a Loch Ness hunt *and* a Bigfoot hunt," Rose said cheerfully. "Never found anything, mind, but it was great fun."

"Have you been on a ghost hunt?" Miriam asked, twisting around to peer between the seats.

"No, they're rubbish," Rose said, and gave Angelus a treat from her pocket.

"That seems a very general statement."

"True, though." She popped one of the dog treats in her mouth, then caught Alice's startled look in the rear-view mirror. "I make them myself. All veggies. Want one?"

"No, thank you."

"Suit yourself."

The main road was a straight sweep through town, in one side and out the other, and the old buildings leaned over the narrow pavements as if jealous of the space they were taking up. Baskets of late summer blooms swung from hooks on walls and frames on the handful of streetlights, and the bright sun lit the small-paned windows of the buildings, making them glitter with delight.

"Ooh, doesn't it look nice?" Miriam said.

"It does," Alice agreed. Whoever had done those flowers had done an excellent job – and kept up to it. As she brought the car to a stop to allow three women in long shorts and hiking boots to drift across the road, she noticed that there weren't even any dead stems in the basket above her. Someone was definitely putting the village's best foot forward.

Other than the flowers, the village's main street was framed by a pub on their left with a sign advertising a riverside beer garden set on the pavement outside, followed by a skinny row of three-storey terraced houses. Just beyond them Alice could see a side road leading onto a stone bridge that rose over a shallow, chattery river, and further along the main road a flower-studded green was hemmed in by the river on one side and the pavement on the other. The right side of the road held another pub, facing the green, and a second side road ambled up a small slope and out of the village again. There was a garden-type shop that looked to be one of those places that sold everything from compost to cooking pans, a small supermarket, and a surprisingly fancy deli/cafe, which was advertising *Beastly Pies* and *Monster Cream Teas.* There was no parking to be had anywhere along the main street, but Rose leaned between the seats and pointed.

"Parking sign up there, see?"

"I do." They puttered through the rest of the little village, which was made up of more grey stone houses with neatly painted window frames and small, well-kept front gardens, and found the National Parks car park on the edge of the buildings, bounded by fields on the far side. There was an automated pay station, and a sign reminding walkers to keep their dogs on leashes, plus a squat block of public toilets, but nothing else – no maps or information boards. Alice supposed that if you ventured this far afield you likely already knew where you were going anyway.

The car park was more crowded than she had imagined, but there were still spaces. She parked between an ageing Range Rover with National Trust stickers in the back window and a small Citroen with a large bumper sticker that read, *My other car is a spaceship,* and turned the engine off.

"Here we are, then," she said.

"Excellent." Rose was already half out of the door, Angelus scrabbling to get out at the same time. A moment later he was dragging her across the car park, intent on decorating the pay station.

"Now what?" Miriam asked, getting out rather more slowly.

"Now we have a look around and see what comes up. It's about time we had our village back."

"It really is." Miriam sighed. "I'm getting very sick of finding journalists lurking at my back gate every morning."

"Is that a euphemism?" Rose asked, rejoining them with a grin.

"*No,*" Miriam said. "And journalists still wouldn't be welcome, even if it wasn't."

"Well, I think we should just go and take a look to start with," Alice said. "Find out what all the fuss is about." She opened the back of her little SUV, and the ladies helped themselves to the bags in the back. She settled her own backpack fairly comfortably on her shoulders, then took out a shopping bag with a picnic blanket and a few essentials in it. "There we are. All set for a picnic, should anyone ask."

"Are we expecting to be interrogated?" Rose asked. Her satchel was slung across her body one way, and one of the waterproof boxes on a strap made out of what looked to be a man's tie in the opposite direction. She looked very laden down, but it didn't seem to be bothering her.

"One just never knows." Alice waited for Miriam to jam a large straw hat on her head, then pick up a shopping bag in each hand. It didn't look like a sensible way to carry things for any distance, but she had learned that it was easiest to let Miriam do things exactly as she chose. It normally worked, after a fashion, and was both frustrating and lovely. She shut the back door, beeped the car locked, then joined the other two women as they walked over the unsealed gravel of the car park and onto the skinny pavement, heading back toward the compact heart of the village.

❧

THE VILLAGE WAS CROWDED, although not as much as the cars parked on the roadside would have led Alice to believe. She assumed most people were out walking – there would be plenty of public footpaths and rights of way out here, skirting fields and cutting through farmyards, as there were through so much of the Dales. Sometimes it seemed there was barely a stretch of valley or hillside when one couldn't spot the bent heads and sturdy legs of dedicated walkers. Of course, given what Rose had uncovered, it was entirely possible a large portion of people were out on the trails looking for cryptids, too.

The green was scattered with people, some admiring the well-kept flowerbeds with ice creams in hand, others paddling in the shallows of the river, and a small group had spread picnic blankets on the grass and were watching small children run back and forth from the water, trailing shouts and rainbows of spray behind them.

"Look," Miriam said, pointing at a sandwich board on the pavement. It was mostly taken up with a blackboard section, but the frame was white and the top had a crest painted on it in deep blue. "*The Eldmere Women's Institute,*" she read. "That's a very fancy board."

Alice inspected it. Someone had written on the blackboard with great care, using chalk pens, *Scones, Cake, Jams. Join us in the Village Hall for a cuppa!* There was a flower drawn under it as well, and an arrow pointing across the road, to where the side road wandered up the slope. "Interesting," she said. "We may have to pop by later."

"Don't bother," someone said, and they turned to see an elderly couple with Nordic walking sticks and large canvas hats sitting on one of the benches closest to the road, eating sandwiches and sharing a thermos flask of tea. "It's all indoors," the man said. "No outside tables at all. On a day like this!"

"Oh, that is a shame," Alice said.

"I'm sure it'd be lovely if one wanted to get out of the sun," the man's companion said.

"On a day like this!" the man said again, waving and dropping pickle out of his sandwich. "Oops."

"You out monster hunting, then?" Rose asked, patting her bag and looking pointedly at the large camera lens protruding from the woman's pack.

The couple looked at each other, then the woman said, somewhat warily, "We had heard there was something like that going on."

"Oh, it's fine. That's what we're up to, too," Rose said. "Worth checking out those reports, right?"

The other woman relaxed, and the man chuckled. "Pretty wild, right? Have you seen the footprints yet?"

"No, but a friend of mine sent some photos. Have you seen them first-hand?"

The man stretched his arms out to indicate size, and his companion clicked her tongue at him. "Fine, fine," he said, bringing his hands closer together. "Still bloody enormous, though."

"And how do we find these footprints?" Alice asked.

"Just head over the bridge and up the hill," the woman said. "There's a footpath sign a few hundred metres up, and if you take that it'll lead you right through the woods to the farm. Getting a bit crowded, though."

The man nodded. "Yeah, we thought we'd come back for lunch. Maybe see if there are any other prints or anything elsewhere. Makes sense, right? No clever beast's going to stick around with so many tourists."

"Quite," Alice said. "Well, we'd best hurry, hadn't we?"

"Good luck," the woman said, around a bite of sandwich.

The sun was hot and intense as they crossed the bridge, and the trees leaning over the wall on the far side offered welcome shade. There was no pavement here, but the roads were quiet other than the occasional walker, most of them laden with cameras or recording equipment, and clothing with more pockets than were really necessary. They wandered up the hill in a companionable silence, listening to the birdsong in the trees and smelling the heavy must of old forest. The trees were big, heavy things, their roots breaching the wall and the tarmac of the road in places, interspersed with smaller saplings trying to make their own way. Sunlight glittered on the leaves above them and tumbled in shafts to the floor of the woods, and Alice thought it was the sort of place she'd rather like to return to at some point when it wasn't overrun with monster hunters.

"Very nice, isn't it?" she said, as they paused for at least the tenth time to allow Angelus to mark the wall.

"Doesn't exactly scream monster central," Rose said.

"It doesn't scream anything," Miriam said. She was frowning around at the trees. Her hat had slipped forward, but with a bag in each hand she couldn't adjust it, and was peering out from under the brim dubiously.

"Do we want it to scream something?" Alice asked.

"Yes. No. I don't know." Miriam peered about. "Something's off."

"Because of the beast?" Rose asked.

"No. Or I don't think so. It feels *empty.*"

Alice watched two women in running shorts jog past, then said, "I take it you don't mean empty of people."

"No. I don't." Miriam was still frowning. "Not human people, anyway. I mean … it just feels *different.* Off. *Missing.* Like … when you get a tooth taken out."

Alice and Rose looked at each other. "It's not going to be like Toot Hansell," Rose said. "We're a bit singular."

Miriam shrugged, sending her hat even lower over her eyes. She sighed, and set her bags down to adjust it. "I can't explain it. But most places you can feel … life, or something. And here it's just very quiet."

Alice didn't answer, even though she didn't quite understand how any place as overrun as this could be termed *quiet*. But she did realise that wasn't quite what Miriam meant, and the more she saw of the stranger parts of the world, the more Miriam's stranger instincts made sense. She wasn't entirely sure she was happy about it, as such things seemed very hard to quantify or to make sense of in any way that she understood, but there it was.

"So you don't think there's a Beast here?" Rose asked.

"I don't think there's anything here at all."

They were all silent for a long moment, and Alice was irritated to find her forearms suddenly rough with goosebumps. Not so long ago the idea that there were no magical creatures in the valley would have been simple fact. She couldn't be bothered by Miriam thinking there wasn't *enough* magic here, could she? Aloud, she just said, "At least we won't have to worry about it involving dragons, if there's nothing here. And it may make it even easier to discredit the journalists."

"I suppose," Miriam said, and picked her bags up again. "I don't like it, though. It makes me feel funny."

"Well, you don't look any funnier than normal," Rose said, and gave her a little one-armed hug. Miriam stuck her tongue out, and the three ladies of the Toot Hansell Women's Institute wended their way on up the hill, toward the possibility of monsters.

Or the hope of them.

5
MORTIMER

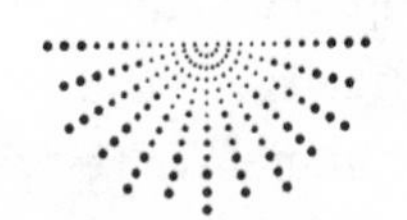

Even a week later, Gilbert's enraged departure from the mount lingered as a sour, burnt-cotton scent, faint but distinct. As Amelia had said, it led them to a swimming hole in the river that was still within the protective borders of the mount, which seemed promising to Mortimer. Surely the young dragon wouldn't have been silly enough to leave on his own, especially considering any retreat from stalking journalists by air would be problematic, to say the least.

The pool was still and quite deep, edged with jumbled boulders and overhanging trees, and a sprite with the skeleton of a trout tucked behind one ear surfaced rather reluctantly when Beaufort patted the water. "What?" she asked, her grey eyes narrow and suspicious.

"Have you seen Gilbert?" Beaufort asked. "Young dragon with piercings—"

"I know who he is. Why?"

"We're just looking for him. We think he was a bit upset."

She removed the trout skeleton from behind her ear and used it to comb her hair, examining the dragons. "Yeah," she said finally. "He was here about a week ago, all wound up. He was fine by the time he left, though."

"When was that?" Mortimer asked.

"A bit after he arrived. What're you chasing him down for, anyway?"

"We need to make sure he's safe," Beaufort said. "Things are a little dicey at the moment. If we just knew he was within the boundary charms, we'd be happy."

"You don't treat him right," the sprite said. "Telling him he's not a proper dragon! For shame."

Beaufort drew himself up to his full height. "I have *never* said that."

"Making fun of him being vegetarian."

Beaufort looked at Mortimer. "We've never made fun of that, have we, lad?"

Mortimer shook his head. He certainly hadn't, especially as he had a sneaking suspicion that Gilbert had a point.

"You don't stop others, though, do you?" the sprite asked. "It's no different, you know. If you just let it carry on. His sister's the worst, and no one tells her to be nice to him."

"To be fair, she's quite scary," Mortimer said. "And she's just worried about him. She's trying to help."

"Then she should support him, not try and make him just like any other dragon." The sprite sucked air through her sharp teeth, shaking her head. "Terrible."

"We will do better," Beaufort said, and the sprite squinted at him.

"Really? Or are you just saying that in the hope that I help you?"

Beaufort huffed. "I have told him to embrace his nature. To swim if he loves it, and never mind the flying. I even tolerate the fact that there seem to continually be stray prey animals wandering around my caverns, even when they roost on my barbecue, and I don't let *anyone* eat them. But I will still try and do better, *if* I can ever find him again. Does that satisfy you?"

She looked at him for a long time as she replaced her trout skeleton behind her ear, then shrugged. "Sure. I mean, I just want him to not come to my pool every week wailing about you all being mean to him. Scares the fish."

Beaufort snorted. "So? Do you know anything else?"

"Not really. *But—*" She raised one webbed finger as Mortimer groaned in exasperation. "I told him that if he really wanted a break from you lot trying to tell him how to be a dragon, he could go over to Meredale."

"Meredale?" Mortimer and Beaufort asked together, then looked at each other.

"Why Meredale?" Beaufort asked. "Where's that?"

The sprite waved a little vaguely. "Two dales that way."

Beaufort nodded as if it were perfectly clear. "And why would he go there?"

"Well, no one else does."

"Why not?" Mortimer asked. "Is it some sort of housing development?"

"No." She stared at them. "How do you not know about Meredale?"

"We've kept very quiet over the centuries," Beaufort said.

"Well, you're making up for that now, aren't you?"

"Possibly," the High Lord admitted.

The sprite chuckled and plucked a handful of moss from the rocks near the bottom, offering it to the dragons. "No? Suit yourselves." She took a large mouthful then said indistinctly, "It's not big – just one little village and a couple of farms. Sort of out of the way."

"That doesn't sound unusual," Mortimer said. Out of the way actually sounded rather nice.

"It's not, in that respect. It's got a river, and some woods, all the usual stuff. But no Folk."

Neither dragon spoke for a moment, then Beaufort said, "You mean no dragons."

"Yes. No dragons. No dryads. No sprites. Nothing."

"That's impossible," Mortimer said. "There's Folk *everywhere.* Even in cities!" He shuddered as he said it – he didn't understand how even humans survived cities. Seeing them on Miriam's television was worrying enough.

"Why?" Beaufort asked. "What happened there?"

The sprite shrugged. "No one really knows. It's just one of those things – no one goes there."

"What – like the Bermuda Triangle or something?" Mortimer asked.

"Oh, people go *there*," the sprite said, giving him a pointy-toothed grin. "They just don't come out again."

"Do Folk come out of Meredale?" Beaufort asked.

"They don't go in in the first place. Not if they're sensible."

"And you sent *Gilbert* there?" Mortimer demanded. "He's just a little dragon!"

"He's three times the size of me, and he was overheating my pool," the sprite shot back. "There's a really delicate balance in here, you know. Besides, it's all just old stories. I reckon it's no different to anywhere else. Overrun by bloody humans and the rivers stinking of fertiliser. He'll be fine."

Mortimer and Beaufort exchanged an uneasy glance, and when they looked back the sprite was gone. Mortimer caught a glimpse of a shadow flashing across the bottom of the pool, heading out into the stream as light and liquid as the water itself, then she was gone.

"What do we do?" he asked Beaufort.

"Find him," Beaufort said.

"But the mount – no one's meant to leave. What do we say?"

"We don't say anything. We just go." Beaufort turned and padded off into the trees.

"*Now?* It's still daylight!"

"We'll stay hidden, lad. We need to get there."

Mortimer broke into a trot to keep up with the High Lord. "But what can possibly happen, if there's no one there to see him? Surely that can't be so bad."

Beaufort looked back at him. "*No* Folk, Mortimer. None. I've never heard of such a thing, and I don't see anything good in a young dragon walking into that."

Mortimer's heart did something complicated and unhappy in his chest.

THEIR PATH through the woods was long and indirect, winding through the hidden ways that didn't even look like paths to anyone other than woodland creatures and certain Folk. They flew when they could, when the roads were distant and the fells steep and unfriendly, and the tracks of humans were of the less-travelled kind. It still made Mortimer's heart work overtime, though, half-expecting to hear a scream of fright from below, or the horrifying *chuk-chuk-chuk* of a helicopter coming up behind them, armed with rocket launchers or nets or giant Tasers, or possibly all three. But no one saw them except the birds, and the sun ran off their scales in the colours of the Yorkshire summer sky, rendering them as nothing but motes in the eyes of any casual observer.

Gilbert must have been much calmer by the time he left the sprite's pool – or he really had attempted flying – as they couldn't catch any more scents of him. But when they were on the ground they asked the dryads, or a sprite, or a passing fox, about Meredale, and the vague directions kept them moving steadily north and east, keeping to higher, more remote ground wherever they could. No one could tell them any more about it. An old fox with one blind eye just shrugged.

"We go there," he said. "The dogs are no worse than anywhere else."

"Do you see Folk there?" Beaufort asked, and the fox fixed him with his one good eye, bright and keen.

"Do Folk always see us?" he asked. "We're all invisible to those who don't look." And then he'd slipped away into the undergrowth, his brush flecked with grey.

It was early afternoon when Beaufort brought them angling down toward the head of a long valley, where a waterfall frothed brightly as it tumbled over a face of grey rock. Below, the waterfall became a river, patchily wooded where it flowed toward a farm and, beyond that, to a small village and more open land. The woods were full and rich below the waterfall, and there was a fat swathe of forest pushing up to the village itself, but the farmhouse sat in more open land, scattered with outbuildings and neatly hemmed fields.

Beaufort landed on the edge of the cliff, peering down to the trees below. Mortimer landed next to him, trying to blend into the rocks. It didn't take much effort – he could feel his scales already greying with worry, and wasn't at all sure how good a job he'd made at being camouflaged on the flight.

"Are we sure this is a good idea?" he whispered.

"I don't think we have any choice," Beaufort said, not bothering to lower his voice. "Gilbert's gone, and this is the best we have to go on."

"But he might just be off having a bit of a quiet time to himself. Like a ..." Mortimer tried to think of the word. Miriam had mentioned it, and while it had had some sort of connotations of floaty white clothes and green juices, it had also made him think of the young dragon. "A retreat," he said triumphantly.

Beaufort cocked his head. "A retreat? He's not been fighting with Amelia *that* much, has he?"

"Not that sort of retreat. A ... restful break, sort of."

"Like we did at Miriam's sister's place? With yoghurt? I rather liked that."

Mortimer squeezed his eyes shut, trying not to remember Beaufort standing on one leg on the patio of a country house, in full view of humans. "Probably not that sort of retreat. I just mean, maybe he wants to be left alone."

"Maybe," Beaufort agreed. "And I understand that, but he is terribly young, and very ..." The High Lord trailed off, searching for words. "Enthusiastic," he said finally. "If he saw something that he wanted to fix – captive chickens, say – he wouldn't stop to think. And we just don't know what's happening in this valley."

Mortimer sighed. "You're right. And especially if he's still upset at Amelia. He'll be doing anything that she wouldn't like, just because he can."

Beaufort snorted. "In my day, that would've meant raiding a market and stealing some barrels of ale, maybe picking a fight with some knights. Now it's rescuing chickens and rehoming rabbits."

"To be fair, I'm not sure Gilbert's an entirely accurate representation of the new generation."

"I'm not sure if that's a relief or a shame," Beaufort said, and peered over the waterfall. "But let's see if he's about, lad. No point twiddling our talons up here." And he slipped off the edge, keeping close to the cliff as he swept down into the cover of the trees.

Mortimer took a deep breath, then followed him, a curious shudder of unease passing through his spine as he dropped into the confines of Meredale, deepening his concern. Gilbert couldn't have got into *that* much trouble even if he had liberated a few chickens. Could he?

❧

IT WAS windless down in the valley, the high hills and old trees trapping the heat. Small creatures moved in the undergrowth, and birds chattered and screamed their alarm at the appearance of dragons. That in itself was odd, Mortimer thought. Normally birds ignored them, satisfied that the dragons were as much a part of the natural world as the trees themselves, and about as likely to eat them (there wasn't much sustenance to be had in a blue tit). But if there really were no Folk in this valley, maybe the birds didn't know that.

Of course, the birds could also have been shouting about the sheer number of walkers about the place. The dragons didn't stick to any of the human paths, of course, just slipped silently among the trees, but even so they passed a dozen or so humans, some alone and others in groups. And, oddly, they didn't seem to be marching toward the waterfall or even sticking to paths themselves, but instead padded through the trees with notebooks and cameras, peering every which way as if they'd somehow got lost within earshot of the river. It was most odd, and the dragons skirted them quietly, keeping themselves hidden in the undergrowth.

Beaufort led the way, Mortimer trailing him, and they walked until the woods thinned and the fields rolled up to meet them, divided by drystone walls and wooden gates and gouged with tyre tracks. The farm was the usual sprawl of old grey buildings and oil-drenched machinery and worn dirt, but, just like the woods, it was busier than seemed normal. People wandered along the river, or in the fields around the farm buildings, the smell of them tangling and layering with the scent of fertiliser and feed and cars and a quiet, bright optimism, as pink and sharp as the thought of cold water at the end of a hot day. There was a collection of tents and cars in one field, and Mortimer wondered if there was some sort of event on, like sheepdog trials. He could smell the soft, drifting whiff of woolly bodies and the sharp, belligerent scent of dogs, among others.

"Anything, lad?" Beaufort asked, and Mortimer knew he meant *any Folk,* which sent a shiver over his scales like a whisper of wind on long grass.

"No. It seems really quiet."

Beaufort *hmm*ed, settling himself on his haunches under the cover of a low, spreading dogwood. They were on the opposite side of the river to the farm, where trees and boulders scattered the land and the slope rose sternly toward the fells above. A handful of alarmed sheep watched them with bewildered eyes.

"Exceptionally quiet, I'd say," Beaufort said. "I thought there'd be a sprite around at least."

Mortimer looked up and down the river, as if expecting one to pop out of the water and wave. "Maybe they're further down, in the village or something."

"They'd have felt us in the water. Seems odd that they haven't come to see what we're doing."

It *was* odd. Sprites knew everything that happened in their rivers and waterways, from the spawning of frogs in a minor pond to the terrible, crushing weight of a tributary dying of pollution or misuse. And since they were so aware of everything, they also tended to want to *know* everything. They were terrible gossips. So not only would they have known the dragons had arrived, they'd usually have come straight over to find out what they were doing.

Mortimer scratched his chin. "No dryads, either. Not unless they were hiding."

"I don't see why they would. They know dragons aren't the ones they have to worry about these days." Even if there had once been a time when fire-breathing beasts were a scourge to the woods, it had been a long time since a dragon had started a forest fire, even accidentally.

"This is very strange," Mortimer said. "I mean, it's not *silent* out here, but it is."

Beaufort looked at him, the sun bright on his old gold eyes. "Something's not right here, lad."

"Gilbert can't have been here," Mortimer said. "Surely it wouldn't feel so *empty* if he had been." He hoped he was right. There was something unsettling about the whole place, the silence of the waters and the trees, and the screams of the alarmed birds.

"I wouldn't be so sure," Beaufort said slowly. "It seems like the sort of place one might disappear quite easily, when there's no one to see you go."

Mortimer stared at him. "So what do we do? How do we find him if we don't even have a scent, and there's no one to ask?"

"We have to search," the old dragon said. "Use our eyes instead. Look for prints." He gave a thoughtful rumble. "It'll be most interesting."

Mortimer looked back at the farm. "You have seen all those humans, haven't you?"

"I'm old, not blind."

Mortimer swallowed a squeak at the growl in the High Lord's voice. "No – I mean, yes, of course—" He swallowed. "I just mean, it doesn't seem very safe for poking around."

"They won't see us."

"We can't be sure."

"No, but it's highly unlikely."

"But not impossible," Mortimer insisted. Once magical Folk had quietly vanished from human knowledge in the centuries past, they had become nothing but myth. And while it was true that they worked at staying out of sight of humans – or passing as them – their greatest protection remained their innate *faintness.* Humans see what they believe they see rather than what's really there. So the faery scooping ice cream in a bright pink van just has a bit of a hunchback, not wings folded under his jacket. The dryad at the market just has remarkably rough hands, not the smooth whorls of old wood on her skin. And the eye slides right off the things the mind can't accept.

It worked very well – unless someone *wanted* to see through the faintness. Someone who was startled enough, or open-minded enough, or, in the case of people like the journalists who were stalking Toot Hansell, fixated enough on uncovering the truth of the world. And while there was no reason to suspect the people wandering around the farm were that way inclined, there was no guaranteeing they weren't, either. And there were so many of them!

"Nothing's impossible," Beaufort agreed. "But unless we've walked into a convention of monster hunters, the odds are very slim, Mortimer. And what would you rather do – just leave Gilbert to it? Anything could have happened!"

Mortimer groaned. *Of course* he didn't want to just leave Gilbert to it, especially as *it* appeared to be a lonely village, empty of Folk and magic. But he was still having nightmares about that journalist Katherine the Terrible trapping him on Miriam's doorstep, even though Beaufort assured him they didn't actually count as monster hunters, any more than the television people whose show had come to a muddy end in the Toot Hansell duck pond. Mortimer wasn't sure why not, though. Because they hadn't tried to behead him and steal his scales, perhaps? He was quite certain that a journalist's camera was every bit as dangerous as a sword, but there was no convincing the High Lord of that.

"Fine," he said. "*Fine.* But can't we at least wait until dark? It seems very silly to be wandering about the place when there's so many people around."

"I think we shall just be very careful," Beaufort said. "No one's looking for us. They're just out enjoying a nice day in the country is all."

It was impossible to argue with the old dragon. And, after all, he was right. Even with all these humans, no one would actually be looking for dragons. But he still opened his mouth to protest, then froze as a couple appeared between the trees, heading upstream away from the farm.

"This wasn't the next sector," the man said. He was clutching a map and a compass, and from what Mortimer could see, the map was upside down.

"We don't *have* to go sector by sector," the woman replied. "Besides, there's so many people in the main woods. We'll have a better chance finding signs out here."

"It's not very efficient, though. I had it all worked out."

"Half of cryptid hunting is instinct."

"And how many cryptids have you found so far?"

The woman muttered something Mortimer couldn't quite catch, and took a small flask from her coat. She had a swig and put it away again before saying, "I shouldn't have even told you about the sighting. This was meant to be fun."

"It's more fun to do things properly. Besides, I was coming anyway. I saw the article too, you know."

"So what're you going to do when we spot the Yorkshire Beast? Ask it to state its taxonomic classification?"

The man scowled. "Well, it'd be a start."

They vanished in the direction of the waterfall, and after a moment Beaufort said, "Would a dragon be classed as a Beast?"

"Maybe," Mortimer whispered.

"And do you suppose this is some sort of Beast festival?"

"Maybe," Mortimer repeated, suddenly aware of how many cameras he could see.

"Oh dear," the High Lord said, and Mortimer just stared at the milling walkers with his chest tightening more and more on each breath.

Monster hunters.

6

DI ADAMS

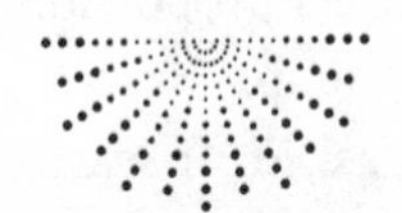

DI Adams stared at Dandy, and the invisible dog stared back. "This is new," she said.

"What is?" Collins asked. The approach to Eldmere from Skipton was a rambling descent from high fells rendered fluffy with heather and populated by Highland cattle with heavy shoulders and curved horns, down into gentler, greener lands scattered with farmhouses and bright gardens and chattering brooks. It had been a slow drive, hampered by creeping caravans and pottering tourist drivers as well as the more usual tractors jouncing between fields, but they'd left the last hamlet behind five minutes ago, and had spotted Eldmere ahead of them, caught in the folds of the land. DI Adams had just been reluctantly thinking how unrelentingly beautiful the whole area was when Dandy had given a howl that had sounded very much as if he were being torn limb from limb. She'd pulled over fast, and now she leaned between the seats, staring at him.

"Did you hear him?" she asked Collins.

"I heard something." He held his arm up and showed her the raised goosebumps. "Or I *felt* it, I suppose? It wasn't like hearing, exactly. It was ... deeper, maybe?"

"He does have that effect."

"Is he alright?"

"He's small." He was. Dandy's preferred size tended to be around Labrador proportions, if much more shaggy and vaguely dirty looking (DI Adams lived with a sneaking concern that he stank, and therefore *she* stank, as Dandy had little regard for personal space, but so far no one had commented. And she had asked Collins). Now, though, the dog looking back at her was terrier-sized at best, and his hair had apparently not shrunk in direct proportion. He looked like nothing so much as the head of a string mop.

"Is small bad?" Collins asked. "I wasn't a huge fan of the angry, horse-sized version."

"He seems worried."

"What does that look like?"

DI Adams reached through the seats to scratch Dandy between his floppy ears. "Very small and kind of whiny." Dandy whined to illustrate her point, then grabbed her hand in his teeth when she tried to pull away. "Ow. Also needy."

"So what does that mean?"

"No idea." She checked the road behind them, waited for a small green VW to pass, then popped the car into reverse and backed up. She kept her speed low, and right at the point Dandy had howled he gave a sudden huff of delight and swelled up to his usual size. She stopped and blinked. She'd never *seen* him change size before, and somehow she still hadn't, even though she'd been looking right at him. It was as if her brain simply refused to accept she'd seen anything. "Huh," she said.

"Huh?" Collins said. "More specific for those of us who can't see the magic dog, please."

"He's popped back to usual size."

"Oh. That's odd."

"I know." She hesitated, then put the car back into gear. "Dandy, I'm really sorry. But we've got to go in."

He whined and shifted position almost as if bracing himself for an attack, and she drove on toward Eldmere.

This time there was no howl, just a whimper that made her heart squeeze. "Sorry," she whispered again, and looked back at the diminutive form of the dandy.

"Did it happen again?" Collins asked, as they continued toward the village.

"Yeah. He's tiny."

"That doesn't seem good."

"No," she agreed. "It doesn't."

THE COOPERS' farm was out of Eldmere on a side road, and they crept their way through the busy streets of the village at not much better than walking pace, stopping to allow groups of people in khaki shorts and hiking boots to stagger across the road in front of them, laden down with cameras and packs. Beasts were evidently very good for business. Somewhere was doing a brisk trade in ice cream, and the pubs were already spilling customers onto the pavements.

Just beyond a terraced row of neat grey houses they turned left onto an old stone bridge with waist-high sides. It was only wide enough for one car at a time, and they had to wait for three men in Lycra to wobble over it on bikes before they crossed. The road plunged them into unexpected forest, cool and green after the open fields on the other side of the village. The stone walls continued, holding back the trees, and as the road rose steadily the wooded slope fell away to the river on their right, and opened onto drives leading to a smattering of old houses in well-established gardens on their left. Further on, the high land to their left grew steeper and rougher, and the woods to the right thickened to something primal and full of promise, before stopping with the same abruptness with which they'd started at the river, cut off from the fields beyond by a stone wall.

"There it is," Collins said, pointing at a drive heading down the slope to the left, separated from the trees by one luminously green field peopled by the cartoonish forms of half a dozen llamas. "Aw. Look at them!"

"They spit," DI Adams said, pulling into the driveway.

"Your dog drools."

"Not with intent."

They rumbled slowly down the unsealed track toward the buildings huddled at the end, the river visible as a bright and chattering waterway not far beyond the farmyard. The drive had been laid with fresh gravel not long ago, filling any ruts and potholes, and as they approached the farm, DI Adams could see why. A little further upriver a field of relatively flat land was full of the bright mushrooms of tents and the curved silhouettes of camper vans and caravans, many of them sprouting striped awnings. There were a couple of buildings in one corner of the field with small windows and solar panels on the roofs that she assumed must be the toilet and kitchen blocks, or whatever else was laid on there. They were of an odd construction, featuring smooth dirt-coloured walls, and there seemed to be a lot of stuff lying around that one could call *reclaimed* or *ready for the tip*, depending on one's point of view. It was busy here too, people in multipocketed shorts and camouflage print T-shirts wandering about showing each other things on their cameras, or poking at tablets, or talking enthusiastically into phones mounted on selfie sticks.

"Whole bloody place looks like a festival," she remarked to Collins.

"Nice, isn't it?"

"What?" She gave him a startled look.

"I like a good festival, me. Though I'm getting a bit old for tents. Glamping's more my style these days."

DI Adams pushed away the image of Collins in shorts and sandals, likely with a hanky on his head, bopping around to trance music. "Nice until someone has to clean it up," she said, and parked between a nondescript BMW and a well-used silver Isuzu pickup truck with a cage on the back.

She climbed out of the car and stretched, then took her jacket from the backseat. There were streaks of Dandy slobber on it, and she showed it to Collins. "Can you see that?"

"Yes. Told you he drooled."

"Dammit. Why can't his slobber be invisible, too?" She looked down at Dandy. "He's still tiny. Maybe there really is a Beast."

"How useful, to have a magic dog that shrinks in the face of danger," Collins said. "I bet a llama wouldn't."

"It might say something about their intelligence, there." DI Adams put her jacket back in the car – it was too hot for it anyway – and turned to survey the farm. "Shall we see if he's home?"

"May as well." Collins led the way across the yard, his hands in his pockets and his bare arms already reddening in the sun.

There was a sign next to the door that said *Please ring bell. If no answer, give us a call!* There were two mobile numbers underneath, and an old-fashioned bell with a clanger attached to the wall. Collins grabbed the clanger and gave it a good rattle, the bell dinging cheerily and scattering rust on his hands. He brushed them off and looked at a chicken that had emerged from under the pickup at the sound of the bell.

"Hello," he said to it.

"Don't talk to the chickens," DI Adams said. "We're still police, you know."

"Yes, but I'm working on the assumption that it pays to be polite to everything these days."

They waited, but no one came to answer the bell. The chicken marched over to them and looked up at Collins intensely, then pecked his shoes.

He moved away a little, and said, "Call them?"

"Shall we have a look around first?"

"Seems reasonable." He headed off across the packed dirt of the yard, the chicken following him and sweat dampening his shirt where it drew tight across his shoulders. DI Adams followed, looking around for Dandy. He'd recovered enough to head off on his own investigations, apparently.

The outbuildings surrounding the house were a mix of old and very old, with the exception of a detached garage next to the house. That looked fairly new and well-insulated, and a large, carefully hand-painted sign above the door declared it to be the home of *Eldmere Llama Treks.* Someone had taped a printed sheet of paper to the door that read, *The Monster House! See the evidence for yourself!* It was locked, and no one answered when DI Adams knocked. She checked the windows on the side, but there were blinds to keep out the curious.

Other than the Monster House, there was a sprawling, custom-built shed of brick and rotting iron with vast rolling doors across the front, one wooden shack with a collapsing roof, and a couple of older, more solid grey stone buildings, their roofs tiled in patchy slate. The largest had wooden double doors to the front and a few small windows pocked around it. A nearly matching sign to the llama treks one hung above the doors and declared the barn to be *Cooper's Petting Zoo*, and a second set of doors on the side of the building was pinned open into a fenced area, where a solitary donkey stood in the sun, eyes half-closed. From inside came the muted grunt of pigs, and the chatter of more chickens. No one appeared when Collins shouted, although the welcome chicken stayed with them.

"Strange," DI Adams said. "Considering he's got a missing wife and about three different businesses going on here, you'd think he might stick around."

"Try the campsite?" Collins suggested. "Maybe he's checking someone in."

"May as well."

The river was down a gentle slope from the farm buildings, and a track, rougher and more rutted than the drive, led to a ford that crossed it. A second track, patchily gravelled but with the worst of the bumps graded out, wound from the farm around to the campsite. There were a number of people in walking gear picking along the banks of the river, eyes on the ground, and just beyond the barn, on ground worn bare of grass by tractors and trailers and feet, they spotted a small shelter made of old blue tarps and paint-splattered scaffolding, and the sort of straps people use on trailers and roof racks.

"That looks interesting," Collins said. He didn't seem to be alone in that assessment – there were a few clusters of people hanging around it, with a mix of intent and impatience that suggested they were waiting for someone to help them. The two inspectors, still followed by the chicken, went to join them.

There was a printed sheet of paper taped to the tarp. *No entrance without authorisation!* it said. *Viewings on the hour.* DI Adams looked at her watch. It was five past one.

"I *know,*" a lanky woman in one of those hats with the flaps that protect the wearer's neck said. "He's late."

"Who?" DI Adams asked.

"Cooper." The woman waved at the farm. "I tried the phone number, and even checked the Monster House, but it's locked. Who knows where he is!"

"What goes on in the Monster House, exactly?" Collins asked.

"It's where he keeps the hair from the Beast. He's got a tablet with the CCTV footage, too, and some other bits and bobs. It's meant to open just after here, but he's late."

"And it's not even like it's his property!" a man in swimming shorts said, and the woman nodded vigorously.

"The farm?" Collins asked, his eyebrows raised.

"No, the *evidence,*" the man said, waving at the shelter. "This is proof of the Beast! No one owns that!"

"Well, it is on his property," Collins said. "You need permission from landowners to view anything on their property."

"Some things transcend the letter of the law," the woman said.

"Not so much," Collins said.

"Spoken like a tool of the establishment," a man in a tie-dyed tunic said, and Collins sighed.

"What's meant to be in here?" DI Adams asked, tapping the blue tarp.

"Paw prints," a young woman with sunburnt arms and purple hair said. "The original ones, from the first night."

"Right. Have you seen them?"

"No – I've seen last night's ones, though. None of them are as good as the first lot, but it's still so obviously a barghest!"

DI Adams wondered if she should be more worried about a mysterious, potentially people-stealing barghest, or Toot Hansell dragons gone rogue. But it wouldn't be dragons, surely. They weren't that silly.

Were they?

❧

DI Adams was just considering whether she could justify pulling one side of the tarp up as a necessary part of police procedure when Collins nudged her.

"What?"

"Someone's up there."

"Where?"

"I just saw them head into one of the sheds, sneaky-like."

DI Adams shaded her eyes with one hand as she examined the constellation of outbuildings, ignoring the woman insisting that the Beast was a wild animal and therefore the property of the people, not some money-grubbing farmer. Collins nodded attentively, but most of his attention was on DI Adams as she tipped her head toward the farm. He nodded slightly, and she hurried up the gentle slope, the sun heavy on her shoulders.

The yard was empty at first glance, the donkey still in his spot, although he'd been joined by a goat who was looking about in a dissatisfied manner. Then there was some eager clucking from inside the barn, and she stepped to the big doors, boots quiet on the soft dirt. A low voice inside said something, the tones vaguely soothing, and she pushed the door open.

"Mr Cooper? DI Adams, North Yorkshire Police—" She broke off as the occupant of the barn gave a yelp of fright, and what seemed like an excessive amount of chickens, four geese, and what she vaguely recognised as a scraggly turkey turned to glare at her. One of the geese blared a warning and charged. She gave her own yelp, slamming the door as the goose bore down on her, and she heard the thunder of its wings on the other side as it attacked the wood.

"Mr Cooper! Please restrain your … birds." She closed her eyes and shook her head slightly.

"He's not here," someone called from inside. It was a male voice, but a little young and wavery.

"Who are you?" she asked the door.

"I work here."

"Can you restrain the birds, please?"

There was no reply to that, and she glared at the door until a familiar voice behind her said, "I did not realise birds were such a threat to law and order."

DI Adams wondered, if she opened the door and jumped aside fast enough, the goose would run out and attack Ervin Giles instead of her. She turned to look at him, and he grinned at her, his hands in the pockets of his jeans and his dark hair messy and flattened by the heat. He was wearing a T-shirt with what she supposed was Bigfoot on it, the text below the picture reading *Social Distancing Since Forever.*

"What are you doing here?" she asked him.

"Covering the Beast phenomenon, then I heard there was a missing persons report. Absolute chaos, isn't it?" He looked around. "Where's Dandy?"

Of all people to share her invisible dog with, it had to be a journalist. And worse, this specific journalist. "He's around," she said, then found herself saying in a low voice, "I don't think he likes it here. He *shrank.*"

"Really?" Ervin looked around the yard curiously. "Maybe there really is a Beast."

"Maybe." She turned back to the door. "Hello? Can you come out—*Bollocks!*" Because there was a sudden, furious *honk,* and the goose came thundering around the corner of the barn, neck extended, and behind it came three others, all blaring their displeasure at having their day interrupted.

Ervin gave a squawk of fright, and DI Adams hauled the barn door open and swung inside, slamming the door so fast behind her that the journalist was only halfway through.

"Hey!" he yelped, squeezing the rest of the way in and pushing the door to.

"Be quicker," she said, looking around the barn. "Hey! You!" It was hard to see much in the shadowy interior after the bright yard outside, but there was someone in the corner, hurriedly covering a crate on the back of a quad bike. "I told you to restrain those birds!"

"Sorry," he mumbled, and as she crossed the barn to confront him, her eyes adjusting, she saw he was only a teenager. He shot her a quick look, then started tucking straps over the crate.

"What's your name?" she asked him.

"Ash."

"Ash …?"

He looked bewildered for a moment, then said, "Oh. Robinson."

"And what're you doing here?"

"Work."

"What sort of work?"

He pointed to the chickens, padding around the floor pecking at seeds. "Feeding them."

She examined him. He still wasn't looking at her, just fiddling with a bead bracelet on his skinny wrist, his skin very pale against his black T-shirt and black jeans. His hair was dark enough that she wondered if it was dyed, and the whole effect was that he seemed to be a face and a couple of arms floating in the shadows. "Is Mr Cooper about?" she asked him.

"The house."

"I rang the bell."

Ash shrugged, and she sighed.

"What about those prints, then?" Ervin said. "You found any others yet?"

The boy shrugged again. "Some."

"Pretty cool. Who found the first lot?"

He stole a quick look at Ervin. "Jake. Mr Cooper."

"What d'you think they are?"

"Dunno."

DI Adams walked back to the door, intending to check if the geese had left the area, and now she heard raised voices drifting into the yard. Ervin turned to say something to her and she raised her hand, easing the door open slightly so she could peer out.

A tall, pale man with his shirt sleeves rolled precisely up his forearms stood in the middle of the yard, looking impassively at a shorter man in tatty jeans and a flat cap jammed down over his red hair. He was wearing a grey T-shirt that proclaimed, *Cooper's Farm, Home of the Yorkshire Beast!*

"I'm trying to help you, Jake," the tall man said, his voice level.

"Oh, sure you are. Just like you were *trying to help* when you had the whole campsite shut down over that rubbish about using stolen materials?"

"There was a complaint."

"There's *always* a complaint! But they're never real. And now Hetty's *missing,* but you're just here trying to tell me to shut my business down again!" The red-haired man, presumably Jake Cooper, jabbed a finger at the other. "Get off my property."

"We both know Hetty isn't missing. It's all—"

"Get off my property!" Cooper took a step forward, and DI Adams pushed the barn doors open.

"DI Adams, North Yorkshire Police," she started, as both men turned toward her. "What's— oh *bloody hell!"* She tried to jump back into the barn as the geese reappeared from where they'd apparently been lurking with intent just out of sight, but Ervin was right behind her and she just bumped into him.

"It's alright!" Cooper said. "They won't—" Presumably he'd been about to say *hurt you,* which DI Adams didn't much believe, but at that moment Dandy streaked across the farmyard, a diminutive ball of red-eyed fury. He growled, and the geese spun toward him, which at least distracted them from DI Adams, but also attracted the attention of three lean working dogs that had been prowling about behind Cooper. One yelped and bolted for the house, and another dived behind Cooper's legs. The third stood its ground for a moment, teeth bared, then dived at DI Adams and Ervin. She sidestepped it neatly as it shot into the barn, but Ervin somehow fell over it, tumbling to the ground with the sort of language that was probably considered setting a bad example for teenagers.

"What the hell?" Cooper demanded, then glared at Ervin. "What did you do to me dog?"

"Nothing! It just attacked me!"

"Serves you right, sneaking around! What're you doing in that barn? That's not for the public!"

DI Adams looked at Dandy. He was panting hard, as if the run had taken a lot out of him, and watching the geese wearily as they hissed and stomped across the yard, posturing like a group of men retreating from a Friday night fight while insisting it wasn't because they couldn't win it, but just because a cop had turned up. Dandy glanced at her, his red eyes dull in the sunlight, and her heart squeezed a little. But Ervin and Cooper were still arguing next to her.

"I was interviewing Ash in there," Ervin insisted.

"As if! He doesn't say enough to interview! You were snooping!"

"I'm the press – don't you want the publicity?"

"Aye, the *right* sort. And I dunno about you!"

The tall man was watching them expressionlessly, his shoulders very straight, and DI Adams unconsciously straightened her own posture as she said, "*Enough.*" Ervin opened his mouth to argue, and she held a hand up to stop him, talking to Cooper instead. "DI Adams, North Yorkshire Police."

Cooper pointed at Ervin. "Arrest him for trespassing."

"Arrest *him* for unsafe dog ownership," Ervin countered. "And unsafe bird ownership, for that matter."

"Is this how you get interviews?" she asked him. "It doesn't seem like a great approach." He subsided, brushing dust from his jeans, and she looked at Cooper. "You do need to keep your livestock under better control, though."

"You were snooping around my property!"

"You called us, remember? Plus you have a campground on site, among other things. You can't have unsafe animals about."

"You shouldn't be snooping," Cooper said, a little uncertainly.

"No, we shouldn't," she agreed, and Ervin gave her an irritated look. "I rang the bell. No one answered."

There was a moment's silence, then Cooper said, "Right. Sorry about the geese."

"That's alright," Ervin said.

"Not *you*. Her."

"Oh, *fine.*"

DI Adams shook her head and looked at the tall man. "And who are you?"

He gave her a vaguely surprised look, as if astonished she were addressing him. "DCI Nathaniel Sykes," he said.

DI Adams almost said something deeply unprofessional, and before she could think of something more suitable to say instead the dogs set up a sudden barrage of barking, and tore off across the farmyard toward the river. She shaded her eyes as she stared after them and very nearly said something much worse, because standing not far from a gate that led into the woods were three members of the Toot Hansell Women's Institute. They were facing down two unfortunately familiar cryptid journalists, looking very much as if they thought they were in a rather more floral version of high noon in a Western.

That sort of thing called for unprofessional language, really.

7
MIRIAM

The woods really did feel terribly *quiet,* despite the chatter of birds and the whisper of a very light wind high up in the branches. There were also quite a lot of non-bird whistles and distinctly human shouting going on beyond the wall, suggesting that the owners of most of the cars in the village were in among the trees somewhere. So it shouldn't have felt quiet, but it did. A different sort of quiet to one that was heard, though. It was the quiet of empty schools and crumbled hamlets. A quiet of *absence.*

"What on earth are they all up to?" Rose asked. She kept trying to peer over the wall, but it was a high affair where it met the road, and Miriam doubted she was able to see much. Not that Miriam could, either, even though she was at least able to see over the top and into the crowded aisles of trees beyond. The woods really were beautifully thick and wild. They reminded her of the tangled forest near Toot Hansell, where the paths ran down to threads and the trees swallowed footsteps, reminding one that some things had persisted longer than memory, and would persist long after one had gone.

"Monster hunting, I imagine," Alice said.

"But what do they think they're going to accomplish, running about like that?" Rose demanded. "They need a *plan.* All they're doing is scaring anything out there into hiding."

"I don't think there is anything out there," Miriam said.

"There certainly isn't going to be at the rate they're going." Rose jogged ahead a few metres as they came up to a small gate in the wall. It was wide enough to permit a wheelchair or a stroller to pass through, and the path beyond it was gravel but smooth enough for all but the most unsteady of walkers. A wooden signpost pointed along the path, with *Eld River* on it, and on the square post beneath the sign someone had cable-tied a rather hastily assembled placard consisting of a sheet of cardboard with printouts inside plastic folder sleeves stapled to it.

Cooper's Farm – the Monstrous Heart of Yorkshire! the printouts proclaimed, and promised camping, homemade scones, and, in the largest text of all, *Proof monsters exist!* There were drawings of capering creatures with horns, fluffy hair, and a varied number of eyes all around the cardboard border.

"They're very well done," Miriam said, pointing at the monsters.

"Maybe, but it's not very precise, is it?" Rose said. "You can't just say *monsters.* You've got to be more specific."

"Do you?" Alice asked.

"Well, yes. It's an entirely different group chasing primitive hominids as are chasing leftover dinosaurs."

"I suppose they were just going for the widest audience possible," Miriam said. "And at least it's not dragons."

"And why would that be any worse?" a new voice inquired, with a faint tone of amusement.

Miriam turned from her critique of the sign to discover a woman in immaculate white capri trousers and a very fetching straw hat looking at them with interest. She had a shopping bag slung over one shoulder, and her trainers were as spotless as her trousers.

"The dragon theorists are the weirdest of the cryptid hunters," Rose said, without hesitating. "Mad as a box of flying frogs, the lot of them."

"As opposed to those looking for ... did you say early hominids and dinosaurs?"

"It's all relative. At least those actually existed at some point."

Miriam looked at Rose with something like wonder. It was as if she'd never once had to argue Walter out of her pear tree.

The woman shifted her bag to the other arm. "So what are *you* hunting for?"

"A picnic spot, mostly," Alice said.

"Speak for yourself," Rose said. "I want to laugh at some amateur monster hunters."

"As opposed to professional ones?" the woman asked.

"They're no fun – as soon as money gets involved, they'll superglue a couple of horns to a hawk's skull and call it a qilin."

"A what?"

"Exactly. Not even the right part of the world."

"I see." The woman sounded more amused than mystified. "You know it's all nonsense, of course."

"It could hardly be anything else," Alice replied, smiling. "But it's a lovely day for an outing, and, as you can see, Rose does know her way around the cryptid field."

"So you *are* an enthusiast."

"An enthusiastic debunker," Rose said. "The world's full of wonderful things, and science is basically magic anyway. I don't know why people need to make things up."

"Exactly," Miriam said, feeling like she should probably add something. "Just look at a sunrise!" The other women looked at her expectantly, and she stared back at them. "It's like magic," she explained, her cheeks hot, and her hat slipped down over her nose again.

There was a pause, and Miriam was painfully aware that her sleeveless top was sticking to her in the heat. Then the woman said, "Quite. Well, there's a rather nice picnic spot at the bottom of the path, by the river, so you're going the right way." She stepped past them, grabbed the cardboard sign, and ripped it off the signpost. Alice and Rose exchanged a glance, and Miriam tipped her head back, trying to see out from under her hat. The woman ignored them, folding the cardboard until she could shove it into her shopping bag – there was more folded card in there already – then took out a multitool and opened the blade, using it to slice through the cable ties.

"Your sign, is it?" Alice asked, her voice mild.

"Of course not." The woman straightened up, folding her multitool and popping it back into her bag. "But it shouldn't be up without authorisation, and all this monster nonsense is just creating *such* a fuss."

"It seems to be bringing a lot of visitors," Alice said. "That must be good for the village."

The woman sniffed. "Not all visitors are created equal. Most of them aren't even paying for parking, let alone spending money anywhere. Just running about making a nuisance of themselves. And this"—she shook her bag—"the monster village of Yorkshire? *Honestly.* It's disgraceful. It's going to turn us into a laughingstock."

Miriam thought the pubs had looked like they were doing a rather good trade, and no one would laugh much at that, but she decided to stay quiet. She set her bags down instead and adjusted her hat. The woman's cheeks had gone a little pink, and she took a breath, glancing off into the woods, then looked back at them with a smile.

"I don't mean *you,* of course. You ladies look as though you understand how to respect a village and its way of life."

"We try," Alice said.

"Quite." The woman adjusted her blouse minutely. "I apologise. You're on your way for a picnic, and here I've waylaid you to natter on about village politics!" She laughed, and it was such a light, infectious sound that Miriam found herself smiling back.

"It's quite alright," Alice said. "It must be very upsetting, all the fuss."

"It is. Cars parking anywhere they like, as if the whole village is some public car park, and just *ruining* the verges. People sticking their cameras everywhere, walking wherever they fancy – and some of them are so *rude.* One of my friends had some strange man poking around her garden yesterday afternoon. When she confronted him, he said he was looking for pixies. *Pixies!* In her *garden!*"

"Oh, he wouldn't want to find them," Miriam said, without thinking. "I hear they're quite unpleasant, really. Best just to put some milk out and hope they leave you alone."

The woman stared at her, and Rose burst out laughing. "Don't mind Miriam," she said. "I'm not sure she even believes in half the things she says she does."

"I do," Miriam protested. "I mean, I believe enough that I put milk out. It doesn't *hurt.*"

Alice smiled and said to the woman, "We're from Toot Hansell. We had a problem with these cryptid journalist types hanging around too, so we do understand."

"They *ruined* the pond," Miriam said. "But then the geese attacked them, which seemed fair." She didn't add that the geese, while undeniably belligerent, probably wouldn't have actually attacked the stars of a ghost hunting TV show if they hadn't been goaded into doing so by a certain sprite who lived in Toot Hansell's waterways and objected to her pond being invaded. The woman in front of them was not the sort of person who'd appreciate that detail.

"We could do with some attack geese around here," the woman said, and smiled at them. "My name's Delphine Harlow. I'm the chair of the local W.I."

"Of course," Alice said offering her hand to shake. "I thought you looked somewhat familiar. Alice Martin, chair of the Toot Hansell W.I. I think we met at the North Yorkshire conference a few years ago. This is Professor Rose Howard and Miriam Ellis."

"Oh, delighted," Delphine said, shaking hands with each of them in turn, then nodded at Angelus without moving toward him. "And who's this handsome creature?"

"Angelus," Rose said, trying not to let the Great Dane get close enough to slobber on Delphine. Miriam didn't even want to think what sort of a mess he could make of those trousers and trainers. Delphine didn't seem inclined to pet him, anyway, no matter how handsome she might have thought him.

"How lovely. I'm sorry, I'm on my way to chat to Mr Cooper right now, but perhaps you'd like to pop by the village hall for tea this afternoon? We've got a little stall there, in the hopes that we can at least make a little money for the village while all the fuss is going on. And it's always lovely to meet fellow W.I. members."

"That sounds wonderful," Alice said. "We'll be sure to do that."

"Excellent." Delphine clapped her hands in a gesture that was part delight, part business-like, and smiled at them all. "Now I'll stop delaying you. Have a wonderful picnic!" And with that she turned and strode off up the road, her cardboard-stuffed bag swinging at her side.

The ladies watched her go, then Alice said, "Come on. Let's go and see what all the fuss is about."

The path was shadowed and, despite the lack of wind down among the trees, cool after the full sun of the village and the steady climb up the hill. It meandered through the trees, heading steadily downward and lit with shafts of luminous light coming through the branches. They didn't pass many people on the path itself, but through the trees Miriam caught glimpses of women in hiking trousers and men in hats with buttons and flaps peering through the undergrowth with binoculars or talking into their phones or snapping photos of the trees and shrubs. They mostly ignored the women, although Miriam heard one sniff and mutter "*amateurs*" as he strode past them with a tripod in one hand and an energy drink in the other.

"They all seem very serious," she said.

"Oh, they are," Rose replied. "I don't know a single other field that takes itself so seriously. They have to, see, because everyone else thinks it's all a joke."

"I'm glad Toot Hansell never got this bad," Miriam said. "Can you imagine? It's been bad enough with the handful we've had poking around!"

"We've been very lucky," Alice agreed. "The timing of this couldn't have been better. I think I might've done something regrettable to the next journalist I saw, otherwise."

"I *did,*" Miriam said. "Or I thought I did. They were lurking at my back door, and I threw the leftover tea and leaves straight out the window and all over them. But it turned out it was a delivery driver, and he was just trying to find somewhere safe to leave a package."

Rose and Alice burst out laughing, and Miriam shrugged. "Well, he should have knocked louder!"

"Quite right," Rose said, still laughing, then yelped as Angelus suddenly lunged forward, tearing his leash out of her hand. *"Angelus!* Angelus, heel! *Angelus!"*

The Great Dane ignored her entirely, galloping down the hill with his long legs going everywhere, heading for the river that was emerging through the trees.

"Dammit," Rose said, and ran after him. Miriam looked at Alice, who hadn't picked up her pace at all. She was just watching the trees and the people drifting through them, her lips pursed slightly.

"Should we help?" Miriam asked, really meaning should *she* help, as Alice's dodgy hip, as well as it had healed, rather precluded running after large dogs.

"I'm sure Rose will have more luck with Angelus than we will," Alice said, still looking around thoughtfully. "It's all most odd, isn't it?"

"The monster situation?"

"Yes. Delphine is *very* down on the idea of monster hunters in her village, yet they really are bringing in money. Even if it's mostly going to the pubs – well, we wouldn't begrudge that in Toot Hansell, would we?"

"Well, no. But we were worried ... *oh."*

"Exactly," Alice said, and smiled at Miriam. "I think it's at least a little possible that our Delphine might be hiding something."

"But ... other dragons? Surely Beaufort would have mentioned them!"

"There are far more creatures than dragons," Alice said. "We know that better than anyone."

"I suppose so," Miriam said, and looked around at the soft green shades of the woods, cut through with golden light. "But then why does it feel so *empty?"*

❧

THE PATH SNAKED down to a half-size gate at the bottom of the hill, made of the same sturdy, weathered wood as the one at the top, and the heat that had been making itself scarce under the trees pounced on them as they emerged into a flood of bright sun. The river was a broad, shallow stream up here, full of rock piles and fluffy green islands just big enough for a couple of ducks to nest on, and it tumbled clear and lively between grassy banks. On this side a huge old willow tree squatted by a rough ford that linked two stretches of farm track, and there was a jumble of buildings a little higher up the hill. Further along the river a multicoloured collection of tents and camper vans flourished like some sort of particularly virulent fungus. There were people sitting in folding chairs outside their tents, and others paddling in the stream with nets and serious expressions, as if they thought they might catch themselves a sprite.

And Angelus was thundering along the riverbank, legs flying. Half a dozen sheep stampeded ahead of him, bleating in panic, and someone was shouting from the direction of the campsite.

"Angelus, no!" Rose shouted, sprinting desperately behind him. "Someone grab him!"

Miriam bolted through the gate without thinking, running to intercept the dog, and more shouts went up along the river. She ignored them, dodged two sheep, and flung herself at Angelus as he barrelled past, eyes rolling and legs flying. She managed to grab him around the chest with one arm and hook her other hand into his harness before he pulled her off her feet and they both tumbled to the ground together. Sheep swerved around them, still running, and Miriam just hoped she hadn't landed in anything too unpleasant. It didn't smell like it, but that'd be just her luck.

"Miriam! Miriam, are you alright?" Rose shouted, and Miriam didn't answer. She was feeling a little winded to be honest, and now there were more people shouting, too, and Angelus was whining unhappily.

"Oh, do be quiet," she told him. "You silly creature." She sat up, still with a solid grip on his harness, and looked up as a handful of people ran up to them.

A man with a large beard knelt down next to her and said gravely, "Don't move. You may have a spinal injury."

"I'm quite sure I don't," she said.

"I'm medically trained," he insisted. "You need to lie still."

Rose made a rude noise as she jogged up to join them. "She's *fine.* You're fine, aren't you, Miriam?"

"I think so," she said, but the man talked over her.

"I'm *medically trained!* Give her some space!"

"I'd rather just get up," Miriam said, and handed Rose the leash.

"You should listen to him," a young woman in leggings and a crop top said. "At your age, falling like that?" She shook her head, making little concerned noises.

"I'm not any age!" Miriam exclaimed, and slapped the man's hands away. "Get off me!"

"She's not making sense," the woman said, looking at the other people who had joined them. "Did you hear her? *Not any age.* I think she hit her head."

"I'll hit *someone's* head," Miriam said, and scrambled to her feet before the bearded man could touch her. "Get away, all of you!"

"She's perfectly fine," Alice said, joining them.

"Yes, shouldn't underestimate this lot," another woman said, the voice horribly familiar. Miriam squinted at her. For a moment she couldn't place her, one of those confused things like seeing your dentist in the supermarket. But then the woman added, "They're bloody deadly with garden implements," and she spotted the man behind her with a camera cradled in his hands.

"You!" Miriam blurted. "Katherine! And ..." she waved at the man.

"Lloyd," he said helpfully.

"Ms Ellis, isn't it?" Katherine said, and grinned. "And, of course, Ms Martin and Professor Howard. How ... *interesting* to find you here, at the site of yet another monster sighting. You do seem to make a habit of it."

"Well, you're here too," Miriam snapped, swiping at the grass stains on her leggings. "Isn't *that* interesting?"

Katherine snorted. "Well, it is my job, Ms Ellis. What reason do you have? Still running your cover-ups, are you?"

"Simple curiosity, Ms Llewelyn. Same as you," Alice said. "And we *were* intending to have a picnic, but I think we'll leave you to it. The whole place seems rather overrun." Her tone suggested that she'd finish that sentence by adding *with riffraff*, if she wasn't making an effort to be polite.

"Maybe we'll join you," Katherine said. "Things seem to just *happen* around you, don't they? Maybe we'll get a dragon popping out of the bushes any minute now."

"Dragons?" the bearded man said, and Miriam jumped. He was very close behind her.

"What are you *doing?* Leave me alone!"

"I'm just here in case you fall. I'll catch you." He gave her what she supposed was meant to be a reassuring smile, then added, "I'd right like to see a dragon."

A murmur of agreement went through the group, and Rose burst out laughing. "You're all bonkers," she said. *"Dragons."*

"I know what I saw," Katherine snapped. "What *we* saw, right, Lloyd?"

"Um."

"Lloyd!"

"I mean, it was really a lot like an iguana—"

"In *Yorkshire?"*

"Evidently you can't even agree among yourselves," Alice said. "I have such faith in your reporting abilities."

"And haven't you ever heard of private collections?" Miriam demanded, moving further away from the bearded man. "Creatures escape!"

"Oh, that is such—" Katherine started, and Miriam shouted over her.

"Will you stop touching me!" She'd dropped both shopping bags when she'd thrown herself at Angelus, and now she snatched up the

nearest – the one with pink flamingos on it – and swung it at the bearded man, a little harder than intended. He yelped as it connected with his hip, giving a satisfying *thunk* that she had an idea might be the thermos of tea.

"*Ow!* What the *hell?* I was trying to help!"

"You weren't listening," Alice said.

"Told you," Katherine said. "Danger to themselves and others."

"*Oi!*" Rose bellowed, jamming both hands onto her hips. "You can take that sort of language and shove it—"

"You can bloody well talk, you little—"

"Angelus, sic 'em!" Rose yelled, and Angelus gave her a puzzled look. It did send everyone scrambling a few steps back, though, and she cackled with delight. "That got you."

"Bloody menace!" the bearded man shouted at Miriam.

"That was assault," the woman in the crop top said.

"I'm not going anywhere," Katherine said, folding her arms. "Where you go, dragons go. I *know* it. You're mixed up in whatever's happening here!"

"We're being harassed," Alice said. "*That's* what's happening here."

"Freedom of the press," Katherine said. "We're not harassing anyone. I've got every right to follow my story, and I *will* find out what you're up to."

They glared at each other, and Miriam was just wondering if she could take a swing at Katherine with her bag and pretend she was still trying to hit the bearded man when three dogs came streaking toward them, low and fast to the ground. They were growling rather than barking, and Angelus gave an alarmed yelp and surged away from them, pulling Rose to the ground. She cried out as she fell, and the bearded man rushed forward, then jumped back again as the dogs streaked between them all.

"Angelus, *run!*" Rose shouted, letting go of the leash, and he took off toward the river, the dogs in pursuit. Rose scrambled up to give chase just as the first of the dogs tried to stop so suddenly that it lost its footing. The other two swerved around it, but a moment later they spun away from what looked to Miriam like an entirely empty patch of plain green grass, and all three of them went sprinting back across the field, whining.

"Oh no," she whispered, because she could think of only one invisible thing that might make dogs react like that, and she was suddenly sure she *was* going to be arrested for assault by thermos.

Or for something, anyway.

8
ALICE

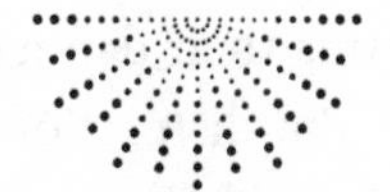

Alice offered Rose a hand to help her up, even as the bearded man took a step toward them. "I wouldn't," she said, and the man gave Miriam a wary look. Miriam glared back at him.

"Are you alright, Rose?" Alice asked.

Rose started to reply but was interrupted by a shout from the direction of the farm.

"Hey!"

They turned to see a red-faced man in a flat cap striding over the grass, the three somewhat cowed-looking border collies slinking after him. Following them were the familiar figures of DI Adams and Colin, as well as a tall man she didn't recognise.

"Interesting," she murmured.

"What the hell are you playing at?" the farmer demanded as he hurried up to them. He pointed at Angelus, who had stopped in the middle of the river. "That bloody dog should be *shot!*"

"I'm sorry, I'm sorry!" Rose said. "He's my dog. I didn't see there were sheep by the tents. I was letting him have a swim. And he wasn't actually chasing them. He was just zooming."

"Zooming?" The farmer turned on her, folding his arms over his chest. "What the hell's that when it's at home, then?"

"He was excited. It's the river. He always gets excited in the water. But look, he's perfectly calm now."

The farmer looked from her to Angelus, still scowling. "I'll be suing you for any damages," he started, and a new voice interrupted him.

"Everything alright here?" the tall man asked. He had soft pale hair and smooth pale skin, and his hands were loose at his sides. "Your dogs causing trouble again, Jake?"

"*No*. Bloody hell – if people would just stop wandering about where they shouldn't, or letting their damn dogs off leashes—"

Rose took advantage of the distraction to run for the river, and Alice frowned at Lloyd, who had his camera raised. She wasn't sure if it was one of those ones that allowed video as well as photos, but he wasn't moving much.

"That's rather inappropriate," she said.

"Freedom of the press," Katherine said again, grinning. "We're not missing a thing you do."

Alice raised an eyebrow. "Invasion of privacy."

"Public space."

"I don't believe it is, actually."

"What's happening here?" the tall man asked.

"Katherine Llewelyn, *Cryptids Today,*" Katherine said, offering him a card, and he looked at it as if it might be infectious.

"*Cryptids Today?*"

"Leading cryptozoology publication in the UK, if not the world."

"Ah," he said, and looked at Alice. "And you are?"

She opened her mouth to answer, and Katherine said, "This lot were part of our story on the Toot Hansell dragons. I reckon they're up to old tricks here."

"You're hoaxers?" the tall man asked Alice.

"Absolutely not," Alice said. "Alice Martin. And we're nothing at *all* to do with these so-called journalists. But who might you be?"

"Terribly sorry." He fished in his pocket and took out a case, slipping a card out of it to offer to her. "DCI Nathaniel Sykes."

"They're not hoaxers," Katherine interjected, holding her hand out for a card, which the DCI gave her with every evidence of reluctance. "They're legit. They are up to something, though."

"Oh? Should I ask what you're doing here?" he asked Alice.

"Having a picnic. Purely a coincidence that this whole monster thing is going on."

"Coincidence my elbow," DI Adams muttered.

The DCI gave her a startled look, but Alice just said, "Lovely to see you, DI Adams."

"You know each other?" the DCI asked.

"And that lot," DI Adams said, indicating Katherine and Lloyd. "They got right in the middle of my investigation a couple of months ago."

"You were *covering up*—" Katherine started, and a shout interrupted her.

"These are so fake," someone called. "What did you use, pound shop monster boots?"

Everyone turned to look, and Alice saw Ervin, the young journalist, just dropping a blue tarp into place on some sort of shelter, watched eagerly by half a dozen monster hunters.

"*Oi!*" the farmer shouted. "You can't just poke around like that! That's my property! What is *wrong* with you?"

"I ask myself that so often," DI Adams said, apparently to herself.

"Oh, you *would* say that," Katherine yelled at Ervin. "You're blatantly working with the cryptid knitting club here. I bet you're trying to get all the stories for yourself!"

A murmur of aggrieved protest went through the crowd, and Alice realised they'd been joined by more of the monster hunters from the river. A man in a long-sleeved orange shirt said, "I quite fancy the sound of that club."

Ervin jogged toward them. "I don't even *write* about this made-up rubbish—" he started, then stopped as the murmur got a little louder. "Well, I don't. I'm a proper journalist. And I'm just saying, they're a bit bloody perfect, aren't they? When does anyone see perfect footprints like that?"

"It was muddy," Katherine said. "And the detail! You can't fake that."

"Rubbish. We're in a drought. And there's like two footprints, then nothing. What happened? Did your monster evaporate?"

"You just don't want to see the truth. You're such a sell-out."

"Yes. That's exactly why I can see that these are *fake*, rather than making up a story to suit my readers."

"They're not bloody *fake*," the farmer said, his face even redder than it had been. "I'll have my bloody dogs on you if you keep this up!"

"Again?" Ervin asked, and Alice wondered what they'd missed.

"Stop," DCI Sykes said, his voice even but firm, and the farmer scowled at him. "Take your dogs back to the house, Jake."

"This is *my* farm—"

"That you are trying to build a business on, correct?"

The farmer opened his mouth to answer, and at that moment someone shouted, "If *he's* had a look without paying, we all get to, right?"

They turned to see a couple of the monster hunters pulling enthusiastically at the strapping on the prints enclosure, and the farmer swore. He ran back up the slope with his wellies thudding dully on the dried earth, yelling, "Leave it! Bloody leave it alone, you vultures!"

"So, picnic," Katherine said to Alice, smiling. She actually had a very pleasant smile, but she was wearing sunglasses, and Alice could only see her own reflection, which was frowning slightly. "What's today's menu, then? Dragon rolls?"

"That's *horrible,*" Miriam said. "What an awful thing to say!"

"It is a bit off," Lloyd agreed, and Katherine glared at him.

"I mean rolls dragons could *eat.* Not ..." She shook her head. "It doesn't matter."

"It does," a blonde woman with close-cropped hair said. "How are we meant to welcome magic into our lives if you're threatening to eat it?"

"I'm *not.* I was talking about *feeding* dragons."

"Well, they wouldn't eat rolls, would they?" a skinny man said.

"They're not going to have evolved to eat gluten any more than we have."

"Oh, come off it, Clive," another man said. "You're not actually gluten-intolerant, you know. *Anyone* would've been sick if they ate six baguettes in one sitting."

"*Six?*" the blonde woman said. "Dude."

"French baguettes are quite small," Clive protested.

"Not really," the woman said.

"They are. They're *skinny.*"

"I still reckon it was the entire round of Camembert that really did you in," his companion added. "And it hasn't stopped you eating that, has it?"

"*Oi!*" the farmer shouted from the enclosure. "If any of you lot want to see foot— *Paw* prints, get a move on! I'll be opening the Monster House next, too."

There was an immediate rush of movement, the monster hunters abandoning the ladies, surging up from the river and the campsite. Rose was just coming back with Angelus, and he gave a yelp of alarm, trying to pull away from her again.

"Angelus!" Rose shouted, somehow managing to keep her feet.

DCI Sykes grabbed the back of the dog's harness and pushed him into a seated position. "He needs more training," he said.

"It's the excitement," Rose said, and Alice wondered if it was something else, considering the way the dog was straining away from DI Adams, and the way DI Adams was staring at the ground in an irritated manner.

"I imagine," the DCI said, then looked at Alice. "Toot Hansell?"

"Yes."

"Yes. A word, I think." He looked around. "There'll be a little more shade by the river." He looked down at Angelus. "Less sheep, too."

"Us?" Miriam squeaked.

"Yes," DCI Sykes said, and turned to lead the way to the tree.

Miriam looked at Alice. "What's happening?" she whispered.

"Something he's going to regret," DI Adams said before Alice could reply. "But I'll try and save us all the hassle." She broke into a jog to catch up with the tall chief inspector. "Sir? A word, please."

DI ADAMS and DCI Sykes were talking just out of earshot, the DCI with his hands clasped behind his back and his head bowed slightly, the inspector standing very straight. They both looked very calm, although Alice could see the faintest frown touching the corners of DCI Sykes' lips.

"What do you think he wants?" Miriam asked, almost whispering.

"Nothing, Aunty Miriam," Colin said. "I'm sure Adams has it all under control."

"But why would he want to talk to *us?* We don't even live here!"

"Because you're known associates of dragons," Katherine said, and Alice frowned at her. The journalists were lingering close by, Lloyd with his camera up and Katherine aiming a phone at them, the fluffy bulb of a microphone protruding from the top.

"Such nonsense," Alice said. "I wouldn't be surprised if *you* were behind all this. Making up monsters to sell your little paper."

"We don't have to make anything up," Katherine said. "We just have to stick close to you."

"That's gone terribly well for you in Toot Hansell so far."

"Out," DI Adams said to the journalists, rejoining them. DCI Sykes lingered behind her.

"Public land," Katherine said.

"You're a public nuisance," she said. "I can arrest you for that."

Katherine scowled and lowered the phone, retreating toward the farm and taking Lloyd with her.

"Now," DI Adams said, and pointed to each of the women in turn, giving their names to the DCI. Her words were short and clipped. "DCI Sykes would like to ask a couple of questions, as he's concerned about this whole Beast thing. Shall we find a bit of shade?"

Alice looked at the DCI thoughtfully. "Why would you have questions for us? We're merely here on a day out."

"It seems a curious coincidence, to choose Eldmere for your day out when there's a fuss about a Beast. Given your own issues with such things in Toot Hansell, I mean. I do keep an eye on the local papers."

Alice examined the tall officer curiously, and he returned her scrutiny with just as much interest.

"Shade," DI Adams said firmly, and led the way to where the willow hung over the bank of the river, creating an oasis of dappled calm beneath it. There were a couple of picnic tables made of untreated wood nestled in the shade, and Miriam promptly dropped her bags on one, kicked her shoes off, and pulled a Tupperware out.

"Lemon slice?" she asked, and offered it to the DCI.

He looked down at her, and at the Tupperware, then said, "Lemon slice?"

"Yes. It's got coconut in. You're not allergic, are you?"

"I … no?"

Alice looked at DI Adams and saw her pressing her fingers to the corner of her mouth.

"The DCI probably doesn't want a lemon slice, Aunty Miriam," Colin said.

"They're very nice," Miriam said, still holding the container out. She gave it a little shake, as if tempting a dog. "Organic lemons. I don't know if they taste better, but because I use the zest I think organic's probably best, isn't it?"

"Yes?" the DCI offered.

"Rubbish," Rose said from the river. She'd taken her shoes off too, and was standing calf-deep in the clear water, the legs of her trousers soaked right up to above her knees. "Organic produce still uses pesticides."

Miriam frowned at her. "Well, I *washed* them."

"I'm just saying – no difference, really."

"They looked prettier," Miriam protested.

"Even after you zested them?" Rose asked, then padded over to them with Angelus' leash unrolling behind her. She took a slice out of the container, and grinned at Miriam.

"I buy organic," the DCI said.

"He would," Colin said, just loudly enough for Alice to hear him, and DI Adams snorted, then coughed over it.

The DCI took a lemon slice, since Miriam was still holding the container out to him, and looked at it dubiously. Miriam offered the inspectors the Tupperware. They both took one, Colin openly grinning and DI Adams trying not to look at anyone.

"If you want to know more about cryptids I can help," Rose said to the DCI. "I've got some contacts. But this whole Beast thing seems very dubious, if you ask me. There's no history in the area. So I'd say—"

The DCI held a hand up, interrupting her. "Professor Howard, I appreciate your input. However, I am not interested in Beasts. I deal with people. People are always behind everything. But I would like to know more about what happened in Toot Hansell. Who might have connections both here and there. Who might benefit from stirring up stories about mythical creatures."

Miriam gave a sudden squeak, and Alice shot her a glance. She had sat down on the grass, and was looking at her empty hand.

"Ms Ellis?" the DCI asked. "Are you alright?"

"What? Yes! Yes, of course!" she said, and wiped her hand on her skirt, giving DI Adams an alarmed look. The inspector was scowling rather fiercely at the ground.

"Do you believe in mythical animals, Ms Ellis?" the DCI asked.

"Of course," Miriam started, then swallowed. "Not. Of course not. How silly!" She laughed, somewhat raggedly, and grabbed a lemon slice, taking a hurried bite.

"No? You were referred to in one article as the village psychic."

"Was I? Well. That's different, though."

"Is it?"

"Yes! I mean, it's just a job. And it's not to do with creatures. It's just feelings and such like. It's not as if I go around hunting for brownies or something. I make brownies if I want brownies." She laughed again, shooting Alice a panicked look, then quickly put the rest of the slice in her mouth. She'd gone very pink, and Alice was sure her hair had somehow become even wilder.

"What are you suggesting, DCI Sykes?" Alice asked. "That Miriam's inventing magical creatures to drum up business?" She gave him a small, amused smile.

"Being mentioned in a cryptid newspaper as being the resident psychic in a hotspot village can't hurt," he said, smiling back. "I imagine such a publication reaches just the right demographic, too."

"That's not true!" Miriam exclaimed, around her mouthful of lemon slice. "None of my clients would *ever* read such drivel!"

"I read it," Rose said. "Mostly to debunk it, of course, but I do read it."

"Yes. Handy," the DCI said. "You would certainly know how best to fake such things. How to reach the ears of the cryptid community."

Alice folded both hands over the top of the walking stick. "One would almost think you were suggesting we're behind all this," she said. "And I should rather like to know why a Detective Chief Inspector is so interested in a little fuss over some fake footprints."

"And I should like to know why three ladies of the Toot Hansell Women's Institute, who have appeared repeatedly in articles written both by cryptid journalists and regular ones, would be here in the middle of yet another ... upheaval."

DI Adams made a small noise that sounded very much like another snort, and Alice said, "It's not a large part of the world, DCI Sykes. And we are retired ladies—"

"Semi-retired," Rose said.

"Self-employed, really," Miriam said.

Alice sighed. "We are ladies with a certain amount of leisure time and wide fields of interest. Of course we're going to look into such happenings so close to home, especially as our own village has suffered rather badly from the attentions of *Cryptids Today*. It rather makes one want to ensure it doesn't happen to anyone else."

DCI Sykes looked at her for a long moment, then turned abruptly to DI Adams. "You've had dealing with these ladies before, I understand."

"I have."

"And?"

DI Adams returned the DCI's gaze steadily. "It's very believable to me that they're here out of curiosity."

Colin snorted rather more loudly than DI Adams had earlier, and scratched his chin.

DI Adams glanced at him, then continued. "I also know they were very disturbed to have the cryptid journalists poking around Toot Hansell, so I find it unlikely they'd be involved in them in any way."

"*Hmm*. Collins? You had something to say?"

"No sir. I agree with Adams."

The DCI looked from one inspector to the other carefully, then turned that pale gaze on the ladies. Miriam squirmed, clutching her Tupperware a little closer. Rose was watching Angelus. And Alice just lifted her chin slightly, returning the DCI's stare. Finally he looked down at the lemon slice in his hand, then took a bite.

"Very good," he said, nodding to Miriam.

"It was the organic lemons," she said, a little faintly.

"Undoubtedly." The DCI nodded to them all, then looked at Alice again. "There's nothing you'd like to tell me?"

"Not at all," she said, smiling. "We're simply here on a day out."

He nodded slowly, then popped the rest of the lemon slice into his mouth. "In that case, please do enjoy your day out, ladies." He looked at DI Adams. "Perhaps we could continue our conversation?"

"Wonderful," she said, and they walked toward the farmhouse together, DI Adams with her hands in her pockets and her shoulders tight. The little group under the trees was silent for a moment, then Miriam let out a sigh of relief.

"That was awful!"

"That was curious," Alice said, still watching the DCI and DI Adams. He was saying something to her, and she was nodding, unsmiling. "Why would he be so interested in this?"

"*Everyone* seems very interested in this," Colin said, and took another lemon square from Miriam. "You really do have to stop turning up at every disturbance in a twenty-mile radius, Aunty Miriam."

"It's not by choice," she protested. "It's all the fault of those journalists!"

"Yes," Alice said. "We're going to need to do something about them."

"No," Colin said.

"Well. *Officially* no," Rose said. "Plausible deniability and all that."

"*No,*" Colin said again, a little more loudly.

"Quite," Alice said, and smiled. Colin frowned at her and started to say something, then Miriam gave a strangled little squeak.

"Ugh, is it that Dandy again?" Colin asked. "Adams said he's been acting weird—"

"He's *tiny,*" Ervin said. He'd rejoined them after hovering at the edge of the shade while the DCI was there. "No idea what that's about. But he's in the river."

"Miriam?" Alice asked. Miriam hadn't paid any attention whatsoever to Colin and Ervin, and was instead just staring over the river with a lemon slice halfway to her mouth. "Miriam!"

"Oh! Sorry!" Miriam said, somewhat indistinctly, and looked around as if afraid to be overheard. She swallowed hard and said, "Um – I don't want to point, but can anyone see anything on the corner of that wall over the river? About halfway up the hill, under the oak tree."

Colin walked to the edge of the river, peering up the slope, and Ervin shaded his eyes to follow his gaze.

"*No!*" Miriam yelped. "Don't look as though you're looking!"

"Oh. Right," Colin said, and retreated to sit on the grass next to his aunt. "Under the oak tree, you said?"

"Yes."

Ervin had kicked his shoes off and was rolling his jeans up. "Might have a paddle," he said, then swore and plunged into the water with one leg still unrolled, and snatched something unseen out of a knee-deep pool. It scattered water all over his shirt and jeans, and he muttered something as he put it on the bank, all while trying to look like he wasn't actually carrying anything. "I do *not* like the new size," he said, apparently to himself, then looked at Miriam. "I see it, though."

"So do I," Alice said, and raised her hand very carefully. Under the oak tree, what looked *almost* like a section of collapsed stone wall raised ... well, a paw in return. Her heart sank. What on earth were they *doing?*

"Fantastic," Colin said. "Just bloody fantastic. Ervin, I thought you said those prints were fake."

The younger man shrugged. "I lied. Seemed sensible. But I didn't think it'd be *our* dragons stomping about the place."

"It seems most peculiar," Alice said. "And *very* unwise." She checked that Katherine was still occupied – she and Lloyd had drifted back toward the tree, but not close enough to overhear. "We mustn't let anyone see them."

Miriam looked around anxiously. "There're so many monster hunters! How can they not see?"

"I imagine that just because they want to doesn't mean they can," Alice said. "But we know Katherine has seen the dragons before. One of us has to get over there and warn them off."

"How do we do that without attracting attention?" Miriam asked.

"Distraction," Rose said, and scratched Angelus behind the ears. "Angelus and I can run off and say we've had a report of something in the woods toward the village."

"A good thought, but the real problem is the journalists, and they'll be watching us," Alice said. "They'll notice if we split up."

Colin took another lemon slice and got up. "You three head off quietly. Leave the journalists to me."

Alice smiled at him. "Well done, Colin."

"Only because I'm still worried about what you meant by *dealing* with them," he said. "But say you go and tell the dragons to leave. What then? They can't exactly fly out in the daylight."

"A very good point." Alice frowned up the slope. Even though she knew the dragons were there, it was quite hard to make them out against the stone. Their camouflage really was excellent, and even more so for anyone who didn't already know how to see dragons.

"There's a road on the moors, just over the top," Ervin said. "They'd have to get out of the valley, but someone could pick them up there."

"Oh, excellent," Alice said. "Miriam, you get the dragons to the road. It's best if we don't all go anyway. It'll draw less attention. Rose and I will go back into town and fetch the car."

"We won't all fit," Rose said. "It was tight enough with me and Angelus."

"Good point." She looked at Ervin. "You'll need to pick them up."

"What? I've only got a Micra!"

"I've had them both in my Beetle," Miriam said. "And it's a proper one, not a new one."

"Still." Ervin looked dubious. "I heard there was a missing person. I was here for *that* story, not more dragons I can't even write about."

Alice looked at Colin expectantly. He avoided her gaze for a moment, then sighed and said, "*Fine.* I'll get you a story."

Ervin grinned. "Sweet. In that case, I'm at your disposal, ladies."

"Well done," she said, and smiled at Miriam. "Are you alright to go up there?"

"Rather that than deal with monster hunters down here." She held her shoes out. "You'll have to take these, though. I do much better without."

"Of course you do," Alice said.

9
MORTIMER

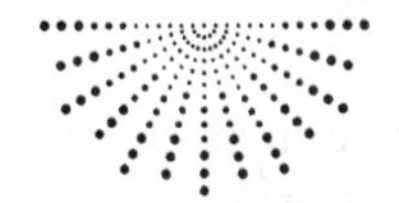

"What're we doing here, Beaufort?" Mortimer asked. "This isn't helping us find Gilbert."

"Shh," the High Lord whispered, and Mortimer curled up on himself as he heard footfalls on one of the seemingly innumerable tracks that carved up the hillside. A track which, as it happened, was far too close for Mortimer's liking. Beaufort maintained that people would assume that this Yorkshire Beast they were looking for wouldn't be anywhere near any paths, which therefore made near a path the safest place to be. Mortimer thought that the Yorkshire Beast sounded rather more clever than they were currently being. At least there was no risk of Beaufort suggesting they move. At this rate they wouldn't be able to move until dark.

"And *I* said," a man's voice drifted through the trees, "I said, well, if you hold with the dragons as pterodactyls theory and Nessie as a plesiosaur, how come there aren't any other living fossils? I'm telling you, they don't have bones like we have. They're all cartilage. Like sharks."

"What about the teeth?" another man asked. "I feel we should've found teeth."

"They don't have them," the first man said firmly. "They just swallow their food whole."

"Okay, Nessie, maybe," a third voice said. "But how could a creature of cartilage manage to live *out* of the water? And fly?"

"They're silicone-based life forms. Like aliens."

"You just said they were cartilage-based."

"*Like* cartilage."

"Alien silicone cartilage?"

"If you like."

There was a rustling noise next to him, and Mortimer opened one eye just enough to see the High Lord shaking softly next to him, his old gold eyes squeezed shut.

"Did you hear that, lad?" the old dragon whispered. "We're aliens now."

Mortimer sighed deeply and thought that seemed alright. Aliens seemed quite sensible about staying away from people, although he wasn't sure about the whole abduction thing. He closed his eyes again. On the other hand, he wouldn't object to *being* abducted right about now.

HIS EYES REMAINED closed ten minutes after the voices had faded away, still discussing the likelihood of all cryptids actually being alien in origin (with one man maintaining that humans were, in fact, the aliens, and one day they'd be taken back to their origin planet where they'd all be dissected as part of an enormous experiment. Mortimer thought that was a rather unpleasant way to view the world). He was quite enjoying keeping his eyes closed. It was peaceful, not spending all his time watching for monster hunters climbing the slopes, and he could concentrate on nothing but the warm smell of rich earth beneath his paws and the whisper of sap moving deep in the veins of the tree above him.

Despite Beaufort's determination to investigate the Beast, the two dragons were still stuck on the opposite side of the river to the farm, where the trees slowly gave way to steeper ground. They had discovered a relatively sheltered spot where the old drystone walls had once merged into a tiny shelter. Both the shelter and the corner of the wall had collapsed long ago, and a large oak tree had filled the gap, along with a rather more recent fence of fat wooden posts and thin wire. The remnants of the shelter made for quite a good hiding spot for two moderately small dragons, especially for one that was having trouble maintaining any colour but anxious grey.

Mortimer had no idea what Beaufort's plan might be. There was no way they could even cross the river until after dark, certainly not here. Further down, past the farm, the woods thickened again, but there was too much open ground between here and there. And if they retreated back toward the waterfall and crossed in the woods there, they would end up with open fields and the overrun campsite between them and the farm. They could, of course, leave the valley entirely, going back the way they had come, but the High Lord wasn't even entertaining the idea, plus there was still Gilbert to think about. So they were stuck. In a way he was rather happy about that. He couldn't see anything good coming from poking around a farm full of monster hunters.

Then Beaufort hissed, "Look!"

Mortimer didn't answer. He didn't *want* to look. Never mind the fact that he'd seen enough monster hunters to last him a lifetime, Beaufort sounded *enthusiastic.* This was not the time for the High Lord's enthusiasm.

"Mortimer, open your eyes."

"I'd rather not."

"No lad, this is wonderful. It's the ladies!"

"Oh no," Mortimer whispered, his eyes still closed. "Oh, that's *not* good."

"Of course it is. And they have bags. I wonder if they've brought a picnic."

"Beaufort, there are *people,*" Mortimer said, trying not to move his lips too much. A squirrel chattered from a nearby tree, and he was quite sure he could actually feel the last of the colour fading from his scales.

"There's no one nearby. Do take a look, lad. They're over the river."

Mortimer reluctantly opened his eyes, at first just enough to check that Beaufort wasn't lying about there being no one around, then properly. Below them the slope fell steeply to the river, a patchily gravelled farm track split in two by it at the ford. Just upriver from the ford was an old willow, its limbs languid and heavy with shade, and beneath it he spotted a small group, all of whom were very clearly looking at the dragons while trying to pretend they weren't looking. Miriam was sitting on the ground with Colin next to her, along with the promised bags, which made Mortimer's belly give a rumble that would've attracted the attention of any roaming monster hunter who heard it. The journalist, whom Mortimer had reluctantly concluded was possibly a reasonable sort, was fishing what looked strangely like a very small dandy out of the river, and Rose had one hand on the back of her monstrous dog.

And finally there was Alice, her silver hair turned gold in the soft light falling through the tree. She raised one hand just slightly, keeping it close to her body, and Beaufort raised a paw in return, just as carefully.

"Oh dear," Mortimer whispered.

Beaufort gave him an amused look. "I don't know what you're worried about, lad. We haven't seen them in a terribly long time. This is lovely."

"It's *not.* How are we meant to even talk to them? There're monster hunters everywhere!"

"I feel quite certain they'll figure it out," Beaufort said, setting himself more comfortably on his belly. "Look, they're up to something already."

They were. Miriam was packing her bags up and trying to give Alice her shoes, for reasons that escaped Mortimer. Ervin was apparently trying to tell Dandy something, but the dandy was just huddled on the bank unmoving, looking like nothing so much as an abandoned, dirty wool hat. There was a moment's more fuss, then Ervin pulled his shoes on and jogged away in the direction of the campsite, leaving Dandy behind, and Colin headed toward—

"Oh *no,*" Mortimer whispered.

"You really need to stop catastrophising," Beaufort said. "Nothing's even happened yet."

"It's *them!* The journalists! Katherine the Terrible!"

Beaufort narrowed his eyes. "Oh, look at that. You're quite right."

"She can see us! She saw *me!*"

"I don't think they're looking," Beaufort said. Colin had confronted them and was pointing back toward the farmhouse, shaking his head gravely, while Katherine the Terrible gesticulated wildly. She was evidently shouting, too, as Mortimer caught the sound of her voice even from here, if not the words. Her companion looked just as unhappy, even if he wasn't being as loud about it. Colin started to herd them away from the river.

"Ooh, here we go," Beaufort said. He really was sounding very enthusiastic, and Mortimer resisted the urge to close his eyes again. Instead he watched as Dandy got up and scuttled – there was no other way to describe it, and for the first time Mortimer felt something like sympathy for the creature – after DI Adams, where she was chatting to an unfamiliar man, apparently oblivious to the activity on the riverbank. Alice, Rose, and Miriam checked on the journalists, who had been herded all the way to the campsite by Colin, then set off for the woods downstream at a relaxed pace.

"Are they leaving?" Mortimer asked. He knew it was very sensible, yet he couldn't help but feel a little disappointed. Especially as he was almost sure those had been picnic bags.

"It would appear that way, lad. But the ladies are very clever. I think it may be a plan."

Mortimer was still trying to decide if that made him feel better or more worried when a little red car went bouncing along the rough track from the campsite, skirted the farmhouse, and headed off up the drive. It pulled right onto the road, heading out of the village, and not long after, a second car bumped up the drive. This one turned left, and

Mortimer saw a man hanging out of the passenger side with a large camera up to his eye.

Colin walked back along the path from the campsite, his hands in his pockets and the sun shining on his short-cropped hair, and joined DI Adams, who was watching the man she'd been talking to heading for his own car. Then they walked up to the farm, vanishing into one of the buildings and leaving only the monster hunters still taking photos of whatever was under the blue tarps, and prowling up and down the river.

The dragons were silent for a while, until eventually Beaufort said, "Well. Perhaps the plan is to pretend they didn't see us?"

"It seems like quite a good plan, when one comes down to it," Mortimer said. "It means they're not drawing attention to us. And they got Katherine the Terrible to leave somehow."

"They really are very clever," Beaufort said, although he sounded a little less convinced than previously.

THERE WAS a small lull in the stream of monster hunters, and Mortimer wondered if they'd taken a break for lunch. The thought of lunch made his stomach rumble again, and he thought longingly of Miriam's picnic bags. Or what he assumed were picnic bags. He supposed he wouldn't know now. He sighed, heavily enough to incinerate a dandelion growing from the rubble, and Beaufort gave him an amused look.

"Bored, lad?"

"No. I just don't like all this hanging around, waiting for a monster hunter to stumble on us."

"They'd have to quite literally do that. I don't think much of the standard of monster hunters these days. I haven't even seen a single lance."

Mortimer looked sideways at the old dragon, wondering if he were joking. Hopefully, but Beaufort was just reclining comfortably amid the crumbled wall, surveying the valley as if it were his own private kingdom.

"I still don't understand why there are no sprites," the High Lord said. "It's a very nice river. Lovely and clean."

"Maybe all the monster hunters splashing about in there have scared them off?"

Beaufort rumbled softly at the back of his throat. "It didn't used to be so easy to scare a sprite." He considered it. "It still isn't, in fact. Think of Nellie!"

Mortimer had to concede that Nellie would likely have called down a whole flock of geese and swans on all the humans poking about in her waterways, and probably set some eels on them for good measure. "There are an awful lot of them, though," he said aloud. "Maybe everyone's just being careful." *Like we should be.*

Beaufort looked at him as if he'd heard the unspoken words, then gave him a toothy grin. "Never mind. We'll get across to check out the farm once it's dark, and make sure Gilbert isn't around. Then we'll be off home for a nice roast rabbit."

Mortimer wished he could be as completely confident that such a pleasant plan would come off as the High Lord seemed to be.

As he was considering how he felt about roast rabbit he glimpsed movement further down the river. He craned his neck, trying to get a better angle, and saw a familiar, robust form wading carefully across the stream, a bag in each hand.

"Is that Miriam?" he asked.

Beaufort followed his gaze, then grinned again. "Told you they had a plan, lad."

Mortimer wasn't quite sure that Miriam splashing barefoot up the bank was exactly a plan, but he had to admit that no one seemed to be paying any attention to her. She'd emerged from the thick woods toward the village and would have been unseen from the farm. He'd lost sight of her himself now, in the folds of rough land. But it wasn't long before she emerged again, padding comfortably along with a straw hat falling over her nose and her bags swinging easily at her side. Every now and then she stopped and looked around, as if enjoying the view, and occasionally she took her phone out and did something with it, as if she were taking photos.

Miriam took her time, but eventually she stopped in front of them, her cheeks and arms pink, and looked up at the oak tree above them appreciatively. "Ooh," she said, rather loudly. "Perfect spot for lunch, I'd say."

The dragons looked at each other. "Are you talking to us?" Beaufort asked quietly.

Miriam gave her head a very small, very urgent shake. "I think I shall picnic right here," she announced, then looked around, her head tipped back so she could see out from under her hat. "*Such* a good picnic spot!"

"There's no one nearby," Beaufort said. "We'd know."

She kept staring about for a moment, then sat down so abruptly that Mortimer thought she'd collapsed. "Are you alright?" she demanded in her usual voice. "What are you *doing* here?"

"Looking for Gilbert," Beaufort said. "What are you doing here?"

"*Gilbert?*" Miriam stared at them. "He's *here?*"

"We don't know," Mortimer said hurriedly. "We were told he might be."

"He's *missing?*" It was hard to know from Miriam's tone if this was worse or not.

"Yes, for about a week now," Beaufort said. He didn't look at Mortimer, but the younger dragon's stomach gave a swoop of shame anyway. A week! Why hadn't he realised sooner?

"Oh dear," Miriam said, and took her hat off to wipe sweat from her face. "Oh *dear.*"

"What's this Beast fuss about, then?" Beaufort asked. "Do you know?"

"Well, we rather hoped it was a hoax," she said. "But it seems there are real paw prints, and Ervin says they're dragonish."

"How does he know?" Mortimer asked. "He can't be sure, can he?"

"He probably can, since he ran around Toot Hansell with us not so long ago," Beaufort said.

"*Ohhh.*" Mortimer squeezed his eyes shut. "Oh *no.* Oh, poor Gilbert!"

"Well, we certainly have to find him," Beaufort said.

"You *can't,*" Miriam said, digging in her bags and bringing out a loaf of bread. "That horrible Katherine—"

"Katherine the Terrible," Mortimer said, eyeing the bread.

"Yes, her and her friend – they're on the hunt. Colin packed them off for now, but they'll be back." She shook her head, staring at the loaf of bread. "And then there's all these monster hunters just running about *everywhere* ... No, you must go."

"We'll go once it's dark," Beaufort said. "We can't fly out now – someone would definitely see us."

Miriam shook her head. "No. We have a plan." She frowned at the loaf. "I've forgotten a knife. I *knew* I'd forget something!"

"I can tear it?" Mortimer offered, and licked his chops quickly. He was drooling.

"Of course," she said, and passed him the loaf, then went back to the bag and took out a large hunk of cheese. She unwrapped it and handed it to him as he tore the bread into thirds. "No, you two have it," she said, when he tried to give a piece back. "I don't think I could even eat. It's all too worrying!"

"It isn't at all," Beaufort said. "We knew you'd have a plan." Then he cocked his head and said, "Quietly now. Someone's coming."

"*What?*" Miriam looked around wildly. "You have to hide!"

"*Shh,*" Beaufort said, and Mortimer flattened himself to the ground, hiding the bread and cheese behind one paw and closing his eyes. He could hear Miriam scuffling with the bags, and over that the sound of approaching boots and the low tones of a heated conversation.

"I'm *telling* you, it's a knucker," a woman said.

"Of that size?" Another woman, her tones a little ragged, as if she were finding the path a little steep and tough.

"You know they expand to fit their environment."

"So that stream is a lot deeper than it looks, you reckon?"

"*No.* Bloody hell. There's a tarn about here, Eldermere? The village takes its name from it. Deep as anything, that one. I looked it up."

"A tarn?" The breathless woman sounded dubious. "They don't get that deep, do they?"

"Eldermere does. Deepest tarn in Yorkshire, if not the country. Sixty-odd metres, and wide as well. Fair few people have vanished in it – bodies never even found. Get a damn big knucker in there easy." She sighed. "I'd love to take a look, but it's on private property, like."

"Well, I suppose it's *possible—*" The voices broke off.

"Afternoon," Miriam said, a little shrilly.

"Alright," the first woman said. "Picnic, is it?"

"Oh, yes. Nice spot, isn't it?"

"Not bad," the woman replied. "You monster hunting?"

"Oh, it's not really my thing." Miriam sounded almost as breathless as the second woman had. "I bet the farmer set it all up."

"It's a theory," the first woman said. "Did a damn good job on those prints, though, don't you think?"

"I haven't seen them," Miriam said.

"Look like big cat prints to me," the second woman said. She took a deep breath and puffed air. "Remember those weird sightings around Leeds? A tiger and a panther, people reckoned. Wonder if it's them?"

"Rubbish," the first woman said. "As if they could live out here and no one notice!"

"Oh, but a knucker can?"

"It's in a *tarn.*" There was a pause, then she added, "Come on, Effie. Cross the river, one more uphill, then it's downhill all the way to the pub."

"Cheeky git," the second woman said, but Mortimer could hear her smile. "First round's on you."

"First round's *always* on me," the other said, and added, "Enjoy your picnic."

"Thanks," Miriam said.

Mortimer listened to the women's boots retreating along the track, leaving behind the trees and the woods and the screeching of the squirrels. He opened his eyes.

Miriam was clutching a little metal cup of tea and nibbling on a lemon slice, looking pink and dishevelled, and otherwise the slope was empty again.

Beaufort peered around, then *hmm*ed. "Knuckers, they think?"

"Knickers?" Miriam asked faintly, passing a Tupperware container to Mortimer. Coconut and lemon scents drifted out of it, like sunshine captured in sugar.

"If one got into a big tarn and grew to fit it, well. They get quite hungry."

"Hungry knickers," Miriam said wonderingly, and Mortimer took two lemon slices then passed the tub to Beaufort.

Beaufort took two, then grinned. "Maybe it's not Gilbert after all, lad. A knucker's a type of water dragon, after all. The paw prints wouldn't be so dissimilar."

"That really would be a relief," Mortimer said, trying to get the coconut out from between his teeth. It was a little ticklish.

"We need to know who it is, though," Beaufort said. "Even if it's not Gilbert, they might need help."

"Well, you can't do it now," Miriam said, reclaiming the Tupperware and packing it back into her bag. "We're walking out of the valley and Ervin's bringing his car to meet us."

"We can't just *leave,*" Beaufort protested. "Something's off here."

"I know," Miriam said. "But if you stay here someone's going to see you. We can get you out, and then we'll come back and look for Gilbert."

"It's not just that, though," Beaufort said. "Do you know, we haven't found any traces of Folk?"

Miriam had stood up, and was settling the bags on her shoulders, but now she stopped. "None at all?"

"No."

"I thought I felt ... something. Or *nothing*, really." They were all silent for a moment longer, then Miriam straightened her back. "But there's nothing we can do when the place is overrun like this. The important thing is making sure no one sees *you.*"

Beaufort grumbled somewhere in the back of his throat, and

looked at Mortimer, who tried to shrug in a way that indicated he shared the High Lord's concerns, but also really didn't want to be Tasered and experimented on by The Government.

Beaufort tapped his claws on the rocks, then finally sighed. "You're right, of course. Our being discovered will help no one. We can regroup and come up with another plan."

"Exactly," Miriam said. "Now come on. Let's get out of here." She turned and started up the rough track where it climbed and switch-backed out of the valley, curling through a mix of grassy swells and the exposed stone bones of the land.

Mortimer took a slow, careful breath and uncurled himself. He hadn't realised how tight his chest had become, but now it felt as if some giant hand were releasing him. Yes. Beaufort was quite right. The ladies *did* come up with the best plans.

10
DI ADAMS

DI Adams was wondering if the north bred particularly tall police officers, or if it was just her misfortune to keep running into them. She was going to get a crick in her neck if she had to deal with DCI Sykes too much.

She was also aware that thinking about how inconveniently tall he was made a good distraction from thinking about the fact that she was quite possibly going to get an earful for not letting him have free rein with the W.I., but it seemed like a reasonable reaction right now. Otherwise she was just going to overthink both what that could lead to and what Dandy might currently be up to, having scared various dogs, stolen a lemon slice, and walked up to her wearing someone's bright pink and orange beanie, which in his current miniature size meant all that was visible was his tail and snout. She'd swiped it off him and left it hooked over the top of a fence post in the hope that it might be reclaimed. The heat was obviously getting to him.

"So, DI Adams. The new detective from London." DCI Sykes had stopped in the middle of the yard, far enough from the paw print enclosure that they wouldn't be overheard, but close enough that they could keep an eye on things. His shirt looked desperately crisp still. Did the man have no sweat glands?

"I suppose," she said. Not that she was exactly *new* anymore. It had been three years since she'd first come up here and encountered Toot Hansell, the Women's Institute, dragons, and other impossibilities.

"We have a different way of doing things up here. Small town policing and all that."

"Yes," she said. "I'm quite aware of that. However, Eldmere is in Craven district, unless I'm mistaken. My Yorkshire geography is a little shaky."

He smiled, just a small curling of his lips, but it crinkled the corners of his eyes and made them slightly less disconcerting. "I somehow doubt that, DI Adams. You strike me as someone who does her research."

"I have been accused of efficiency."

"Horrifying."

"Apparently so." She regarded him steadily. "DCI Taylor told us this was our case, and as it's not actually your district, I have to ask why you're so interested."

"Call it professional curiosity." He thought about it. "And personal connections."

"Personal connections?"

"Yes. My family are from Eldmere, and if anything happens here, I tend to get a call."

"But not from Mr Cooper."

There was no change in his expression, but DI Adams thought she caught the faintest hint of disapproval in his tone. "No. Jake Cooper's from away, so I assume it didn't occur to him."

She nodded. "Well, I understand that you want to look after your village, sir, but Collins and I have this under control."

"Are you sure? I've heard that you two spend a lot of time in Toot Hansell, and here you have half the Toot Hansell W.I. wandering about. Seems odd, don't you think?"

"Craven's not that big an area, sir. And Toot Hansell's not so far from here."

He nodded, looking over at the paw print enclosure, where Cooper was collecting money from the monster hunters. "I just do question where all this came from. And maybe Toot Hansell doesn't mind such things, but this is a quiet village."

"I'm sure it'll all blow over. Right now I'm more interested in a missing woman," DI Adams said. "And I'd quite like to get on with interviewing the farmer rather than watching you question ladies of a certain age over organic lemon slices." As soon as she'd said it she wished she could take the words back. DCI Sykes might not be *her* DCI, but he was still a DCI. But, to her surprise, he laughed. It was a very small laugh, and he looked as startled by it as she was. He coughed.

"Of course. Thank you for indulging me. Would you mind if I sat in on your interview with Cooper?"

"I would, actually. Since you know him."

He nodded again, and handed her a card. "In that case, DI Adams, I shall leave you to get on with things. Efficiently."

"Thanks," she said, tucking the card into her phone case.

"And should you turn up any evidence regarding the Beast hoax, I would appreciate it if you let me know. I can disseminate the relevant information on my own time, just to clear up all the fuss."

Something about that made DI Adams uneasy. She wasn't sure if it was simply the fact of someone casually dropping *disseminate* into conversation with supposedly positive connotations, or the protectiveness over Eldmere. She understood wanting to look after places that mattered, but there were limits. One couldn't just appoint oneself the protector of a village. But she just said, "Of course."

He held out his hand and they shook, his skin smooth and cool against hers. She was uncomfortably aware that her own palms were sweaty with the heat, and that hand cream was something her mum gave her every Christmas but that she never used.

"A pleasure to meet you, DI Adams."

"Ah … likewise," she said, and watched him walk back across the farmyard toward the nondescript BMW, his stride long and his gaze shifting from the river to the woods to the crowded campsite near the drive. It wasn't a gaze that missed much. Only once his car had vanished up the drive toward the road did she turn her attention back to the group by the tree.

She almost immediately wished she hadn't. Not because they were doing anything in particular, but because they weren't there, and that made her sure they were up to something. Again.

She started toward the river, intending to see if she could spot anyone, then stopped as a red Nissan Micra jounced past on the track from the campsite. Ervin was driving, and he raised a hand briefly but didn't stop. She watched him go, frowning, then turned to see another car leaving. She let it pass, Katherine glaring at her out of the driver's side, and looked at a very small and very wet Dandy who had just joined her.

"What's going on?" she asked him quietly, but he only whined. "Yeah, me too," she said.

BY THE TIME Collins ambled up to her, his head pink through his short-cropped hair and his shirt sticking to him in places, Cooper had left the paw prints and led the little crowd to the Monster House, leaving the yard quiet again.

DI Adams gave Collins a wave that was intended to mean *what the hell?*

"You don't seem to be in your happy place, Adams," he said.

"I'm not sure I have one anymore," she said. "Work was my happy place. I like arresting people. It relaxes me. But Yorkshire has entirely ruined it."

"That's harsh. Placing a lot of blame on the white rose there."

"Fine. *Toot Hansell* has ruined it. I'm not sure the W.I. shouldn't be classed as a terrorist organisation."

"Assault by lemon slice?"

"Something like that."

He rocked on his heels gently. "It's a fair point. At least I packed the *Cryptid Today*-ers off. The W.I. were muttering about *dealing with* them just now."

DI Adams had a momentary, horrifying vision of the ladies of the W.I. wrapping Katherine in pork pie pastry and dropping her in a river somewhere. Although she supposed the pastry would dissolve, but knowing the W.I. they'd have some special, slow-dissolving pastry, prepared just for this very occasion. "I still hold out hope that I'll get to arrest them one day."

"Hope springs eternal."

"So what are they up to?"

Collins looked around, then lowered his voice as he said, "The dragons are here."

"*What?*" DI Adams swallowed, aware that she'd almost shouted. "Seriously? This was them?"

"I'm not sure on that account. It seemed unlikely that they'd be so silly after evading notice for however many centuries. But Ervin reckons the paw prints are legit, and it looked like Mortimer and Beaufort over the river."

DI Adams pinched her forehead. "And so what's happening?"

"I told Katherine that we had an open case here and I'd do her for interfering if she didn't clear out for a bit. Ervin's off to pick up the dragons on the other side of the hill, and Aunty Miriam's gone to take them up there."

"Miriam?" DI Adams was having trouble seeing her trekking cross-country.

"Oh, yes. Barefoot all the way." Collins grinned.

"Right. And the other two?"

"Ah. Gone?"

She glared at him. "Gone where?"

"Does it matter? They're dealing with the dragons. They're not in any danger. That leaves us free to do our actual job. Nice, right?"

DI Adams started to argue, then stopped again. It was true. The monster hunters might be a risk to the dragons, but not to the W.I. And if they were keeping the dragons away, *they'd* stay away too. "Huh," she said, and straightened the front of her shirt. "This might not be so bad."

"I wouldn't get used to it."

"Good point," she said with a sigh, then looked down at Dandy. He looked even smaller than before, if that was possible, and appeared to be trying to become one with her leg. He was still very wet, and now so were her trousers. "What's up with you?"

"Nothing," Collins said, then followed her gaze. "Oh, him."

"He's being weird."

"The invisible dog's being weird. Imagine."

"I think he's even smaller than before."

"He'll vanish entirely if this keeps up."

DI Adams shook her head. "Maybe small is cooler in the heat. Come on. Let's see what Cooper's got to say for himself." She headed toward the garage, keeping a wary eye out for the geese while the pint-sized dandy scrambled to stay close to her heels and the sun burned her arms.

The crowd at the Monster House had already thinned out, and as DI Adams and Collins headed for the open doors of the garage they could see a couple of workbenches with boxes set out on them. Jake Cooper was standing next to them holding a tablet, the display turned toward a couple who were peering at it closely.

"It doesn't look like anything," the woman said. She had smears of sunblock on her bare shoulders, but her neck looked red under her bun.

"It really doesn't," the slope-shouldered man next to her said. "Could be anything, that."

Cooper sighed. "I'll rewind it again." He turned the tablet back toward himself, tapping at the screen with a frown on his face. The sunlight from the door turned the red hair that escaped his hat into a beacon.

"Nah, don't bother," the woman said. "Next time at least put some effort into things."

"This is *real,*" Cooper insisted. "It was really hard to capture on CCTV, is all. It made the camera go all a bit glitchy. I reckon it's a defence mechanism, like."

"Sure," the man said. "And you only have two paw prints because, what – it was doing a handstand in your yard?"

"It was the only part of the yard that was wet! A drum busted—"

The woman waved dismissively. "Look, good on you. Fools and their money and all that. But *we* know what we're looking at, don't we, Sid?"

"We run a course," Sid said proudly. "*Cryptids: Sorting Fact from Fiction.*"

"Exactly. And those paw prints? Made by 3D printed boots, I'd say."

"The technique's in our course," Sid said.

Cooper had been staring at them, and now he slammed the tablet down on a workbench so hard that DI Adams feared for the screen. "*Get out!*" he shouted, flinging one hand out toward the door. "*Out!* And you can pack up and take your bloody tent with you, too!"

"We've paid for the weekend," the woman protested.

"And we just got the tent set up nice," Sid agreed.

"If you're not out in twenty minutes I'll put my tractor right through your damn tent," Cooper said, taking a step toward them. His hands were in fists at his sides, and his face was a startling shade of red.

The woman stepped back. "We'll tell *everyone* what a scam this is!"

"Yeah!" Sid said. "And your bloody Monster House is a right rip-off for five quid!"

"It's *free* with the camping," Cooper shouted at them. "How can you complain about *free?*"

"Mr Cooper," DI Adams said. "A word, please."

"Oh, don't waste your time, love," the woman said. "It's a right bloody scam." She turned and headed for the door. "Come on, Sid. Let's pack up and go to the pub. This is an absolute *joke.*" She strode off, Sid following in her wake and looking a little perkier at the mention of the pub.

Cooper took his hat off and wiped his forehead, his shoulders slumping. "Bloody public," he said. "Someone wanted to know if they could race the llamas earlier. As in *ride* them."

"You don't ride llamas?" DI Adams asked.

Cooper put his hat back on and stared at her. "*No.* Of course not!"

"Right. What do you do with them, then?"

"Walk them," he said, in a tone that indicated she was asking silly questions.

"Of course you do." She looked at Collins, who shrugged. "Have you heard anything from your wife, Mr Cooper?"

"No," he said, the anger falling away like a dropped scarf. "Nothing. I'm just … I'm trying to keep busy, like."

"I understand she was *meant* to be missing initially?"

"Ah, yes." He cleared his throat, checking the yard for anyone who might overhear. "It was … the Beast's been good for business, you know?"

"And you thought it might be good for business if people thought the Beast had taken someone?"

He gave an awkward little shrug. "It's exciting, isn't it? And, I mean, she were going to come back in two days with all sorts of stories – she's really good with stories, Hetty – so it wasn't like anyone was getting hurt."

DI Adams *hmm*ed, and picked the tablet up. There was a video frozen on the screen, and she hit play. The picture resolved into the farmyard, rendered in the grey shades of deep night. A chicken wandered through, and a moment later something came jerking across the screen, pixelated and out of focus. It could have been anything – a person, a horse, a glitch in the recording. She handed it to Collins and looked at Cooper.

"So she was meant to come back yesterday?"

"Yes. Early morning." He took his hat off again and rubbed his hair, a nervous, unconscious movement. "I went to pick her up at the hut up by the tarn – it's all private round there, no walkers – but she wasn't there."

"Have you asked family? Friends?"

"Of course." He settled his hat back on his head. "No one's heard from her. The mobiles don't work up there – it's patchy all around the valley – and we didn't leave a car, just in case anyone did get nosey."

"So she had no way of contacting anyone if anything went wrong?" DI Adams asked. "That doesn't sound very safe."

Cooper stared at her for a moment, then went and picked up a small radio unit from a desk in the corner and set it in front of her. "We use these for the llama treks. It's how we keep in touch in case *something goes wrong.*"

DI Adams looked from the radio to the farmer. "So where's hers?"

"That is hers," he said. "It was at the hut. She wasn't. Her things are gone, as well."

There was a pause, and the inspectors exchanged a glance. "How have things been at home?" DI Adams asked. "Any arguments? Disagreements?"

"Nothing," Cooper said firmly. "She were really excited about the Beast, and us getting some more business. One in the eye for some people around here, I tell you!"

"What do you mean by that?" Collins asked, handing the tablet to DI Adams. The video was paused on what looked rather like a tent caught in the act of being blown away. She frowned. She supposed, with a bit of imagination, it might look like a dragon. Imagination, and also a reason for a dragon to be prancing across a farmyard on their hindlegs with their wings out like a ballet dancer.

"We've had some pushback on things," Cooper was saying. "It's a small place. Hetty's dad bought this farm from Gerald Harlow, who had a bit of a problem with the horses and needed the money. Turned out his family had no idea he either had a problem or was intending to sell, and it seems no one's quite forgiven us for being the current farm owners."

"What sort of pushback?" Collins asked.

Cooper rubbed his mouth. "Just obstruction, really. The bloody W.I. protest any planning application we put in, and one of them's always out on the paths checking to see if we've done anything they can report to council. Which we *never,*" he added firmly. "Oh, and the local supply store won't run us an account, and only one of the pubs will even serve us." He shook his head. "Hetty's dad didn't even make it to sixty. Had a heart attack and fell in the damn tarn, and I swear it were the stress. It'll do me at this rate!"

"That sounds like a lot," DI Adams said. "Are you sure Hetty mightn't have wanted a break from it all?"

Cooper snorted. "Not Hetty. She basically forced her mum to keep the farm when her dad died, and took it over as soon as she could pay it off. Her mum's down on the south coast, playing bingo in the sun, and Hetty's never missed a day." He gave them an amused look. "I'd've been happy being a postie. I *was* a postie. But Hetty was going to work herself to death, so here I am."

Collins put his hands in his pockets and rocked on his heels gently, somehow making himself smaller as he said in a quiet voice, "It really can be a lot, this sort of life. Did Hetty ever struggle with her health at all?"

"I don't think she's had even a cold in about five years."

"Mental health?" Collins asked, still in that same quiet, almost confidential tone.

Cooper actually laughed. "I've never met anyone more level than Hetty."

Collins nodded. "Sometimes even those closest might not know. Have you noticed any changes in her behaviour at all? Trouble sleeping? Drinking more than normal, perhaps?"

Cooper recoiled as if Collins had spat at him. "*No*. I mean, no. She were just fine when she left the other day. And we talk, you know? Proper talk. I'd've known."

There was silence in the garage then, until someone said brightly, "Jake, dear? Do you have a moment?"

They all turned toward the voice, startled, and spotted a woman in spotless white three-quarter trousers smiling at them. She was right at the corner of the door, and DI Adams had a sneaking suspicion that she'd been standing just outside for a while without them seeing her. Beyond her, Dandy lay in the dust of the yard with a chicken *buk*-ing at him furiously. His head hung low, and DI Adams wondered if he was sick. Not that she could do much if he was. She didn't fancy turning up to the vet with an invisible dog. She turned her attention back to the new arrival.

"*No,*" Cooper snapped. "I'm talking to the police about Hetty."

"Oh, dear. I am sorry," she said, and lifted a shopping bag. "I brought you a little shepherd's pie. I didn't think you'd be eating properly without her."

Cooper scowled at her. "What, you think she did all the cooking or something?"

"No, dear. I just think it's a trying time, and one mustn't forget to eat."

He nodded and said, in a tone that suggested he already knew, "And what's in the other bag, then?"

The woman just kept smiling as she came inside and set both bags on the desk. "I did tell you that those signs weren't authorised. I told both you *and* Hetty. Such things have consequences."

DI Adams peered at the bags. All she could see was a bunch of torn cardboard and cut cable ties. She looked at Collins and he shrugged. "Excuse me, Ms …?" she trailed off expectantly.

"Miss," the woman said, and offered a slim, well-manicured hand, the nails neatly trimmed and a delicate gold chain on her wrist. "Delphine Harlow, chair of the local W.I."

"The W.I.," DI Adams said, keeping her voice even and ignoring Collins as he gave what sounded very much like a snort.

"Yes, the Woman's Institute, dear." Delphine squeezed her hand and released it. "Maybe you don't have that where you come from."

"Oh, I imagine there's quite a few in London," DI Adams said. "Detective Inspectors Adams and Collins. I was just wondering what you were doing here."

"Looking after our own, of course," Delphine said, and favoured Cooper with another smile. "We do that here."

"More like snooping," Cooper said, and shoved the bags back at her. "I don't want your *pie.* And I've told you before – you're not welcome to just pop by whenever you want."

"It's public land, dear."

"Not here it isn't. Get back on the footpath and do your snooping from there."

Delphine tipped her head to one side and gave him a sorrowful look. "I *am* sorry about Hetty. Her dad, then her. It's terrible. And I don't blame you for being upset. If there's anything at all the W.I. can do, you just let us know." She looked at the two inspectors. "Lovely to meet you, detectives. Do pop by the hall for a tea later. Refreshments for law enforcement are always complimentary."

Cooper waved her off impatiently, and once she was out of earshot, heading toward the river, he looked at the inspectors. "You see? She just walks right on in like her family still owns the place!"

"How annoying," DI Adams said.

"It really is." He ran his hands back through his hair. "Anyway – you'll want to see the hut, right?"

"We will."

"I'll take you up. Just give me a minute – Ash! Bloody hell, there you are."

Ash eased through the door, keeping close to the wall. He glanced at Delphine's retreating form, shrugged eloquently, and picked at the skin around his thumbnail. The welcome chicken followed him in and looked about quizzically.

"Took your time," Cooper said. "You get everyone fed and watered?"

A small nod.

"Good. I need you to close up here and cover the prints. Next viewing's at five until five-fifteen, alright? No exceptions."

Another nod.

"If anyone comes to camp, just show 'em where everything is. I'll sort payment later."

Nod.

"Call me with any questions."

Ash gave a final nod and crept back out into the sun, keeping his head down as he headed toward the prints enclosure, the chicken trailing behind him.

"Right." Cooper looked at the two DIs. "I'll just get the dogs in the truck – you coming with or following me?"

"We'll follow," DI Adams said, and let the farmer hurry off across the yard, the dogs emerging from the shade to join him. There was no sign of Dandy, and she looked at Collins. "Thoughts?"

He shook his head. "A weird one. We'll need to talk to her friends, see if she was telling them anything she wasn't telling him."

"Hut first, then we'll get on it," she said. It sounded practical, and formulaic, and *logical* – like actual police work. She smiled as she unlocked the car.

As long as they ignored the dragons and monster hunters, of course.

11
MIRIAM

Miriam was wondering if not wearing her shoes had been quite the right idea. She had yet to meet a pair of shoes that agreed with her quite as much as bare feet, and always felt a little regretful that she didn't live in the sort of climate that would allow her to go shoeless permanently. However, as they climbed steadily out of the valley the slopes were shrugging out of their coats of grass, exposing rockier, harder terrain beneath, and in places it was becoming difficult to find soft ground. She kept going, though, the sun hot even through her hat and her top sticking to her back with sweat.

She wasn't quite sure when they actually crested the edge of the valley itself. There was no clear ridge to mark it, no sense of abruptly being *out.* But the land opened up before them with a sudden sense of openness, higher peaks visible in the distance, and their slope became more of a plateau, stretching away in shades of green and brown and grey, while the sky pressed tight and blue above them.

"Are you alright, Miriam?" Beaufort asked, as they crossed a little-used farm track, barely more than a suggestion of wheel ruts left under a heavy coating of grass.

"Yes, thanks," she managed, shifting her grip on her bags. She probably should have left them with Alice, but she'd been quite right about the need for a picnic. One should always be prepared for hungry dragons.

"We could follow the track for a bit?" Mortimer suggested. "It'll probably lead to the road anyway."

"It's far too exposed," she said, scrambling up a small bank on the other side and trying not to sound too out of breath. "Someone—*Ooh!*" She'd just sunk ankle-deep into boggy ground, strangely out of place on the dried-out slopes. She peered back at the track, and now she could see water seeping along at the edges of the road. "It is a bit sodden up here, though."

Beaufort joined her, sinking almost to his elbows. With the tussocky grass sprouting all around him, he bore more than a passing resemblance to a lurking alligator. "We can't be too far from the tarn. We should go and take a look."

"We're meant to be meeting Ervin," Miriam reminded him.

"A road likely goes to the tarn," Beaufort said. "And we can at least see if there's traces of a knucker anywhere. If there is, they might know if Gilbert's been around, too."

Miriam looked at Mortimer. He'd scrambled up the bank too, and was staring at one mud-caked forepaw rather distastefully. He wasn't quite as grey as he had been when she'd first spied them, and he'd taken on greens and browns in places, but there was still no sign of his own lovely royal blues and purples. Now he put his paw back down, sinking into the mushy earth, and said, "Those hunters earlier said the tarn was private."

"So?" Beaufort said. "*We* haven't seen any signs, have we?"

Miriam tried to give him a disapproving look, but he was grinning so toothily it was impossible. "Alright," she said. "We do need to know if Gilbert's around, don't we?"

"We certainly do," Beaufort said, and waded off across the boggy ground.

Mortimer looked up at Miriam and said, "I'm not sure if I'm more worried about monster hunters or telling Amelia her brother's still missing."

Miriam considered it as she struggled after Beaufort. "I think I'd be more worried about Amelia," she said finally. "If she thinks anyone's mistreated Gilbert I see razed villages in our future."

Mortimer returned to a more washed-out shade of grey. "That's a very good point," he managed, and picked up his pace.

❧

THE BOGGY PATCH seemed to go on for far longer than was reasonable, in Miriam's mind, and by the time they reached a rambling drystone wall and found a stile to clamber over her legs were slicked with mud up to mid-calf, and her toes were numb. It might be unreasonably hot for a Yorkshire summer, but the water was too deep and too old to be bothered by such things.

The far side of the wall revealed a jumbled, welcomingly grassy slope, all ups and downs and the odd rocky outcropping, and she sat down on a handy boulder to fish the thermos out of her bag. Mortimer sat next to her while Beaufort wandered on a little, his head high as he sniffed at the still air. They hadn't seen anyone since they'd left the valley, but that wasn't to say there wasn't anyone out here. Someone could be in the next dip in the hill and they'd have no idea.

"Tea?" Miriam asked, and offered Mortimer the thermos cap, half-full of tea.

He looked at it dubiously. It looked like an egg cup next to his paws. "No, thanks," he said. "It hardly seems worth it."

"I suppose," Miriam said, and took a sip herself instead. It was still hot but had that mysterious thermos taste everything seems to get, even in stainless steel. She was just digging the lemon slices out when Beaufort padded back to them.

"I've spotted something," he said.

"The tarn?" Miriam asked, offering Mortimer the Tupperware. He took a slice, trying to avoid scattering mud from his paws all over them.

"No." Beaufort's voice was oddly quiet. "Come and take a look."

Miriam looked at the old dragon, seeing deep, angry red tinges to his snout, out of place against the soft camouflaging colours the dragons had been using to blend into the hills, and threw the rest of her tea away, replacing the lid hurriedly and gathering her bags again. "What is it?"

"I'm not entirely sure," Beaufort replied, and led them to a small rise. Miriam could see the edge of the tarn glittering not far away, and a track snaking down to a little stone hut crouching on its shore. Between here and there were more folds and angles of land, old walls prowling here and there along them, patched with the tussocks of bogs and feathered with heather. A kestrel wheeled above them, and pipits flitted and dived in and out of cover. Away to the left somewhere there must be the main road, and she supposed there must be other farms or houses hidden up here somewhere too, but it felt vast and empty and strange, the *absence* she'd sensed in the valley lent weight by the lack of everything else. It made the breath catch in her throat and her chest squeeze.

"Are they *pumpkins?*" Mortimer asked, startling her.

"What?"

"It does look like it," Beaufort said. "But what are they doing just sitting out there?"

Miriam looked around, trying to find where they were looking, and finally spotted a small, windowless stone hut, half-hidden by a growth of luminously yellow-flowered broom and nestled up to a stone wall. It looked fairly solid, the door missing but the slate roof still complete. And outside it stood a neat pile of five or six large, green-tinted pumpkins.

"I can take a guess what they're doing," she said. "I don't think any human would have dragged a bunch of pumpkins up here for fun."

"But where did he get them from?" Mortimer asked. "Has he been raiding gardens? Is that where the paw prints came from?"

"More to the point, why are there so many?" Beaufort said. "Because he can only really carry one or *maybe* two pumpkins."

Miriam shaded her eyes, trying to glimpse movement through the open doorway of the hut, but she couldn't from this distance. It did seem odd, though, that there were so many there. "Shall we have a closer look?" she suggested.

"We shall," Beaufort said. "But do you see the tracks?"

"What tracks?" She looked around, suddenly seized by the idea that there was a giant, hungry knucker about who had stolen Gilbert and was about to steal them too.

"The tyre tracks," he said, and pointed with one paw. She followed his gaze and saw where they'd gouged the softer ground as they made their way up to the hut. The terrain was too rough for even a 4x4, but a quad bike could make it.

"Oh," she said softly. "Is someone *keeping* him there?"

"I think we best find out," Beaufort said, and stalked down the slope with his wings trembling above him. Miriam and Mortimer exchanged a glance and followed. She wasn't quite sure if it might be better for the young dragon if someone *was* keeping him there. She didn't really fancy seeing an angry High Lord.

❧

THE SCRAMBLE DOWN to the hut didn't take long, and a few minutes later they were lurking behind some tussocks, the dragons with their bellies to the ground and Miriam crouching next to them. She'd considered lying down, but the ground felt damp, and she didn't fancy having a soaking wet belly for the rest of the day. There was still no movement from the hut, or in the hills around it.

"I'll go and have a look," she whispered. "You stay here."

"That's no good," Mortimer said. "What if he really is being held against his will? His captor could be there!"

"Only if they walked here," she said, then thought about it. "Or, I suppose, if someone else dropped them off. But they're not going to be sitting in the hut in the dark, are they?"

"Then we'll all go," Beaufort said.

"Someone might see you," Miriam pointed out.

"You just said there probably wasn't anyone there."

"Oh." She wrinkled her nose, thinking. It felt wrong to have the dragons come with her to potentially confront a dragon-napper, but it was true there didn't seem to be anyone around. "Alright," she said. "We'll all go."

She shifted her grip on her bags as she stood up, glad she hadn't drunk much of the tea. The thermos gave the bag a reassuring heft. They crossed the soft ground toward the hut cautiously, skirting the piled pumpkins, which Miriam could see had definitely been nibbled at, but by something small. The top ones were immaculate, though, and the twists of their stems were still green. Whoever had picked them apparently hadn't had any riper ones to choose from.

Beaufort approached the hut, his teeth showing, and stopped to one side of the door, looking at Mortimer. The younger dragon edged a little further away from the hut, trying to stay out of sight – in case whoever was inside got past Beaufort, she supposed. She took a deep breath as Beaufort started to prowl forward, then marched straight past him and stopped in front of the door.

"Hello?" she called, trying to sound like she'd just popped by the abandoned hut to be neighbourly. "Anyone in? I seem to have got myself off the path somewhat."

There was a long, empty pause, in which Miriam could hear the pipits calling to one another, then there was a rush of movement out of the hut, accompanied by a screech. Miriam jumped back, giving her own little screech, then stopped as the movement resolved into a chicken. It ignored Miriam entirely, rushing instead toward Beaufort, but stopping before it got too close. It *buk*-ed warily, tipping its head to one side then spied Mortimer and rushed toward him instead. He started to back up, but the chicken stopped before it reached him.

"*Buk?*" it offered.

"Hello?" he said, and his snout immediately flushed an embarrassed lilac. He glanced from Miriam to Beaufort. "I mean ... I know it can't reply."

"Well," Beaufort said, padding forward to peer into the hut. "Pumpkins, a happy chicken – I don't even need the scents to know Gilbert *has* been here."

"What can you tell from the scents?" Miriam asked. "Was he captured?"

Mortimer joined them at the hut door, and they stared in at the packed dirt floor. In one corner someone had piled up four beanbags, and a couple of large blankets were laid over them. One was lightly singed on the corner.

"If he was, he was quite happy about it," Mortimer said. "Or, no. Not happy, but ..." he hesitated, snuffling quietly at the air. Dragons scent emotion as much as physical scent, and after a moment he said, "He was confused, mostly, I think. It's all muddy greens, rivers after storms, that sort of thing. He wasn't scared, though, was he?" He looked at Beaufort.

"No," Beaufort agreed. "A little sad, maybe, and a little angry, but not scared."

"A little sad, a little angry, and mostly confused," Miriam said. "Oh, poor Gilbert. How awful."

"Well, it's hardly *awful,*" Beaufort said.

Miriam shook her head and looked at the chicken as it pecked her bag. "Of course it is. He left the mount because he argued with Amelia so much that he felt he couldn't be there, and then he was here all on his own with only a chicken for company, wondering what sort of dragon he's going to be. That's very hard for any creature."

Beaufort gave her a startled look. "Wondering what sort of dragon he's going to be? He's a *dragon.*"

"That's like me saying, *I'm a human*. It doesn't mean anything. It's just what shape we are. What matters is who we decide to be, and it's very hard to do that when you don't feel you fit anywhere."

The High Lord considered it, then said, "I've never even thought about that."

"One doesn't, when one has always known how one fits," Miriam said, and set her bags down. The chicken looked up at her hopefully, and she fished out some of the seeds that had fallen off the bread. The chicken clucked in delight and pounced on them.

"So how do we find him?" Mortimer asked, looking around. "Do we wait?"

"We can't," Miriam said. "We have to meet Ervin."

"And Gilbert's not been here for a couple of days," Beaufort said. "Wouldn't you say, lad?"

Mortimer looked around, his snout wrinkled. "I suppose," he said.

"Might he have gone home?" Miriam asked.

"And just left the chicken on her own?" Mortimer asked. "That doesn't seem right."

Beaufort padded up to the pumpkins, then started to scout around. "Give me a hand here, lad. Maybe we can pick something up."

Miriam sat down on a bit of drier ground and fished as many seeds as she could find out of her bag for the chicken, who gobbled them down then settled in the sun next to her. It didn't take the dragons long to regroup and join them. "Anything?" she asked.

"Nothing useful," Beaufort said. "There's scent scattered everywhere."

"Anyone other than Gilbert?"

"Yes, but it's very faint. It must be whoever's been bringing him pumpkins."

"Or whoever took him *away* from the pumpkins," Miriam pointed out, then wished she hadn't. It was an awful thing to have out in the open.

"We don't know anything happened to him," Beaufort said. "Those monster hunters are complete amateurs."

"The ones we've seen," Mortimer said, and there was silence for a moment.

Miriam got up and brushed her skirt off. "We have to go," she said. "I don't have any signal on my phone, and we need to get you out of here."

"You go," Beaufort said. "Mortimer and I will stay and see if whoever's been supplying Gilbert comes back."

"But Gilbert's been gone for a couple of days, you said. Which means anything could've happened since then. No." Miriam shook her head. "Whoever's been bringing him pumpkins probably knows he's gone and isn't coming back, anyway. Let's go home and figure this out."

Beaufort gave a low rumble of frustration. "We *just* missed him."

"I know," Miriam said. "But something very strange is going on here, and I don't think you should be wandering around until we know what it is. It's far too empty here." She shivered, looking suddenly over her shoulder as if half-expecting someone to be sneaking up on her with a cartoon net. "We can't lose any more dragons."

The High Lord looked like he might want to argue, then he sighed. "Alright. Let's go. We can come back tonight and have a good look in the dark."

"Oh, good," Mortimer said. "That sounds *wonderful*."

THEY STRUCK OFF AGAIN, roughly in the direction of the tarn, the chicken *buk*-ing along behind them anxiously. Every time she fell too far behind she'd screech in frustration, and eventually Miriam picked her up and tucked her inside one of the bags, where she clucked happily. Miriam wouldn't have minded someone tucking *her* inside a bag and giving her a lift the rest of the way, if she were honest, but there was no chance of that. So she just padded on, sticking to the grass wherever she could and checking her phone every so often to see if she had a signal. Finally, on a ridge above the tarn, a message dinged in from Ervin.

Where are you?

Going to tarn, she sent back.

Why? I said road.

She *hmph*ed, and put the phone back in her pocket. "Let *him* find his way to the road over all this," she said.

"What's that?" Beaufort asked.

"Nothing."

They emerged at the rocky shore of the tarn about a quarter of the way around its shore from the solid stone hut that the track led to. There was a silver pickup and a smaller black car parked next to it, and when Miriam shaded her eyes and peered across the water at them she was almost sure that it was Colin and DI Adams standing there talking to the red-haired farmer. She almost considered shouting to them, but that seemed quite likely to get her in trouble for something – trespassing, maybe – so she just headed along the shore with the dragons padding on ahead.

By the time they'd made their way around the edge of the tarn to the hut, the DIs and the farmer had both left, grumbling back up the track, and not long after a little red Nissan jounced its way to meet them, Ervin clinging grimly to the wheel. He parked in front of the hut and climbed out.

"Thanks for warning me that the farmer was down here," he said. "I think he'd have shot me for trespassing if Adams hadn't said she'd asked me to take photos of the crime scene."

"Crime scene?" Miriam asked.

"Yeah, apparently the wife was staying here before she vanished," Ervin said, wandering over to try the door of the hut. It was locked, and he peered in the windows instead. "Not much to see."

"Not much to smell, either," Beaufort said. He was standing elbow-deep in the tarn. "It's very deep and very old, and very, very empty."

"No knucker?" Miriam asked.

"Barely a minnow," the High Lord replied and waded out. "It's the same as the village."

"Same how?" Ervin asked, then cocked his head. "Do you hear a car?"

"*Yes,*" Mortimer said. He'd been inspecting the hills warily, and now he sat straight up. "It could be the farmer coming back."

"In the car!" Miriam said. "Quickly!"

Both dragons rushed for the car as Ervin opened the back door and hurriedly threw an old coat across the seats. "*Try* to stay on that, can't you?"

Miriam dug in her bags. "I've got … yes! I've got a picnic blanket still!"

Ervin looked at her blankly. "You carried that all the way out of the valley?"

"Well, one never knows when it might come in handy." She shook it out and flung it over the dragons. "Lie still!"

"That's not going to work," Ervin said. "It's not a bloody invisibility blanket. There's blatantly something very large under it."

"That doesn't matter," she said impatiently. "It could be bags of rubbish."

"Why would I have two dragons' worth of rubbish in my back seat?"

"Well, laundry then. Just as long as the dragons lie still, why would anyone think there's anything important under there?"

"It's very hot," Beaufort said, sounding slightly muffled. "I mean, we *like* hot, but there may be some smouldering issues with the blanket over our heads."

"Oh, good," Ervin said, and shut the door on them. "Let's go. We'll squeeze past on the track rather than wait for anyone to look in the car."

Miriam hurried to the passenger's side and clambered in, popping the bags at her feet as Ervin started the engine and swung the car around, gravel crunching under the wheels.

"Try not to set my car on fire till we're past whoever's coming, alright?" he said, and pulled onto the track.

It was a one-lane affair, hemmed in on one side by a crumbling wall that protected them from the steep slope to the tarn, and on the other by patches of old wall interspersed by stretches of ditches or high banks or simply flat land. Trees started to crowd around them as they climbed, and as they came around a curve they met a Land Rover rumbling the other way. Ervin jammed on the brakes, and the driver of the other vehicle did the same. There was a pause, and Miriam stared at the man in the Land Rover. He stared back, his pale face set in disapproving lines, and she wondered what on earth DCI Sykes was doing up here. He indicated to them to stay where they were, then backed up until he could pull onto a lower part of the bank. He rolled his window down as Ervin edged past.

"What are you doing here?" he asked. "This is private property."

"Taking some photos of the tarn for the detectives," Ervin said.

DCI Sykes frowned, and looked past him at Miriam. "That seems rather unorthodox. And Ms Ellis – you're here too."

"Um, yes. I was …" She trailed off, unable to think of any reason at all she should be there, and painfully aware of the heat of the dragons behind her.

"I needed someone to hold a couple of lights for me," Ervin said.

"Oh! Yes," Miriam said. "I do like helping."

The DCI nodded, still examining them with that disconcerting gaze. "I'm setting some traps. Terrible problem with ferrets around here."

"Is there?" Miriam said faintly.

"Ferrets?" Ervin asked.

"They eat the birds' eggs. There are five endangered waterbirds that nest here, and I volunteer to protect them." He frowned at them. "I hope *you're* here with the approval of the landowner."

"Like I said – special request from DI Adams. I think the lab guy couldn't get here right away or something."

The DCI's frown deepened. "How careless."

"We should go," Miriam said. "Good luck with the ferrets."

"Quite," the DCI said, and Ervin gave him a nod then squeezed past and continued up the track.

Miriam twisted in her seat to check behind them, but the Land Rover was quickly lost in the turns of the land. "That was strange."

"Very," Beaufort said, shaking the blanket off and sitting up. "I've never heard of using a goat to catch ferrets."

"What?" Ervin asked.

"There was a goat in the back," Mortimer said. "I could smell it."

"Huh," Ervin said. "Maybe it's some sort of bird-guarding goat."

"Are there such things?" Miriam asked.

"Emotional support goat?"

"Now you're being silly."

"*Buk.*"

"Is that a *chicken?*" Ervin yelped.

"Well, obviously," Miriam said.

"Right," Ervin said. "The goat seems less strange now."

Miriam petted the chicken, who had climbed onto her knees, and wondered about goats and traps and poor lost dragons. She didn't like the feel of any of it.

12
ALICE

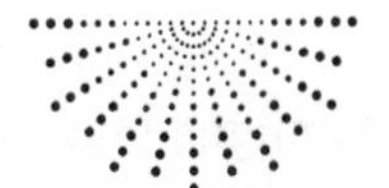

Alice nodded pleasantly at a couple on the way up the hill to the farm as she and Rose let themselves out of the gate and back onto the road. The couple were wearing matching *I Love Nessie* T-shirts, hefty walking boots, and the sort of trousers that zip off into shorts, and they both looked distinctly hot and discomfited.

"I'm telling you, we should have stayed by the river," the woman said. "Everything needs water. It'll come down there eventually."

"With so many people around? Rubbish. I don't think it's even in the valley anymore. We should be looking up on the moors."

Once they were out of earshot Rose said, "She's right, of course. Camping out at the water source is the best way to spot anything."

"There's almost as much water in this place as Toot Hansell," Alice said. "But at least we know the dragons are nowhere near any of it."

"It still doesn't make sense," Rose said. "What on earth are they thinking, hanging around when it's this busy?"

"I'm sure we'll find out," Alice said. "But the important thing is getting them out so that we can prove how *very* mistaken Katherine Llewelyn is, and how clearly she's been staging these hoaxes both here and in Toot Hansell."

Rose grinned. "Do you have a plan?"

"I have the beginning of one. If we're working on the assumption that the paw prints are real but everything else is fake—"

"We are," Rose said.

"Then if we prove the rest is fake, we can certainly argue the prints are. All we need to do is show that Katherine *knew* that, and is working with Cooper to perpetrate the hoax."

"How are we going to show that?"

"That's the bit we need to work on. But you know plenty of people in the field. Any who'd be keen to do some debunking?"

"Probably," Rose said. "It might take some time, though. They'd want to take stuff back and test it, and we'd have to get it off Cooper to do that."

Alice nodded thoughtfully. "And we need this done sooner rather than later, I'd say. I think we shall need a little get together tonight to chat some ideas through."

"Excellent," Rose said, and pulled out her phone, then frowned. "Ugh, the signal around here really is terrible."

"Never mind. We're almost to the village."

It wasn't long before they emerged from the trees and crossed the bridge into Eldmere. The afternoon sun was still high and bright, and the village green was, if anything, even more crowded than when they had left. There were more coolers and bare chests about now, and someone in a dinosaur suit was posing for photos in the shallow water of the river. Two men in bright yellow T-shirts were selling bottles of monster repellent from a couple of cardboard boxes, and a woman stood next to them making huge bubbles with a wand. Alice thought the monster repellent looked a lot like a cheap spray bottle of the sort she used for misting plants, with a home-printed sticker on the side.

The pubs were doing a good trade. The picnic tables outside the one across the road from the green were crammed with people in walking boots and red faces, clutching pints and showing each other cameras or phones. They glimpsed the riverside beer garden behind the other pub as they crossed the bridge, and it was equally crowded, umbrellas sprouting from wooden tables all across the bank.

"It really does seem to be very good for the village," Alice said. "I can't imagine they're ever anywhere near this busy usually."

"Yes, Delphine might be in the minority with her *this is bringing the tone down* thing."

Alice nodded, and wondered if they had maybe been harsh, trying to chase the monster hunters out of Toot Hansell. Maybe they should have thought more about what business it might bring in. But there was a real risk to the dragons, and she couldn't justify that by the deli selling a few extra sandwiches. It did make her wonder again about what other motives Delphine might have, though.

She pointed at the W.I.'s sign as they walked along the edge of the green. "We should pop our heads in. See if we can find anything out."

"If anyone knows anything, it'll be the W.I." Rose petted Angelus' head absently and he looked at her adoringly, his eyes almost level with her chest.

"Exactly," Alice said, and they crossed the road, following the arrow on the sign into a side street that led them up a gentle slope lined by grey stone buildings that quickly gave way to fields. The village hall was a small building sandwiched between the graveyard and a row of five terraced houses that climbed up the hill in neat steps, roses clambering over the front of three of them, another with its door framed by well-trimmed bay trees, and the third looking almost determinedly overgrown and scruffy among its neighbours. The door to the hall was open, and there were flowers in vases at the door, as well as a small, round woman who waved at them cheerily as they approached.

"Tea? Coffee?" she called, while they were still two doors down. "We have some *wonderful* elderflower cordial!"

"I wonder if it's anything like Gert's," Rose said to Alice in a low voice.

"Hopefully not," Alice said. "I'm driving." She smiled at the woman. "Tea would be wonderful."

"Oh, good." She looked at Angelus warily as they stopped outside the hall. "He can't come in, though."

"Aw," Rose said, and rubbed Angelus' ears.

"Shall I bring you something out?" Alice asked.

"No, don't bother." Rose looked back down the road. "I spotted someone I know. Meet you back at the car?"

"Of course," Alice said. "Will you call Gert about tonight? I completely forgot." She smiled at the friendly woman. "I was distracted by afternoon tea."

"More people should be distracted by afternoon tea," the woman said. "Rather than all the other things they keep being distracted by."

Alice couldn't argue with that, and she stepped into the cool of the village hall. The thick stone walls kept the heat of the day out, and the windows were flung open onto the garden, but the sound of birdsong and bees was muted and distant.

Delphine came forward as Alice's eyes were still adjusting to the dimmer light, and she clasped Alice's hands in her own. Alice managed not to pull away, and arranged her face into something she hoped suggested that she was friendly, but not so friendly one should go about just touching her for no reason.

"You came!" Delphine said, smiling. "How wonderful. Ladies, this is Alice Martin, from the Toot Hansell W.I. I told you I ran into her earlier?"

There was some friendly nodding and calls of welcome, and Delphine finally released Alice's hands.

"Can I get you a cup of tea?"

"I'd love one. I hope I'm not too late?"

"No, no. You're very welcome." Delphine looked toward the door. "Where are your friends?"

"Still enjoying the sunshine," Alice said, and followed Delphine to one of a collection of tables corralled by stalls of cake and biscuits and jams and flowers. There was a large, hairy man with a small, sleek dog at one table, the man carefully spreading jam on a scone, and at another a woman was leaning back with a bottle of cold water pressed to her forehead while two small boys scoffed chocolate cake and argued about something that might have been a video game, a TV show, or a new organism, by the name. Alice wasn't particularly up to date with what young people were interested in.

"I'm surprised you're not set up outside," she said to Delphine as they took a seat at a small table by a window, the air warm and heavy with scent as it drifted in.

"Far too hot," Delphine said. "We wanted to create a bit of an oasis from all the disturbance in the village, and it's terribly loud out there."

Alice tipped her head. There was some music bouncing away somewhere, but over it she could hear shouts from the river and a few people cheering, as well as the steady hum of humanity that rises in any busy space. It reminded her of being in school when summer was creeping closer, desperately slowly and full of promise, and being crushed with a curious mix of deep longing to be out and away, and an intense yet unfocused sadness that one was missing out on something wonderful happening just out of sight.

But she wasn't here to sit in the sun, so she took her backpack off and hung it on the chair, then looked around. "Where do I get—"

"Oh no," Delphine interrupted. "Trudy's getting us some tea and scones." She took a seat, straightening her trousers slightly, and a woman with a mane of thick grey hair ferried a teapot and plates over to them.

"Thank you so much," Alice said. "You really needn't fuss so."

"It's no fuss," Delphine said.

"But I can get it myself."

"It's really fine," Trudy said, blinking a little too quickly in the dim light as she set a jar of jam on the table. "Can I get you anything else? Water? More milk?"

"No thank you," Alice said, even though she'd have rather liked a water. She didn't like the feeling of being waited on in a village hall. She wasn't out at a restaurant. Delphine just nodded and checked the teapot.

"Won't be a moment."

"Of course. Has it been busy?" Alice asked.

"Not as much as we'd have liked."

"The pubs seemed busy when we came past."

"It's that sort of demographic," Delphine said, arching her eyebrows. "It's a shame, but what can one do? The sort of people who go out chasing monsters probably aren't that concerned with a nice cup of tea."

"I suppose," Alice said, taking a scone from the plate. She wasn't very hungry, but it wouldn't do to look as if she'd come in just to be nosey. "It can't carry on like this, though, can it?"

"One would hope not, but it seems that every day there's some new *discovery.*" Delphine sniffed, checked the pot again, and poured them each a cup. "Utter nonsense, of course."

"Oh? You don't believe in any of it?"

"Complete tosh," Delphine said, looking at Alice levelly. "Wouldn't you agree?"

"More things in heaven and earth and all that," Alice said, smiling.

"Well, quite." Delphine's expression didn't alter. "But some things *shouldn't* be real, should they?"

Alice hesitated, then laughed softly. "I don't think we get to decide that."

"Don't we?" Delphine picked her cup up. "Surely we get to decide what we entertain in our villages."

"To a certain extent, I suppose," Alice said. "But that's not the same as deciding what's real or not, is it?"

Delphine was silent for a moment, taking a sip of tea before answering. "I understand that you had a similar problem to our current one in Toot Hansell."

"Not on this scale," Alice said.

"But you did have all these journalists, didn't you? And this idea of *monsters* lurking about the place."

"We did. They seem to have moved on."

"Yes." Delphine put her cup down. "To here."

Alice cut a scone in half neatly and set her knife down on the edge of her plate, then smiled at Delphine. "It's most unfortunate, and you do have my sympathies. But I'm sure they'll lose interest in here before long, too."

They looked at each other, both smiling, and the moment stretched long and syrupy. Then one of the small boys hit the other, and they both started shouting, and the mother slammed her bottle onto the table and shouted, "Can you not behave for *just five minutes?*"

The answer was evidently no, and Alice turned her attention to her tea as Delphine got up and went to calm things down. She wasn't quite sure what the other woman was suggesting. That the Toot Hansell W.I. had sent the journalists here? Or that they knew about dragons, or monsters of some sort? She looked around and caught Trudy's eye, waving the other woman over.

"Do you need more tea?" Trudy asked. She was still blinking too much, and Alice wondered if she had an eye issue.

"No, this is wonderful. Lovely scones, too."

"Oh, yes. It's Delphine's recipe."

"I must ask her about it. But I just wondered if you'd had problems like this before."

"The kids? Yes, it's the heat. They're all a bit grumpy."

"No. The fuss over the monster. Anything like that?"

"Oh no." Trudy wiped her hands on a tea towel that was hanging over her shoulder. "We're a very quiet village, usually. We don't like this sort of thing." Her nose wrinkled, as if she were speaking about unspeakable acts on the village green.

"Of course." Alice let her go, then got up and wandered over to the flower stall, examining the potted gerberas and bouquets spilling sweet peas and cornflowers out of the confines of their waxy paper and vases. "Beautiful work," she said to a woman who was counting up change in a small tin.

The woman looked up and gave her a shy smile. "Thanks. They're all from our gardens."

"Oh, how lovely. I'm Alice."

"Caitlyn," the woman said, her smile widening

"Lovely to meet you." Alice looked along the tables. "I do like your potholders there. So practical."

"They are," Caitlyn agreed, straightening a patchwork one in subtle shades of pink. "We find the practical things sell quite well. Bibs and so on."

Looking at the neat piles on the tables, the sales didn't seem terribly good currently. "We've branched out into less practical things," Alice said. "Just for variety. We seem to end up with an awful lot of kitchen witches and dreamcatchers, but they sell well. Oh, and fairy doors to put on trees in the garden. Very popular, those."

"Oh, we wouldn't do those," Caitlyn said, her smile fading. "Nothing like that."

Alice raised her eyebrows. "Oh?"

"It's not really the done thing, is it? Anything pagan like that."

"I'm not sure you'd call fairy doors pagan."

"Well, magic, then."

"Why ever not? It's just a bit of fun."

Caitlyn stiffened. "I suppose it depends what you call fun."

"What sort of fun's this?" Delphine stepped up next to Alice. "Terribly sorry. I think they were trying to see who could get the most chocolate cake in their ears."

"Who won?" Alice asked, and Delphine frowned at her. Alice smiled, not even sure why she'd asked the question. Something about all the *properness* in here seemed to be making her channel Miriam.

"Shall we finish our tea?" Delphine suggested. "They've gone now, so it should be more peaceful."

"Of course." Alice followed the other woman back to the table, wondering if she'd be banned if she slurped her cup. It was surprisingly tempting to try.

❧

BACK AT THE TABLE, Alice dutifully asked Delphine about her scone recipe, and made appreciative noises regarding using yoghurt for a more tender crumb and grated butter for ease of working. But mostly she tried to keep an eye on the other women in the hall. As well as Caitlyn and Trudy, there was the short round woman with her short curled hair from the door, a tall skinny woman with stooped shoulders drifting in and out of the kitchen with very little enthusiasm, and a sixth woman bustling frantically about the hall, although as far as Alice could see all she seemed to do was pick up one cup, move it to another table, pick something else up, move it to a chair, then come back to the cup again. There was nothing about any of them that suggested they were accustomed to dealing with monsters, but then, she supposed no one would guess that from looking at the Toot Hansell W.I., either.

The big man and his small dog got up and meandered out the door, and Alice brushed crumbs off her fingers. "I should go and let you pack up," she said.

"That's not necessary." Delphine said. "I'm sorry if I rubbed you up the wrong way earlier. I didn't mean to imply you were somehow responsible for the journalists coming here and making all this fuss."

"Of course not. I didn't imagine so."

They both regarded each other for a moment, and Alice wondered if she should just ask. Just say, *so, do you take tea with monsters? Is that why you won't have anything to do with magic on your stalls? So as not to draw attention?* Not that she meant the dragons were monsters, of course, but one wouldn't want to ask leading questions.

But then Delphine tapped her fingers on the table lightly and said, "This whole fuss is just very *exasperating.* One needs to take care of one's village. To protect it from such things."

"The monster hunters?" Alice asked.

"The monster hunters. The journalists. The implication that *creatures* could be lurking in one's own backyard."

Alice nodded slowly. "Because of the disruption it causes?"

"It's not right." Delphine inclined her head slightly. "Nice villages like Eldmere and Toot Hansell don't deserve such things."

"I see your point." Alice didn't, actually. She still couldn't tell what the other woman's meaning was. It could be simple outrage at the invasion of the village, or it could be more, and there was no way to tell unless she just *asked*. But something didn't sit right. The Toot Hansell W.I. were fiercely protective of the dragons, but they delighted in the silly, playful magic of fairy doors and toadstool houses all the same. Because magic matters, whether in the imagination or in the world, and seeking to quash it felt less like a way of protecting it and more like a way of banishing it. So she just smiled at Delphine and said, "I really must be off. How much do I owe you?"

"Oh, don't be silly. It's been such a pleasure meeting you," Delphine said. "I do hope you're able to pop back soon."

"Well, thank you," Alice said. "I'm sure we'll be back before long."

Delphine walked her to the door and waved her off, and she went with the uneasy feeling that she'd missed something. But there was nothing more she could do right now.

She was almost at the corner of the main street when she looked back and saw Delphine still standing outside the village hall. She'd been joined by the tall, broad-shouldered form of DCI Sykes, and they were both watching her. Delphine raised her hand and waved, and Alice waved back, then continued on to the main road. When she looked back, they were both gone, presumably inside. It wasn't so odd, if the DCI came from here. He could well know Delphine, or any of the other ladies of the W.I. There was no reason for her to feel uneasy about the way they'd both been watching her. And she certainly hadn't given anything away as to what she knew about dragons. *That* she was sure of.

ROSE WAS WAITING at the car when she got there, Gert leaning next to her. Alice had a moment of dislocation, as if she'd lost hours in the dozing heat of the hall.

"Gert?"

"Ay up, Alice. How was the tea?"

"Stewed and strained," she said, beeping the car open. "What are you doing here?"

"Libby – that's my nephew's partner's sister's cousin – is running a nice line in frozen ices, and she suggested we bring some tees down."

"Teas?"

"T-shirts." Gert was wearing a rather pretty strapless sundress that showed off her broad shoulders and muscled arms, but she took a luminously yellow T-shirt from her bag and shook it out. In stark black print it read, *I survived the Yorkshire Beast!*, and there was a large, taloned paw print under the text.

"I see."

"Yeah, our Flip – that's my second cousin's brother-in-law's girl – whips up any design you want, quick as you like." Gert inspected the shirt critically. "I should be wearing it, for advertising, like, but it's so damn hot."

"It is," Alice agreed. "Has Rose filled you in?"

"She has. We're doing a roaring trade here, but Murph can handle it. I'll come back with you and we can rally the troops. I've got a couple of ideas already if we're talking framing journalists."

Alice raised her eyebrows. "*Discrediting* them, not framing them. There's no crime, as such."

"Techniques are all the same. Plant the evidence and tip off the cops." She thought about it. "Or, in this case, the monster hunters, I suppose."

"Well, yes. I suppose." Alice pulled her phone out of her pocket. "Let me just see how Miriam's getting on." She put it on speaker so that the other two could hear as they huddled together on the pavement, but the call went straight to voice mail without even ringing, and she hung up without leaving a message. "Or perhaps not."

"She'll be right," Rose said. "She can't get in any trouble with Beaufort and Mortimer there to look after her."

"I suppose not," Alice said, putting the phone back in her pocket and looking at Gert. "Right. Everyone in, then. The sooner we can get this done, the better."

"You'd do well in academia," Rose said. "It's all about discrediting some poor sod to further your own career."

"Harsh," Gert said, settling comfortably into the passenger seat.

"In this case, warranted," Alice said, and pulled the car back onto the road, bound for home.

13
DI ADAMS

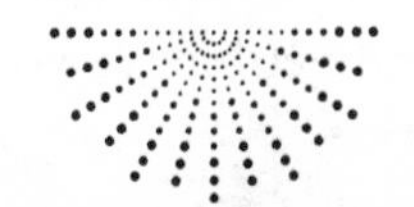

The hut by the tarn was nothing more than one room with a couple of windows punched through the thick walls to either side of the door, which had been secured from the outside by a hasp and padlock. DI Adams stood in the middle of the dusty stone floor and looked at the air mattress tucked into one corner of the room. There was a sleeping bag rumpled on it, and a decent-looking pillow. A small camp stove huddled at the opposite end of the space, framed by a burnt pot and a green plastic cooler. She turned on her heel slowly, glimpsing the tarn through the cobwebs on the windows. There wasn't exactly any furniture to throw over or plates to smash, so all she could go on was the dust on the floor. It was barely disturbed, just trails of footprints heading between the door, the stove, and the bed. If anyone had had a scuffle here, it had been very civilised and entirely bloodless.

She walked back to the door and leaned out to look at Cooper. "Where's the bathroom?"

He blinked at her and pointed at the tarn. She made a face. Even in summer, she didn't fancy a dip in those waters.

"Toilet?"

He pointed at the tarn again.

"Really?"

"We're going to turn it into an Airbnb as soon as we get the money together," he said, kicking his wellies into the rough ground. "Composting loo and solar shower, same as the campsite."

"Good to know," DI Adams said, and looked at Collins as he came around the corner of the hut. "Anything?"

"No signs of struggle that I can see."

"Right." She looked back at the hut again. "Well, there's nothing in there. We can call Lucas and get him to go over it properly, but let's make sure it's worth it first."

"Worth it?" Cooper demanded. "Hetty's *missing!*"

"And we're going to find her," Collins said, ducking into the hut and leaving DI Adams outside with the farmer.

"Yes," she said, trying for the same reassuring tones as Collins.

"Then call your Luke or whoever! Do your job!" His hands were in fists at his sides, and she looked from him to the tarn thoughtfully.

"Calm down, Mr Cooper," she said.

He snatched his hat off his head and twisted it so hard she was surprised it didn't rip in two. *"Calm down?* My wife is *gone* and no one believes me! You're as bad as that bloody Sykes and Delphine!"

"You did say it was a deliberate disappearance to start with."

"It *was!* But just because it started that way doesn't mean it's what's *happened!* She's *gone!*"

DI Adams nodded and said, "There's no evidence of a struggle, Mr Cooper. So either she walked out on her own, or she met someone she knew." She looked at him, her eyebrows raised.

"I don't know. It's not like there are cameras. But I was the only one who knew she was out here. This is private property, and there are no walking tracks around the tarn. No one could've even seen her."

"And her phone didn't work out here."

"No, I told you."

She examined him as Collins emerged from the hut. "So, let me make sure I'm clear on this," she said. "No one's seen your wife since Tuesday, when you brought her up to an abandoned, toilet-less hut next to a very large tarn and left her. And you didn't report her missing to us until today."

"It were Tuesday night," he said. "We had to make sure no one saw us."

"Right," she said, and watched him expectantly. He just looked at her blankly. She sighed. "Do you see how this doesn't look very good for you?"

"What?" He stared at her, his hat still clutched in both hands. "What d'you mean?"

DI Adams and Collins looked at each other. "Never mind," she said. "We'll get someone to go over the place."

"Good," he said, and straightened his hat out enough to fit it back on. "I need to get back. Ash's a good lad, but he's not really the welcoming face of Cooper's farm."

Collins snorted. "I don't know. He's pretty suited for a monster farm." Cooper almost smiled at that, and Collins added, "He worked for you long?"

"A few years. His parents don't mind, it's not child labour or anything. He just helps out about the place, and I give him some pocket money and the use of the quad bike when he wants to go brood on the moors or whatever. Mostly he just seems to like the animals." Cooper looked at the tarn. "She wouldn't have just run off, you know? We're good. I know we are."

"Good to know," DI Adams said, almost to herself. She was looking for Dandy. He hadn't been in the car when they left the farm, but that wasn't so unusual. Just as he had his own ways of navigating walls, he had his own ways of finding her. But he wasn't here. There was no Dandy drifting along the shoreline, or sniffing around the corners of the hut in the hopes of frozen peas.

The suggestion of a smile vanished, and Cooper said, "Wait. You're suggesting I did it!"

"I'm not suggesting anything," she said, scanning the shoreline. She was almost sure she'd seen movement. "But the fact remains that you were the last to see her, and intimate partner violence is the most common cause of—"

"DI Adams is bad with people," Collins said, cutting her off, and she blinked at him, then at Cooper, who had gone very, very pale.

"Yes, I am," she said hurriedly. "I'm very efficient, though."

Both men stared at her, Cooper in something like horror and Collins with a look that suggested he was biting the inside of his cheek.

"Shall we go?" she suggested, after the silence had gone on far too long for comfort. "I think we've seen all we can here."

"Good plan," Collins said, and patted Cooper on the shoulder. "You head home. Send us a list of all Hetty's friends and family and their contact details, alright? We'll be back to see you tomorrow."

Cooper looked from one to the other, then said very quietly, "Okay." He headed back to his pickup, and Collins looked at DI Adams.

"What?"

"Do you actually think he did it?"

She sighed. "No, not really. If he's clever enough to make money off the whole monster thing, he's clever enough to have *some* sort of alibi in place."

Collins tucked his hands into his pockets and looked across the tarn. "I think you're right. Creepy sort of place this, isn't it?"

DI Adams took her keys from her pocket. "I definitely wouldn't want to be out here on my own with no phone or car. Taking things a bit far, that."

"Not much of a camping person, are you, Adams?"

"I've done it."

"Really?"

"When I was about ten, Dad got it in his head to buy a caravan off a friend. He dragged us all up to Scarborough. In *autumn*. The caravan leaked, the stove didn't work, and we got stopped by the police for the indicators not working .... I don't remember how many times. Definitely twice. It took us ages to even get to the campsite, and then it turned out the kitchens were shut for the off season and the showers only worked on solar. In the rainiest week for something like twenty years. It kind of put me off."

"So you have been up north before."

She scowled at him and opened her car door. "It doesn't improve." She checked the shore of the tarn once more before they left, but there was nothing. No Dandy. No monsters.

She'd never thought she'd miss an invisible dog.

❧

THEY CAUGHT up with Cooper halfway back to the road, where he'd met Ervin's red Nissan Micra nose to nose on a corner, and was currently threatening to set the dogs on him for trespassing and harassment. DI Adams swung out of the car and hurried to intervene.

"I asked him to take some photos," she told Cooper. "Quicker than waiting for our lab tech to make it out here."

"But he's one of those journalists," Cooper protested.

"I'm not one of *those* journalists," Ervin said. "But I'd've thought you'd like them getting the word out on your monster and all, anyway."

"Too bloody nosey by half," Cooper said. "That Katherine keeps trying to follow me any time I go anywhere. Turned up down here the other day." He glared at Ervin, and he raised his hands.

"Here by request," he said, and pointed at DI Adams. "She said."

"I did," DI Adams said, and waved Cooper back to his car, then scowled at Ervin. "Try not to keep getting in altercations with my suspects, will you?"

"I feel more like I'm being altercated *at*."

"Of course you do."

There was some back and forth with the cars as they tried to squeeze past each other on the narrow track, then they were rumbling back up toward the road above.

"Good timing there," Collins remarked as they followed the pickup back toward Eldmere. "Might've been a bit awkward to explain why my aunt had just turned up at his private tarn with two dragons in tow."

DI Adams sighed. "I used to investigate proper crime back in

London, you know. Not deal with people's aunties popping up with dragons."

"We've got a missing person. That's proper."

"With dragons. Why is everything in my life *with dragons* these days?"

"I blame it on your magic dog," Collins said, glancing into the back seat. "What size is he now?"

"He's not here."

"What? He's always here."

"No. He was at the farm, but doesn't seem to have caught us up."

"Oh." Collins was silent for a moment, then said, "Do you want to go back to Cooper's and look for him?"

DI Adams hesitated. She *did* want to, but that was silly. Dandy always vanished off on his own little missions then reappeared again. Just because he was small didn't make it any different. "No," she said aloud. "Let's head into the village and see how things are looking. Decide if we need to call some uniforms in before DCI Sykes decides to restore public order off his own bat."

"He could just walk around frowning at people. That'd calm everyone down quick enough."

"He's really not that bad."

"You only think that because you're also terrifyingly efficient."

"Possibly," she said.

It didn't take long before they were dropping back into the valley, the shadows lengthening and the light taking on richer golden hues as the long afternoon crept on. They passed Cooper's farm and slipped over the bridge back into the village, which was at least as busy as it had been earlier that afternoon, if not more so. Walkers and monster hunters in everything from sandals and fairy wings to army surplus boots and what looked alarmingly like night vision goggles poked along the river or crowded the pavements outside the pubs, and the level of noise from the pubs themselves had definitely ratcheted up a notch or so. A woman with one of those rolling shopping bags was wandering around the green selling sandwiches and bottles of water, and an ice cream truck was parked in the bus stop. It was doing a brisk trade.

"Looks alright," Collins asked, as DI Adams pulled into the car park and found a space. "Certainly doesn't seem like there's about to be a battle between the cryptozoologists and the sceptics or anything."

"It does look alright. But we may as well have a look around, see if there's anything interesting happening."

"Interesting as in mildly illicit drug use?" Collins asked, climbing out of the car and examining the green across the road. "Because I think I can see some of that from here."

"Interesting as in anyone who might know what happened to Hetty Cooper."

Collins nodded at a sandwich board on the edge of the green. "We could start there."

"No," she said immediately.

"The W.I. always know what happens in their village," he said. "Besides, there's obviously a bit of history between Delphine Harlow and Cooper. Let's go and find out about it."

DI Adams made a noise that was rather close to a growl, but headed for the side road the sign was pointing up anyway. All roads lead to the W.I., it seemed.

❧

SOMEONE WAS BRINGING in the sign outside the village hall as they strolled up the street toward it, and DI Adams let herself have a small moment of disappointment that they hadn't been ten minutes later. But as they approached the door a round woman came out to pick up the vases of flowers from the step and immediately gave them an enthusiastic wave.

"Hello, hello! You're just in time – we've still got a couple of slices of cake left, and the kettle's not packed up yet!"

"Coffee?" DI Adams asked hopefully.

"Of course! We've got some of that lovely stuff in the packets that froths up just like a cappuccino. It's so fun!" She ushered them inside, and DI Adams swallowed a groan.

"Never mind, Adams," Collins said in a low voice. "There's still tea."

DI Adams supposed there was, and as her eyes adjusted to the dimmer light inside she spotted tables being packed away and jars of jam and homemade chutneys being stacked into well-depleted boxes. Women with neatly set hair and floral skirts and sensible shoes bustled around with cloths and plates and Tupperware, and she had a horrible flashback to her first encounter with the Toot Hansell W.I., in a very similar hall. But this wasn't Toot Hansell, she reminded herself. *All* W.I.s couldn't be that bad.

She straightened her shoulders and turned to the woman who had shown them in, intending to ask for Delphine, when a sharp voice cut across the room.

"Police! You're the police from the farm!"

DI Adams swung toward the voice and found Delphine coming in the back doors of the hall, the garden a framed swathe of colour and texture in the doorway behind her. "DIs Adams and Collins," she said.

"Perfect timing," Delphine said. "I would have asked DCI Sykes, of course, but since you're here ..."

"How can we help?"

"You can remove these journalists from my hall."

"We're not in the hall," Katherine called from the doorway, and grinned in at them. Lloyd leaned in next to her and snapped a photo, making one of the woman squawk at the flash.

"That's still hall property," Delphine snapped. "They're refusing to leave," she added to the DIs.

"What're you doing?" DI Adams asked Katherine.

"Well, W.I., you know. I figured the Toot Hansell lot were hiding dragons, so this lot must be hiding the Yorkshire Beast, whatever that may be. Probably dragons again."

"Honestly, she's completely unbalanced," Delphine said. "She's upsetting everyone."

DI Adams looked around at the other women in the hall. They didn't look happy, exactly, but they were just continuing with their work. Even the woman who'd screamed at the flash was packing up jams placidly again.

"I'm just doing my job," Katherine said. "There's something going on here. You can't hide the truth forever."

Delphine scowled at her. "*You're* what's going on here. Making up all these ridiculous stories about dragons and beasts and completely *ruining* my village. I won't have it!"

"Well, you're certainly being a nuisance," Collins said, and pointed to the door to the street. "Come on. Let's leave the ladies to pack up in peace."

"You should arrest them," Delphine said. "It's harassment. And slander."

"I will take that into consideration," Collins said.

"We've not done anything wrong," Katherine insisted. "We're just doing our jobs."

"Amazing how often that excuse has been used for terrible things," DI Adams said.

Katherine glared at her, then, to DI Adams' surprise, nodded. "Fine. Come on, Lloyd."

"Right," he said, and ambled after her as she headed to the front door. "Thanks for the scone."

"Quite alright," one of the women said, then ducked into the little kitchen when Delphine glared at her.

DI Adams watched Collins escort the journalists out, then looked at Delphine. "I realise you're packing up, but might we have a word?"

She smoothed the front of her blouse. "Yes, of course. Always happy to help the police." She gestured to a folding table that was still set up, and as they sat down the round woman from the door bustled up with a cup of frothy coffee.

"There we go," she said breathlessly. "Enjoy!"

"Thanks," DI Adams said, staring at it suspiciously. Then she looked back at Delphine. "How do you know Mr Cooper?"

"Jake? Oh, he moved here ... maybe ten years ago? The farm's Hetty's, of course, but he seems to have adapted alright."

"Do I understand the farm was previously in your family?"

"That's right. My older brother sold it to Hetty's father."

"Must be hard, seeing someone else on family land."

Delphine tipped her head, then smiled. "I see. No, DI Adams, it is not. I have done everything I can to welcome the Coopers – Hetty's family, you understand, Jake took her name – as have all the village. And I know that Jake is suffering right now, but every friendly gesture I make is rebuffed."

Collins had come back in while they were talking and sat down, a catering cup of tea looking very small in his big hands. "Such as tearing up his signs?" he asked.

"They were both unauthorised and very tacky. We don't need these *monster hunters* here."

"Are you speaking for the whole village?" DI Adams asked. "Only the business seems good for the pubs and so on."

"I'm speaking in the best interests of the village."

"That's not the same thing."

Delphine sighed, the sigh of a woman being very reasonable and searching for new ways to express herself to someone who was evidently a little slow on the uptake. "People are very short-sighted, Detective. They just see some extra money coming in and think, oh, why not? They don't think of the long-term impact on the image of our village. Imagine if we became known as some sort of monster attraction? How tacky!"

"So there isn't that much resistance to the monster hunters in the village as a whole."

"As I said, people are very short-sighted. But those who've had their gardens invaded by strangers, and cars parked over their driveways, are hardly as keen as the pub owners and Jake Cooper with his scruffy little campsite." Her cheeks had gone quite pink.

Collins had been looking at his phone, and now he looked up and said, "And how has that scruffy little campsite impacted your business, Miss Harlow?"

DI Adams leaned over as he tilted the phone toward her. *Luxury Glamping Pods,* it read, and there were pictures of a row of cabins nestled among flowerbeds and kissed with sunlight. The pods looked rather like the upturned hulls of fishing boats sitting on the ground, their wood-tiled roofs curved all the way to the ground.

"Not at all," Delphine said. "Entirely different clientele." Her hands were clasped on the table, and DI Adams could see the skin whitening under her fingers.

"Must be irritating though," Collins said. "Looks like you were the only camping option around here previously. Everything else is B&Bs."

"*Glamping.*"

"Of course." He looked at DI Adams.

She had a sip of deeply unsatisfying coffee, and said, "Did you have much contact with Hetty Cooper?"

"Not so much. I invited her to join the W.I., but she wasn't interested." Delphine sniffed slightly, and DI Adams felt sure Hetty had made a wise choice there.

"When did you last see her?"

"Oh, I don't know – when all this monster nonsense started up. I went to talk to them about it. So ... last weekend, I suppose?"

"And do you have any idea where she might have gone? Any friends you know of?"

"Different circles, Detective Inspector," Delphine said, and smiled tightly. "Is there anything else? We *were* just packing up."

DI Adams looked at Collins, and he shrugged. She pushed her cup away. "Thank you for your help, Miss Harlow. We'll be in touch if there's anything else."

"Of course. Any time."

Delphine escorted them to the door, as much, DI Adams felt, to make sure they were gone as to be polite. The frothy coffee enthusiast waved them off enthusiastically as they headed back toward the main road.

"That didn't get us far," Collins said. "Other than feeling much happier about our W.I."

"They're not *my* W.I."

"Better than that lot," Collins said, tipping his head to the hall behind him.

"True," DI Adams admitted, glancing back. Delphine was at the door, talking on her mobile as she watched the inspectors leave. There was a moment's pause, where DI Adams felt something frosty worm its way across her spine, then Delphine waved, her smile bright. DI Adams nodded back. "Why is it that I want to arrest every W.I. I come across, though?"

"You may want to talk to someone about that."

THE FESTIVAL-LIKE ATMOSPHERE of the village was intensifying as they headed back toward the car. An impromptu band had sprung up on the green, consisting of two guitars, a ukulele, and someone beating on an empty cooler box. Some small children in bare feet were dancing happily, but no one else seemed particularly interested, although there were plenty of people around. Quite a lot of them were a little worse for wear from sun or alcohol or a combination of the above, but everyone seemed to be sharing a vague sense of monster-based camaraderie. There was a lot of good-natured arguing about monster identification, but none of them looked likely to come to blows. There was mostly just a lot of quoting articles and semi-scientific papers at each other, and they heard a man shout in an aggrieved sort of way, "But not *every* witness can be lying!"

"Well, *he's* not police," Collins said, rocking on his heels in time to the cooler box beat, and DI Adams snorted.

She examined the board outside the pub opposite the green. *Monster Sharing Platter,* it suggested, as well as *Creepy Cocktails* and *Beastly Baps.*

"Embracing the concept," Collins said.

DI Adams nodded. "It looks like Delphine may be in the minority, not wanting the Beast thing to continue."

"We need talk to some of them," Collins said. "See how much of this feud is in Cooper's head and how much is real. And if anyone knows anything about Hetty." They looked at each other, then Collins added, "Tomorrow morning would probably be better, though. It's *heaving.*"

"There is that." DI Adams examined the green again, still waiting for Dandy, then said, "I think we get a couple of uniforms down here tonight, just to keep an eye on things, and we start phoning some of Hetty's friends and family. We can re-interview Cooper tomorrow and see what other details we can shake loose."

"And now we go to Toot Hansell and make sure all dragons have cleared the area?"

"*Go?* Do we really have to go? Can't we just call?"

"They'll have decent coffee."

She scowled. "*Better. Better* coffee, not decent coffee."

"You're going to have to start drinking tea, Adams. I keep telling you."

"And I keep telling you that is never going to happen."

He snorted, and they walked back to the car through the happy, bouncing crowd of monster hunters, while the Yorkshire summer afternoon slowly melted into evening.

14
MORTIMER

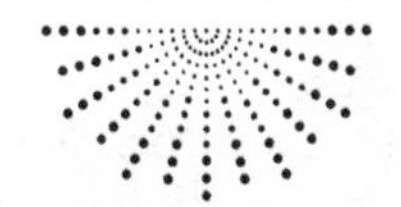

"It's okay! You can come in!" Miriam waved urgently from the side of her house, and Ervin looked back at the dragons, still trying to stay as low in the car as they could.

"How bad's my back seat?"

"You take the corners too fast," Beaufort said. "We had to use our talons, or we'd have been thrown all over the place."

Mortimer gave a little mumble of agreement. The corners had been *very* fast. The straight bits had been even faster, as it happened, and he had only hung onto Miriam's bread and cheese through sheer willpower. He could still feel it at the back of his throat, threatening to break free.

Ervin opened the back door and Mortimer slid straight out onto the pavement. "Hurry up," the journalist said. "Straight into the garden. Anyone could be watching!"

Mortimer managed to find his feet and scuttled through the gate into the chaos of untrimmed grass and wildflowers and cheerfully chaotic flowerbeds at the front of Miriam's house. She petted his shoulder as he padded around her and into the relative safety of the back garden. *Relative.* Katherine the Terrible had seen him here. He looked around anxiously, just in case Miriam had missed a journalist lurking in the apple tree or something, but he couldn't see anyone. A moment later Beaufort caught up to him.

"Come on, lad," the old dragon said. "Time for tea, I'd say."

"I'll put the kettle right on," Miriam said, leading them into the kitchen. "Ervin? Do you want one?"

"I think I'd rather something stronger after having dogs set on me, farmers threatening me, and having to cart dragons all across the Dales."

"That's exactly what tea's good for," Miriam said, pulling familiar, big soup mugs out of her cupboard. The whole place smelled of the memory of winter wood smoke, and fresh-cut grass, and flowers from the garden, and something earthy and vibrant and *Miriam,* and Mortimer took a deep, slow breath, then sat down in front of the AGA cooker, closing his eyes.

"Are you alright, lad?" Beaufort asked.

"Almost," Mortimer said, and looked up at Miriam as she patted him on the shoulder.

"A tea will sort you out," she said. "And I've got some summer fruit cake."

"That will definitely do it," he said, and closed his eyes again, soaking up the solid, familiar feel of the stone flagged floor beneath him and the late afternoon sun coming through the deep-silled windows to drench his scales, and only half-listening to Miriam as she told Ervin where to find the catering-size teapot in the top of the pantry, and how many plates to put out on the table, and did he think they should set up in the garden or in here?

"This is not my area of expertise," he said, and Mortimer opened one eye to see him staring doubtfully at a pile of unhemmed cloths. "Are these the napkins?"

"They're cleaning cloths. Look at them!"

"Right." He took a second pile from the same drawer and inspected them. They didn't look terribly different, to Mortimer's eyes. "These ones?"

"Yes. Now, inside or outside?"

"I really don't know," the journalist said, looking at the dragons helplessly.

"Outside," Beaufort said. "It's still very hot, and it'll stop us overheating everything.

"Oh, well done, Beaufort," Miriam said. "Of course. Outside!" she said to Ervin.

"Right," he said, and wandered out with the napkins in one hand and some plates in another.

"He's not so bad," Miriam said to the dragons. "Just needs a little direction, is all."

"I understand completely," Beaufort said gravely, and Mortimer watched his scales flush with his own deep colours, rising against the grey like an incoming tide.

❧

THE NINE OTHER ladies of the Toot Hansell Women's Institute arrived in ones and twos, bearing Tupperware containers and plates and, in Gert's case, four large bottles of elderflower cordial. The garden table was quickly overloaded, and Ervin was sent to get a folding card table from Miriam's unused dining room. He took a while about it, and when he came back he took a chair and moved it next to the dragons.

There was much fussing with tea and plates, and Mortimer wrapped his paws around his third soup mug of tea and took a cheese scone off his plate, closing his eyes as he ate. It was *delightful,* and all the more so because it had seemed for a while there that they would never be able to sit in Miriam's garden for tea and cake ever again.

Finally Alice clapped her hands lightly and said, "Ladies? Are we ready?"

"I think we've been ready for ages," Priya said. "Honestly, this journalist thing has gone on long enough!"

"*Cryptid* journalist thing," Ervin said, then looked at his mug when everyone's gaze turned to him. "Just to be clear," he mumbled.

"Should he be here?" Rosemary asked. "He could be a plant. Carlotta, what did you do to plants back in the old country?"

"I don't know why you insist on thinking I should know such things. But we'd probably put his delicate bits in boiling oil. If I was to guess."

Miriam offered a plate of Bakewell slice around. "Ervin has been very helpful."

"If you're vouching for him, then you'd have the same punishment if he proves to be a plant," Carlotta said, pouring herself a generous dose of Gert's cordial and topping it up with sparkling water.

"I don't even know who I'd be a plant *for,*" Ervin protested, then yelped as a tabby cat with ragged ears leaped onto the table next to him. "Oh, not bloody you!"

"Nice," the cat said, his voice a rough rasp.

"You wiped my brain," Ervin said, carefully not looking at the cat.

"It was an improvement."

"Hush, Thompson," Alice said. "You're not being helpful."

"I'm a cat. I have no requirement to be helpful. But I did see that the old bat signal went out—"

"*Excuse me?*" Gert said, folding her heavy arms and glaring at the cat.

"Bat signal? Like Batman? Do you not watch movies?"

"I think it was the old bit we're not so happy about," Teresa said. "Very rude, that."

The cat narrowed his eyes. "It was a manner of speaking. It wasn't directed at you, but it does fit, you realise?"

Beaufort growled, and Thompson gave him a sideways look. "Jeez. Everyone's touchy today."

"Try to be a civilised creature," Alice said to him.

"Because you humans are so good at it?" Everyone looked at him, waiting, and he sighed. "Sure, sure. Is there any salmon?"

"There will be," Alice said, and waved at Miriam to sit down again. "Don't run after him like that."

"I'll trade you in," the cat said.

"Fickle monster," Gert said. "I still can't believe I let you sleep in my bed, and all the time you could *talk.*"

"It was a nice bed," Thompson said with a shrug. "But what's the emergency?"

"Twofold," Alice said, looking around the table. "Firstly, Katherine Llewelyn has a new target in Eldmere."

"That's good, though, right?" Jasmine asked. "If she's moved on from here, then we can go back to normal, right?" She smiled at Mortimer, and he gave her a toothy grin back. She'd baked some sort of sesame bun things, and he could feel the oil of the seeds coating his gullet.

"Until she comes back," Rose said. "It could be a diversion, waiting for us to relax our guard so she can rush back in and catch us."

Mortimer looked around the garden, the oil suddenly tasting rancid at the back of his throat.

"Quite," Alice said. "And she's very determined. She's not going to forget that she saw Mortimer."

The sesame bun seemed to be trying to make a reappearance, and he swallowed hard.

"So what do we do?" Pearl asked, leaning over to top up Mortimer's mug. "If she's just going to keep coming back, what *can* we do?"

"Discredit her," Alice said. "We make it very clear to everyone that she's setting up the monster sightings, and that the same thing happened in Toot Hansell."

"Okay," Teresa said. "We can figure that out. But what's the second part of the problem?"

Alice looked at Beaufort, and he sighed. "Gilbert is missing," he said quietly.

There was an immediate chorus of responses.

"What?"

"How?"

"Oh, poor Gilbert!"

"Did someone hurt him?" Gert demanded. "I'll bloody have them!"

"That is *unacceptable,*" Priya said. "Who would *do* such a thing?"

Beaufort waved his paws. "We don't know that they have. It seems he and Amelia had a little falling out"—understanding murmurs washed around the table—"and we can't even be entirely certain that he's in Eldmere."

"I think we can," Mortimer said, and lifted one forepaw. Cuddled against his chest was the chicken, and she *buk*-ed at him irritably.

"And then there were the pumpkins," Miriam said. "There were all these pumpkins and blankets and beanbags in a hut up on the fells, but no Gilbert."

"So he may have *been* in Eldmere, but then left," Beaufort pointed out.

"He wouldn't have just left the chicken out on the fells," Mortimer said. "A fox could have got her."

"*Buk-buk!*"

Thompson squinted at the chicken. "Any scents?"

"Nothing to follow."

"And this is our little flight-challenged Gilbert?"

"Exactly," Mortimer said. "So I don't see how he can have just left."

"Huh." Thompson yawned. "He does have a bit of an emo thing going on. Have you checked he's not joined some sort of dryad poetry group? That'd be his style."

"*Buk!*" the chicken said sternly.

"There's no dryads in that valley," Beaufort said. "There's nothing."

"Interesting."

"Someone must've been helping him," Jasmine said. "How else would he get the beanbags and so on?"

"We did wonder that," Miriam said.

"So maybe they moved him?"

"But why leave the pumpkins and beanbags behind?"

No one spoke for a moment, then Alice said, "Because they were in a rush. Whatever happened, they had to hurry to get it done. Which means someone had discovered Gilbert."

"Or the person who discovered him did the moving," Priya said. "They forced him to go with him somehow."

"*Buk.*"

Mortimer stared at the chicken. "Gilbert's a pacifist. If they threatened the chicken, he'd have done whatever they wanted."

"*Buk*," the chicken said, and nestled closer to his chest, her head drooping.

"Bloody vegetarianism," Thompson said. "It's a slippery slope. Start eating carrots and the next thing you know you're giving up the magical secrets of centuries to protect a damn chicken."

"I don't think it was the vegetarianism," Mortimer protested.

"I do." Thompson stretched and shook himself, scattering hair all over a plate of delicate feta pastries.

"Do you mind?" Alice asked, moving the plate.

"Not really. Look, I'll go and check out this place. Where is it?"

"Eldmere. It's a couple of dales over," Beaufort said. "Do you think you'll have more luck than us, though?"

Thompson tipped him a wink. "Us cats have our ways. But I don't know it."

"I'll show you on maps," Alice said, picking up her phone.

"That's no good. That doesn't *mean* anything. What's near there?"

"There's Eldermere tarn."

"I don't know that, either."

"It's not so far from the B6160," Rose said.

"You know that's not even a road name, right? It's just numbers."

"Well, this is useful," Gert said.

They stared at each other for a moment, then Thompson said, "You'll have to drive me over there."

Alice sighed. "Well, you'll have to wait. I imagine the DIs will turn up before long, and we'd all best stay put until then."

"Why are they involved?" Thompson asked.

"There's a missing person," Miriam said, and the cat broke into huffing laughter.

"*Of course* there is. If I was ever going to talk to humans, I'm glad it was you lot. Endless entertainment." He sat down and started grooming himself, until Alice moved him off the table and looked at the rest of the W.I.

"The missing person is for the DIs to deal with. The journalists are our side of things."

"I can help," Ervin said. "I can write an exposé of the whole thing. I just need a few good photos, and enough evidence to show that she *could* be faking that she can't do me for libel. But if I throw enough *it appears* and *according to sources* in, it doesn't need a lot."

"Well done, that man," Carlotta said, and winked, raising her glass to him.

"Yes, very good," Alice said. "Now, we need to put this plan into action as quickly as possible."

"How quickly?" Pearl asked.

"Tomorrow."

"Tomorrow?" Rosemary said. "That's not much time to do *anything,* Alice."

"I realise this. But the longer we leave it, the greater the risk that the monster hunters in the village will stumble on real evidence – or on Gilbert."

"We can do it," Priya said. "We've a good track record for last-minute events. Remember when the pub kitchen caught fire and we served seventy-six guests out of the hall kitchen with three hours' notice?"

"I can't forget it even when I try," Jasmine said with a shudder. "I still don't know how my custard *exploded.*"

Rose patted her arm. "Neither do I."

Gert nodded. "It's doable. I can call in some help if necessary. We've already got a presence in Eldmere."

Mortimer wondered what a *presence* was, exactly. It sounded vaguely threatening, but the ladies were all nodding approvingly.

"What about Gilbert?" Miriam said. "Who's dealing with that side of things?"

"We are," Beaufort said. "We'll go back as soon as it's dark and keep hunting. We must be able to find *something.* He can't have just vanished."

"We'll go with you," Alice said.

Mortimer and Beaufort looked at each other, and Beaufort gave a delicate little cough. "Not that I don't appreciate the offer, but …" He trailed off, while the ladies looked at him expectantly and Thompson looked up from licking cream off a scone with his ears pricked, waiting.

"Night vision," Mortimer said. "You don't have any."

"Yes," Beaufort said. "Also wings. We'll be able to cover more ground."

"I wasn't suggesting we scramble about the fells with you," Alice said mildly. "I do recognise that we have *some* limitations."

"Wow," Thompson said. "Anyone seen any flying pigs recently?"

Alice ignored him, looking at the dragons. "We will drive you there and bring you back, and so minimise the risk of anyone seeing you."

"And we have to stay in touch," Miriam added. "It's been so hard, because you don't have mobile phones or anything, and the whole flag system really didn't work, and so there's just been no way to communicate. And with all the monster hunters about we *need* to be able to stay in contact."

"Oh," Beaufort said. "I suppose that would be fine, then."

"Of course it will," Alice said. "I'll take Thompson to the village and show him the farm and so on. I imagine you'll want to start from the hut you found, so Miriam can take you two up to the tarn."

"I will?" Miriam squeaked. "At *night?* In Betsy? I don't know if she'll make it!"

"I'll take them," Rose said, then frowned as a chorus of *no* went up around the table. "What?"

"I'm sure it wouldn't be any good for your car either, dear," Alice said, and smiled at the dragons.

"It doesn't sound any good for anyone," someone said from the path, and Mortimer dropped a berry-studded slice of summer fruit cake into his tea, slopping it everywhere.

"DI Adams," Alice said. "I was wondering when you might join us."

"Just in time, by the sound of things." She walked up to the table, followed by Colin.

"Where's your monster?" Thompson asked, peering around the garden with the hair on his spine already lifting. Mortimer sympathised.

"Not here."

"Good call," the cat said.

"Coffee?" Miriam asked, jumping up and almost knocking her chair over. "I'll get a pot on."

"Only if it's no trouble," DI Adams said.

"No, no, be right back." She rushes off toward the house, and Ervin followed to find more chairs.

❧

"YOU WILL NOT – *will not* – go back to Eldmere tonight, alright?" DI Adams' voice was level, but there was a small tic under her eye that had started up at about the point Mortimer had shown her the chicken and explained about the hut. She took a sip of coffee and sighed. "Lovely coffee, Miriam, thank you."

Alice frowned. "That's rather unreasonable, DI Adams. Gilbert's there somewhere, and night is the best option for the dragons to look for him."

The inspector looked at the dragons. "You do have wings."

"I had rather the same thought myself," Beaufort said gravely.

Alice tipped her head. "But Gilbert doesn't fly, plus us driving the dragons there means less chance of them being seen."

DI Adams took a piece of coffee cake and looked at Colin. He rubbed the back of his neck, then said, "One missing person is enough. And that tarn is on Cooper's property, so you really shouldn't be out there without permission."

"*Can't*," DI Adams said. "*Can't* be out there without permission."

"I meant that. Also DCI Sykes is still lurking around, so if you run up against him he might just arrest you because he feels like it."

"Sykes was out at the tarn this afternoon," Ervin said. "Talking about setting traps for ferrets."

"What?" DI Adams asked. "You saw him?"

"We met him on the track as we were leaving."

"And he didn't do you for trespassing?" Colin asked.

"No, I said Adams told me to take photos, and that Miriam was helping me."

"And he didn't question that?" DI Adams asked, and took her phone out as if expecting to see a message or call from the DCI.

"Not really."

"He said he worked protecting wild bird nests, and was setting traps to catch ferrets," Miriam added.

"He just volunteered that?" Colin asked.

Miriam and Ervin both nodded, and the DIs looked at each other with matching mystified expressions.

Then Rose said, "Rubbish. It's basically September. Nothing's nesting at the moment – or nothing anyone's worried about, anyway. And no one's worried about ferrets, except the potential for cross-breeding with polecats. American mink, maybe, but I've not heard of them being a problem up here."

"He said there were five different endangered species nesting around the tarn," Miriam said.

"Then he has no understanding of bird life cycles at all," Rose said.

"We saw him in Eldmere, too," Alice said. "It must've been before you saw him at the tarn. He was talking to Delphine after we left the hall."

Mortimer could smell creeping, grey-scaled concern drifting off the inspectors, an uneasiness that made him almost as uncomfortable as Dandy usually did. And now he had to admit that the *absence* of Dandy was making him uncomfortable.

"Dodgy doings," Gert said.

"Yes," DI Adams said. "And even more reason for you to stay well away from him and Delphine. *We* will get to the bottom on this." She pointed at Colin, then back at herself. "Us. Got it?"

No one spoke, until Thompson said, "One would think you'd give up trying to tell them what to do at some point."

DI Adams glared at him, and Colin said, "We could post someone on the road out of here, you know."

"The thought has crossed my mind," DI Adams said. "I was just hoping to talk sense into everyone."

Alice looked at her watch and nodded. "You're right. It's very late, and it'll be dark before long. We shall stay put."

"What?" The word seemed to burst out of Miriam. "We can't! Poor Gilbert—"

"We will deal with Gilbert," Beaufort said. "It's much easier for us, and I'm sure we'll be just fine flying. No one will see us."

Miriam frowned. "I don't like it."

Mortimer didn't, either. Not that he liked the idea of the ladies being at risk, either, but the thought of going back to those strange, empty fells made his paws itch.

"I wish you agreeing with me made me feel better," DI Adams said. "I'm not sure it does, though. What are you up to?"

"Nothing you need to worry about." Alice smiled at the inspector. "We will be going back tomorrow, however. Because the journalists must be forced to stop hunting dragons. However, we will stay away from Delphine and DCI Sykes."

DI Adams started to say something, and Colin said, "Short of house arrest, that's as good as we can hope for."

"Even house arrest doesn't work," Thompson said. "You should know that by now."

"She was under protective watch, not house arrest," DI Adams muttered, then sighed. "But fine. Let's leave it at that." She drained her cup of coffee and got up. "Don't go running about the fells tonight, and please try not to get arrested, kidnapped, stuck in monster traps, or provoke any monster-based riots, alright?"

Alice smiled. "We will try our best, Detective Inspector."

DI Adams turned to leave, then stopped and looked at Mortimer and Beaufort. "While you're out there," she said, "can you keep an eye out for Dandy?"

"I noticed he wasn't with you," Beaufort said. "Where did you last see him?"

"Eldmere. And he was very small."

"We will do what we can to find him," the High Lord said. "Won't we, Mortimer?"

Mortimer shivered, but nodded. "Yes. Of course."

"Thanks," DI Adams said, then she and Colin made their way out of the garden, Colin clutching two Tupperware containers Carlotta had filled and pressed on him. DI Adams' gaze shifted across the garden constantly, looking for a shadow that wasn't there.

"Interesting," Thompson said. "I mean, personally I think the Dandy can stay lost, but I'm up for checking out this Eldmere."

"We said we wouldn't tonight," Miriam said.

"*We're* going," Beaufort said. "We really do need to find Gilbert."

"Not alone," Alice said.

"Yes, alone. It takes less time to fly there than to drive, and if we find Gilbert one of us will come back and get you. Won't we, lad?"

"Yes," Mortimer said, even though he didn't much like the idea of flitting about Eldmere with monster hunters below. "We can do that."

"You just deal with the monster hunters," Beaufort said. "No one's looking for a couple of dragons up on the fells."

Alice frowned at him, then sighed. "I suppose it does make more sense than us driving you."

"Exactly." Beaufort grinned. "And you won't get in trouble with DI Adams."

Mortimer thought of the missing dandy and wished that was the worst of their worries.

"*Buk,*" the chicken said, and pecked his shoulder reassuringly.

"Thanks," he said with a sigh.

15
ALICE

Alice took a careful sip of her elderflower cordial and added some more sparkling water. Gert really did make very tasty cordial, but one didn't want to have too much of it. Not when one had a full day of debunking monster hunters ahead.

"Well," she said, as Miriam padded barefoot out to the table and sat down opposite her. "We need a plan for tomorrow."

"Do we trust him?" Teresa asked, pointing at Ervin.

"I'm very trustworthy!" he protested.

"I don't know. I think your dimples let you get away with too much."

"They are very nice dimples," Carlotta agreed.

"I can't help that," Ervin said.

Alice clasped her hands on the table. "He has proven himself to be quite reliable so far."

"We'll just threaten him with Thompson if he misbehaves," Beaufort said, grinning.

"No," the journalist said.

"Oi," the cat said. "I was just doing my job. *And* helping you lot out."

Alice supposed he had been, at that. It appeared that Thompson was the representative of some mysterious council of cats that policed the division between the humans and magical Folk. One way they did that was by being able to *suggest* to humans that they hadn't seen anything out of the ordinary. She was sure it was some sort of hypnosis, even if Thompson got sniffy at the term. However, it didn't always take, and the more exposure one had to the Folk world, the less chance that they could be made to forget it. The young journalist had been subject to such suggestions, but it hadn't lasted, and had simply left him with a strong aversion to cats. Or to Thompson, anyway.

"Did you ever do your suggestion thing on Katherine and Lloyd?" she asked the cat now.

"Couldn't," Thompson said simply. "Those two are deeply invested in cryptids. It's what they do."

"It doesn't mean they really believe it, though," Pearl said. "Remember those monster hunters from the telly who tried to find the bottom of the pond? They didn't believe *anything.*"

"Katherine the Terrible does," Mortimer said, plucking at his tail. "She *saw* me."

"That was unfortunate," Miriam said, and patted his shoulder.

"So that's out," Alice said. "And I suppose you can't exactly do some sort of mass hypnosis— sorry, *suggestion*, on everyone in Eldmere?"

"Absolutely not."

"How helpful."

"Maybe it'll all just blow over," Jasmine suggested. "If there's no new evidence, I mean."

"It's possible," Rose said. "There are periodic fusses about cryptids all the time. This is kind of a big one, though."

"And what if someone really does have Gilbert?" Mortimer asked.

No one spoke for a moment, and Alice tapped her fingers on the table, trying to understand how all the pieces fitted together. "I'm sure we're missing something."

"Marbles?" Thompson suggested, and she ignored him. Gert flicked one of his ears and he bared his teeth at her.

"Are we sure the paw prints are real?" Rose asked.

"Yes," Ervin said. "Sure as I can be, anyway."

"Alright. But on the forums they're saying the rest of the stuff in his Monster House is clearly faked." Rose tapped her phone where it sat on the table. "That suggests *he* doesn't have access to Gilbert, otherwise he'd have scales. He wouldn't be bothering painting horns and dying wool."

"So he found the prints and is blagging the rest for the money," Gert said. "Fair play."

"Which could mean Cryptid Kathy and Co are just there for the story. They might not know anything else," Ervin said, looking at the dragons.

Alice frowned. "And Delphine being so upset over it? She won't even have fairy doors in her markets, it appears."

"How boring," Miriam said, making a face.

"Some people are just very uncomfortable with magic," Beaufort said. "Even the suggestion of it is too much for them. You humans were very wound up about it for a few centuries there."

"I suppose," Alice said. It made sense, and she was probably reading far too much into Delphine's reaction to the idea that there were more things in the world than she appreciated.

"There were some very late witch hunts around here," Jasmine said, frowning. She pulled her phone out. "I was reading about it."

"Sounds like good bedtime reading," Rosemary said.

"I wanted to know more about the history of magic in the area," the younger woman said with a shrug, not looking up from her phone.

"Alright, Alice," Gert said. "What's our plan, then?"

Alice took another sip of cordial. "The dragons find Gilbert. We prove that the entire monster hunt is faked."

"How?" Rose asked.

"That's what we need to work on."

"I'll put the kettle on again," Miriam said.

"Have you got anything stronger?" Gert asked. "To keep the chill off, like."

"I'll look," Miriam said, and headed for the house.

"Here it is," Jasmine said. "*The last witch trials in England are rumoured to have been conducted by the Association of Ladies Against Rogue*

Magic (ALARM) in North Yorkshire. Officially they disbanded in 1743, but reports continued of ALARM still being in action throughout the nineteenth century. They were known, among other things, for destroying gargoyles on churches despite their intended design being to ward off evil, as well as believing all cats to be agents of chaotic magic."

"Fair," Thompson said.

"Does it say where in North Yorkshire they were?" Alice asked.

"No. Apparently they grew more and more secretive before finally vanishing. Science was in and witch hunting was very much out well before the end of the nineteenth century."

"Have you heard of them?" Priya asked the dragons.

"No," Beaufort said. "But we were very disconnected from humans through those days. The early witch hunts were the tail end of Folk having anything to do with humans. Dragons had already pulled back and become legends, but even the sprites and dryads went into hiding once they realised humans were quite happy to burn and drown each other over having a chat with a stream or a tree. No one wanted to be responsible for that."

There was silence for a moment, broken only when Miriam came back with a bottle of whisky in one hand and the big pot of tea swinging from the other. "What?" she asked, looking at the silent group. "What's happened?"

"Nothing," Alice said. "Just talking about witch trials."

"Ugh." Miriam put the pot on the table and handed Gert the bottle. "*Humans.*"

"My thoughts exactly," the cat said.

IT WAS, in the end, not a complicated plan. But the best plans didn't need to be. In fact, it was better if they weren't complicated at all. Less moving parts meant less things to go wrong. But as Alice walked home through the twilight shadows the image of Delphine standing on the doorstep of the Eldmere village hall with DCI Sykes, watching them leave, niggled at her. Although there was no reason to think that it was at all connected to the journalists or Gilbert in any way other than the fact that the village *was* rather overrun. She would have hated for Toot Hansell to have suffered the same fate, and she supposed she would have also called Colin and asked if he could do anything about moving people along before they stumbled on the dragons.

Which brought her back around to suspecting that Delphine had ulterior motives for wanting the village clear of people. But was that motive Gilbert, or another creature, or was there nothing at all? Alice supposed she could just be projecting. It was hard not to, when one knew there were dragons running about the place.

She sighed, and looked at Thompson, padding next to her with his tail up and his ragged ears twitching. "I hope we're going about this the right way."

"Self-doubt? That isn't like you."

"I'm sure we're doing the right thing as far as exposing the hoax. It's Delphine that's worrying me. I can't shake the idea that she knows something. And with poor Gilbert still missing …"

"Maybe he joined a dwarf band?" Thompson suggested. "They get into some pretty serious rock music. Heh."

"Stop being smart. This is serious."

"I will always be smart, but fine."

Alice frowned at him as she let them in the front gate. "You don't get any more endearing, you know."

"Neither do you. And that's a quality, not a deficit."

She shook her head. "I can see why ALARM were worried about cats being agents of evil."

"Agents of chaotic magic, it was. And, look, I can see why the W.I. make you nervous. You have inside information about just how devious they are. But do you really think they know about dragons?"

Alice dug her keys out of her bag as she considered it, then said, "I don't know. They – or Delphine at least – just seem so against the monster hunters. More so than you'd think would make sense if they're just being a bit of a nuisance."

Thompson shrugged. "Then they'll be happy you're helping clear the village of hoaxers, won't they?"

"I suppose."

"I know. Do we have any of that cod left?"

"We?"

"I live here too."

Alice sighed as she stepped into the calm, familiar scents of her kitchen. "And I still don't know how that happened."

"No one ever does," the cat said comfortably.

ALICE SPENT the time until midnight reading up on Eldmere, for all the good it did her. There was very little to be said about it that she could see. There were the usual mentions of walking tracks and fêtes, and apparently it was in the Domesday Book, which meant it had been around right back in 1086. But there was nothing else of interest that she could find, no matter how she poked around on the internet. The Eldmere W.I. was listed on the main W.I. site, of course, but there was nothing else of interest there. She wasn't sure what she'd been hoping to find. A listing of "monster-keeping" in their interests, perhaps? But it did pass the time, and at midnight she shut her laptop and got up. It was now technically tomorrow, so she was following the letter of her promise to DI Adams, if not the sentiment.

"Come on," she said to Thompson, who had been snoozing on the sofa next to her. "Let's go and see what you can find."

He yawned and blinked at her. "Gilbert in a beret, doing spoken word poetry on the edge of a lake. That's my guess."

"That would be handy," she said, and grabbed her keys from the hook by the door as she led the way out of the house.

The roads were dark and empty, but with the moon nearing full the fields were painted in shades of silver and charcoal, waterways turned to glittering veins of mercury where Alice glimpsed them in the rolls of the land. It was a quick, easy drive without cyclists or walkers to worry about, and between the vast stretch of star-dusted sky above her and the otherworldliness of the moonlight, she felt like an explorer in a Jules Verne novel, stepping out into an undiscovered and unimagined world.

Well, except for Thompson, who spent the drive coming up with other possibilities for where Gilbert might be.

"He's joined a cult."

"A cult?"

"Yes. The vegetarianism was the first sign things were wrong."

"Do Folk have cults?"

"Folk are every bit as silly as humans, in their way. Maybe he's run off to sea. He always liked swimming more than flying."

"You're entirely ignoring the fact that we're almost sure he was at the farm. Unless there's some other dragon wandering about leaving paw prints everywhere."

Thompson yawned noisily. "He probably went to break out some sheep or something."

"That's the first sensible thing you've said."

"I still like the idea of him in an emo band."

Alice wasn't exactly sure what an emo band was, but she wasn't going to let on to a cat that he knew more about human pop culture than she did. So she just pointed through the windscreen and said, "That's the edge of the valley there."

"Weird. I thought I knew the area pretty well," Thompson said, putting his paws on the dashboard so he could peer at the road. "I don't—" he sneezed and gave Alice a startled look.

"Bless you," she said, and he sneezed again, his eyes wide.

"Stop," he said.

"What?" She took her foot off the accelerator.

"*Stop.* ***Stop!***" He flung himself back into the seat, as if shying away from an oncoming collision, and Alice jammed her foot onto the brake.

"Thompson?"

But he was gone. Somewhere between falling away from the dashboard and hitting the seat, he'd simply *gone.* And while Alice was unpleasantly familiar with the ability of cats to vanish and reappear at will – shifting, Thompson called it – this hadn't seemed like that. She checked the back seat, then peered through the rear window, half-expecting to see him sitting by the side of the road, but it was empty.

"Thompson?" she tried again, but there was no response. She shifted into reverse and backed up to around the point just before his first sneeze, then put the handbrake on and got out. The night air was softly cool, the scent of grass and earth still warm from the day heavy about her, and she could see sheep drifting in the fields to one side, and to the other long, undisturbed grass.

But there was no cat.

"Well, this is unexpected," she said to the night. Nothing replied, so she got back in the car and found somewhere to turn around. She didn't drive home immediately, though. She just sat there, watching the night and wondering about the valley of Meredale. What had Miriam said? That it was *empty.*

Maybe there was a reason for that.

ALICE CHECKED HER WATCH, then knocked smartly on Miriam's door. She was rewarded by a shout inside, and she opened the door to find Miriam still pulling on a giant green cardigan festooned with haphazardly attached crocheted flowers. Her hair was unbrushed and managed to look both flattened and bushy, and she fumbled the kettle on as Alice set a plate of muffins on the table.

"It's barely light," she said. "You didn't even give me time to get dressed!"

"I know," Alice said. She had tried to sleep, but it had been a very unfruitful exercise. She had eventually got up and gone digging through the internet for any mention of the Association of Ladies Against Rogue Magic. She hadn't been able to find anything more than the little bit of information Jasmine had given her, but she knew she wasn't terribly good at such things. She had sent a message to Jasmine as early as she had dared, asking her to look into it. The younger woman would be much more effective. Now she pushed the plate of muffins toward Miriam. "Breakfast?"

Miriam looked at the muffins, then at Alice. "What's going on? We weren't meeting for another two hours."

"They've got sunflower seeds in them," Alice said. "Your favourites."

"Sunflower seeds aren't anyone's favourites, Alice. They're very plain. I like *sunflowers.*"

Alice nodded. "But the seeds are good as well."

"Have you slept at all?" Miriam asked, ignoring the muffins as she muddled about with the tea and the pot.

"Not really." Alice rubbed her forehead. "I've lost Thompson."

"What? How?"

"I got almost as far as Eldmere—"

"*Alice.* Only the dragons were meant to go last night!"

Alice waved a hand impatiently. "Yes, yes. But something happened when we got close. Thompson just *vanished,* and he hasn't come back."

"It wasn't just one of his usual cat vanishings?"

"No. I thought maybe he'd be home when I got there, but there's been no sign."

Miriam pushed her hair off her face and took cups from the cupboard to the table, anxious creases on her forehead. "Did you argue?"

"No more than usual. But Miriam, he shouted for me to stop, and it was as if something was *hurting* him."

Miriam stared at Alice. "Like … like he'd hit an electric fence?"

"Maybe. I don't know."

Miriam fetched the milk from the fridge, then just stood there, frowning. Alice wanted to lean over and slap her hand lightly, to tell her to *focus* and hurry up, that this mattered somehow. But she just couldn't quite articulate how. Something here would bring everything into focus, if they could just work it out. But there was no rushing Miriam. It would just fluster her. So Alice folded her hands on the table and waited, while the thin morning light gathered strength and began to spread warmth across the world.

Miriam put the milk on the table, poured the tea and picked up a muffin before she looked at Alice, and said, "You mustn't laugh at me."

"I never do," Alice said, perfectly honestly.

Miriam tipped her head slightly, then smiled. "You don't, do you?"

"Of course not. You may have some funny ideas, dear, but they always make some sort of sense. You're very wise, in your way."

"That may be nicest thing anyone's ever said to me."

"I shall stop being nice if you don't tell what you're thinking, though."

Miriam snorted. "Alright. When we drove into Eldmere, and when we left, I felt a ... a *frisson,* I suppose. Like a cat walking over your grave."

"I see."

"And it's not nerves, or anything like that. It's an external thing, like when you stand somewhere that something monumental has happened, and you can hear the echoes of it somewhere down deep, where we're all still small creatures hiding in the dark."

Alice considered it. "So something monumental happened there? But why don't we know about it? And why would Thompson vanish?"

"I said it's *like* that. Maybe it's not the memory of anything, in this case. Maybe it's magic. I feel little sparks of it sometimes when Mortimer shows me a particularly good bauble, or when Beaufort growls. There's an *otherness,* you know?"

Alice thought she might, but she wasn't sure. This was very much Miriam territory, not hers. "Could it be to do with why you felt the woods were empty?"

"Yes," Miriam said immediately. "Yes, I think so. Maybe there's something that keeps Folk out, and we humans just aren't developed enough to feel it properly."

"But the dragons could get in and out just fine."

"Dragons are very old and *very* magical. Maybe they have more resistance to it." Miriam considered it. "Dandy got into Eldmere, but then he was acting very strangely, and now he's vanished. So perhaps it acts differently on different kinds. Thompson's just a cat, and is really very young in the scheme of things, so maybe he couldn't go through it at all."

"Then where is he?" Alice asked. "Wouldn't he have come back here?"

Miriam considered this while she ate a piece of muffin. "This is very good," she said after a moment. "I do like the sunflower seeds."

Alice smiled at her, then said, "What about Gilbert, then?"

"Maybe something else happened. Maybe there are other ... *traps* for creatures that make it past the barrier." Miriam stared at her plate as if the muffin had suddenly sprouted legs. "Maybe there really are hunters in there."

They were both quiet for a moment, then Alice said, "Perhaps passing the barrier triggers something. It takes longer to catch up with the bigger creatures, but it snatched Thompson up right away." She thought about it. "That seems very magical for a place determined to keep magic *out,* though."

"Maybe it's all about the type of magic," Miriam said. "You know, like all those people who protest affordable housing. Houses are fine, but not *affordable* ones."

Alice nodded slowly. "That sounds very accurate, dear."

"And *awful*. Who would do that? Who *could* do that?"

"I would only be guessing," Alice said. "But I can think of someone who would most certainly *want* to."

Miriam stared at her, then popped the last bit of muffin into her mouth and got up. "I'll get dressed. What about the rest of the plan?"

"Oh, we'll need that more than ever," Alice said, and picked up her phone. "I'll make some calls while you get ready."

She had her thumb hovering over the dial button when she suddenly looked around the bright kitchen.

"Miriam," she said. "Shouldn't the dragons be back by now?"

Miriam turned from the door to the hall and looked at the floor as if startled to discover there were no dragons taking up half the room.

"Oh no," she said.

16
MIRIAM

They set off for Eldmere in a small convoy just before eight. The heat barely seemed to have dissipated in the night at all, and it was the sort of Saturday that chased people out of cities and towns into the nearest patch of green land. Cars were already puttering along every road, packed with families trying to get ahead of the crowds and festooned with dogs hanging out of windows, the drivers going far too slowly and taking up more than their fair share of the skinny lanes. Walkers in frayed shorts and old trainers, maps hung around their necks, looked sideways at others in spotless high-performance hiking trousers and the sort of boots one needed an instruction book to get into, all of them vying for the best footpaths and tutting at each other at gates. The cyclists had multiplied exponentially, and motorbikes grumbled and revved at the congestion, while the sheep watched it all with bland yet nervous indifference.

Miriam looked over her shoulder at the white van following them. Gert was leaning out the window shouting at a red-faced man in an Audi convertible, who was refusing to get any closer to the wall on his side of the road.

"Move *over*, you numpty!" Gert shouted. "You think you're the only car on the road?"

"I *can't* move over, you ridiculous woman! There's no more road!"

"Do you not know how verges work?"

"This car does not go on verges."

"It bloody will if it wants to get past my van!"

"Oh dear," Miriam said. "Should we do something?"

"No," Alice said, checking the rear-view mirror. "He'll survive."

"His car might not," Jasmine said from the back seat.

"It's a very silly car," Miriam said, but Gert was squeezing past the man, who shouted something that made a woman walking with two children turn to her son and say, "This is how you don't behave, alright?" The boy nodded, and Gert gave him a thumbs up as she sailed after Alice. Rose and Priya were in the front seat with her, both of them laughing, and behind the van was Teresa's car, ferrying Pearl, Carlotta and Rosemary. Miriam felt vaguely more at ease having the other women with them. Sometimes there was a certain safety in numbers. Not that she was staying with them for long – Ervin was already in Eldmere, and she was going with him to look for the dragons. She would rather have gone with Alice, but Alice said she needed to stay in the village, and that she was sure Miriam could manage the young journalist perfectly well. Miriam supposed she could, but she wasn't sure she really *wanted* to.

"Tell Miriam what you found out, Jasmine," Alice said now, as the road opened up a bit more.

"Ooh, yes. So, I did some more reading on ALARM – the Association for Ladies Against Rogue Magic. And it's still active."

"What?" Miriam twisted in her seat to look at Jasmine. "Really?"

"Yes, only it's called LAAB now – Ladies Against Antisocial Behaviour."

"I don't like the sound of that any better."

"No. It seems to be a bit neighbourhood watch-ish, but more ..." Jasmine hesitated, searching for the right word.

"Unpleasant?" Miriam suggested.

"Intolerant?" Alice offered.

"Possibly both of those. There's quite a bit on one forum about a branch in Cumbria that basically forced the owners of a new campsite out of business because they were clothing optional."

"Still witch hunting, then," Alice said.

"I suppose." Jasmine scrolled through her phone. "There's no central site that I can find, or a list of where there are branches of it – it's kind of secretive."

"I do wonder why," Alice said, raising one eyebrow. "Anything connected to Eldmere about either of those?"

"Not that I've found. But Eldmere has a weirdly high rate of accidental deaths."

"Oh?"

"Yes. People drowning in the tarn, having their tractor roll over on them – someone even somehow got sucked into quicksand? I didn't even think quicksand was quite real. I thought it was just in books."

"Anything in common with the deaths?"

"Not sure yet," Jasmine said. "So far they all seem to have recently moved to Eldmere, though."

"Dangerous place," Alice said.

"Seems so. But apparently the ALARM villages were the safest places in the country back in witch hunting days."

"Unless you were a witch," Miriam said.

"Well, yes. Or anything else magical. Iron was buried in the hills to keep the faeries out, and the rivers were poisoned to kill the sprites, and there weren't even any healers or herbal remedies allowed. In order to join the association you had to be either recommended by a member or have a letter from an actual witch hunter promising you weren't a witch."

"Keeping faeries out is sensible, but the rest seems very unnecessary," Miriam said with a shiver. She'd only had one encounter with faeries, but she had no desire to repeat it. They were less glitter and sparkle, more teeth and claws.

"It would explain why there's no Folk in the valley," Alice said.

"Do you really think there's still an ALARM in Eldmere?" Miriam asked.

"Maybe. Or it might just be the memory of it." She glanced at

Miriam. "But we do have two missing magical creatures. Three, if we count the cat."

Miriam nodded slowly and leaned back in her seat. "Five. We don't know where Mortimer and Beaufort are."

There was silence after that, as they headed for Eldmere and its silent hills, haunted by the threat of something far more fearsome than the Yorkshire Beast.

❧

ERVIN WAS LEANING against his car, which was pulled onto the verge at the beginning of a long line of parked cars leading into Eldmere. He straightened up as Alice pulled in behind him, and watched Gert and Teresa rumble past, giving them a bemused wave. He bent to look at Alice as Miriam climbed out.

"What are you lot up to?"

"If you'd stayed last night, you might have known," Alice said, smiling.

"Leeds is a long drive from Toot Hansell," he protested. "And here. Plus I had some work to do."

"Miriam will fill you in," Alice said, as Miriam took her shopping bags from Alice's car and Jasmine climbed into the front seat. The bags were laden with vegetarian sausage rolls and solid slices of fruitcake and anything else that she thought a young, hungry dragon might need. She'd been up very late baking it all, which had made Alice's early morning call even more unwelcome.

Miriam and Ervin looked at each other dubiously. "Put it in the boot?" he offered, opening the back of the car.

She dropped the bags in, wishing she were going into the village with the others, and looked at Alice. "What if we have no mobile reception again?"

"Just find Beaufort and Mortimer," Alice said. "We'll deal with the village and the journalists."

Miriam nodded, and Ervin said, "Find them? I thought they were coming back to yours."

"They never turned up," Miriam said.

"That's not good." Ervin rubbed a hand through his dark hair. "Are we sure there's no Beast?" He said it with a smile, but it was a half-hearted thing.

"I'm starting to side with DCI Sykes on this," Alice said. "I rather think this might be all human." She looked at Miriam. "Don't worry about anything except the dragons. We'll be absolutely fine here."

"Alright," she said, and waved as they pulled away, heading for the village. She looked at Ervin. "Is that what you're going dragon hunting in?" He had evidently made it home to change, but he was still in jeans and trainers, which she didn't feel were particularly practical for hiking around hills looking for dragon-nappers.

"Me?" he asked. "What about you?"

She had reluctantly put a pair of hiking boots on, as she supposed there was no guarantee all the terrain would be good for barefoot walking, and the boggy bits would pose a serious threat to trainers. She'd also swapped her bright skirt and leggings for the darkest ones she had, in the hope that they'd be less obvious on the fells. That meant a lovely deep burgundy for the skirt and dark blue with a glittery finish for the leggings. She also had a boring black walking coat in case of a sudden change in the weather. She couldn't remember buying it. Someone must have given it to her.

"Do you even have a jacket?" she asked the journalist. "The weather can change terribly quickly on the fells. Most people get in trouble because they forget that."

"I've got a hoody in the car," he said, and scratched his chin. "Shall we go, then?"

"Alright."

They headed off rather stiffly, creeping through the village, which was even busier than it had been the day before. The pavements were crowded with families as well as groups of monster hunters, and Gert's yellow monster T-shirts had proliferated like some sort of curious pollen. There were signs everywhere too, rough things printed on A4 paper and stapled to the wooden posts of fences and taped to the very few streetlights. Miriam spotted a round woman with curly hair painstakingly removing them, as well as a couple of girls with gangly, pre-teen legs under their big yellow shirts sticking more up at a rather quicker pace.

"So what's the plan?" Ervin asked.

"Find the dragons," Miriam said. "And as quickly as possible."

"I mean with all your shirts and posters. That's you, isn't it?"

"Distraction," she said, and waved at the road. "Just hurry, can't you?"

"I can talk and drive at once."

"I'd rather you didn't. It's very busy."

Ervin snorted, but just swung over the bridge and headed out of the village again, picking up speed as the walkers thinned, then vanished as they passed Cooper's farm. Miriam checked her seatbelt as they accelerated through the twisting roads out of the valley, thinking she maybe shouldn't have insisted he hurry up *quite* so much.

❧

THE ROAD to the tarn had a gate at the top, a red and white *Private No Entry* sign attached firmly to the middle of it. Miriam got out to let them through, averting her gaze from the sign as if that might mean they were less likely to be noticed. But other than a pack of cyclists burning past with their heads down and their alarmingly toned calves pumping rhythmically, they got through without being seen, and a moment later were bumping down the track toward the tarn, Ervin wincing every time the raised ridge in the middle of the road scraped the undercarriage of the car.

"I'm going to have to get a different car if this keeps up," he said.

"Alice had to," Miriam said. "Although that was probably also because we got the other one stuck on the fells. She didn't want a repeat."

"Oh, great. Good to know."

"It wasn't our fault. Thompson was telling us where to go, and I don't think he quite understands the limitation of cars." Miriam hesitated, then added, "And it wasn't as bad as the time someone blew up the brakes on her new car."

"*What?*"

"They put some device thingy on them and triggered it while I was driving. It was *awful.*"

"I bet," Ervin said. "I hadn't realised life in the W.I. was quite so dangerous."

"You should have seen the exploding baubles. *They* were dangerous."

They jounced on a little further in silence, then he said, "I really hate that I can't write about this stuff."

"No one would believe you anyway," Miriam pointed out.

"I *know.* It sucks." He rubbed a hand through his hair and gave her a dimpled grin. "But also I don't want to end up unemployable and sectioned, so I'll keep quiet."

"And Gert might set Thompson on you."

"Or Walter might come after me." He shuddered. "I still have nightmares about the drooling."

Miriam laughed, then straightened up in her seat as the tarn came into view, the surface a flat sheet undisturbed by wind and reflecting the sky above. "Here we are." She'd half hoped to see the dragons sitting on the shore waiting for them, even though she knew that was impossible. They'd have been home that morning if that were the case.

The track twisted and turned and bounced a little further before finally delivering them to the shoreline and the hard-packed, grassy area next to the hut. Ervin stopped well back from the water, and they both stared at the tarn. It looked darker from this angle.

"I don't like just leaving the car here," he said. "If anyone comes down they'll see us straight away."

Miriam opened her door, letting in a slow roll of hot, still air that started her sweating almost immediately. "No one should really be down here."

"No one except that Sykes and his fake ferret traps, and Cooper with his dogs."

They looked at each other, then she said, "Right. I'll start looking for the dragons. You take the car back to the main road and be ready to pick me up."

"I can't leave you. That's just as likely to get me bitten by Walter."

Miriam squared her shoulders and raised a finger, trying to channel Alice, and in that moment there was an explosion of movement from the tarn, the surface shattering and water surging upward. Ervin yelped, grabbing the steering wheel as if he were about to drive off immediately, and Miriam swallowed some very unsuitable language as the movement resolved into a grey, pony-sized dragon scrabbling ashore and shaking his wings off, then running to meet them. The chicken appeared out of the reeds on the shore and ran after him, squawking in disapproval.

Miriam scrambled out of the car, scanning the hills as she did. "Mortimer! *There* you are! What on earth's happened? Why didn't you come back?" She stopped, one hand on her chest, as he looked up at her with wide amber eyes. "Where's Beaufort?"

"It was a trap," Mortimer said.

"The ferret traps?" Ervin asked, climbing out of the car.

"Yes. I mean, no, they weren't ferret traps—"

"But they were his traps," Miriam said, her hands clenching into fists at her chest. "It was *him.*"

"I think so. We were just about to give up when we found this cage up on the fells with a live goat in it. I told Beaufort not to go in, but he was sure he could get out again, and he wanted to release the goat in the hopes it might tell us something." Mortimer swallowed. "Only the cage shut on him and he *couldn't* get out, and the goat kept fainting, so it couldn't tell us anything at all."

"Where is he now?" Ervin asked. "Can we see if we can get him out?"

Mortimer shook his head. "It's locked. You need a key. And we couldn't bend the bars or even burn them. I tried *everything,* and then it was daylight, and ..." He trailed off, his voice shaky, and Miriam patted his shoulder as reassuringly as she could. She wasn't sure how well it worked, as her hands were shaking from a mix of fright and a boiling fury that was churning in her belly. How dare that Sykes do this to *dragons? How dare he?*

"Maybe with hands—" Ervin started.

"Don't be silly," Miriam said sharply. "You've seen Mortimer's craft-dragon-ship. If he can't open the lock, we can't either."

"Craft … dragon …?"

Miriam ignored him. "We have to tell Alice. Or DI Adams. Or someone." She checked her phone, but there was no more reception now than there had been the day before. "It's almost ten already. Sykes hasn't been back?"

Mortimer shook his head. "I've been here since it got light, waiting for you."

She nodded. "Then Sykes could be back any moment. Mortimer, we'll go to the trap and make sure if he does turn up he can't do … whatever he's planning to do." The very thought made a tight band of pressure pop into existence over her forehead. "Ervin, you head back to the village until you can get some reception and tell … well, *everyone.* We're going to need tools or something to get Beaufort out, and we have to keep Katherine away, and we have to catch this horrible Sykes, and we have to—" She stopped, spots dancing in her vision.

"Miriam?" Mortimer said.

"Do you want to sit down?" Ervin asked, sounding as if he were far too close to her.

"No! No, I need … I need a cricket bat." But she sat down for a moment in the passenger seat anyway, taking deep, shaky breaths until the spots started to recede. When she looked up again, Mortimer and the chicken were both staring at her, the chicken with her head to one side and Mortimer with his eyebrow ridges drawn down. Ervin was rummaging in the back of the car, and a moment later he reappeared and handed her an aluminium baseball bat.

"What's this?" she asked.

"I do on occasion find myself in not great places for my stories," he said. "It's only from Sports Direct, but it seems alright. Never had to use it, mind."

She stood up and swung it a couple of times. It felt lighter and more fluid than the cricket bat, even if it was a touch longer. "Oh," she said, and gave him a slightly wobbly smile. "Thank you."

"Sure. Just tell Colin I tried to stop you from running off over the moors in search of a rogue police officer. That way at least I only have Thompson and Walter to worry about."

"Okay." She thought about it. "You didn't try to stop me, though."

"I'm not quite that silly." He climbed into the driver's side. "Go on, then. Let's get on with this."

Miriam slammed her own door, and by the time Ervin had headed carefully back up the farm track, the little Nissan jouncing enthusiastically, she and Mortimer were already striding through the tussocky grass that fringed the tarn. Mortimer was still terribly grey, and the chicken was clucking anxiously where she rode on his shoulder, but Miriam walked with her back as straight as she could, the baseball bat resting on her shoulder while she thought about Sykes – about *anyone* – putting a dragon in a cage.

She shifted her grip on the bat and thought she might have to get one for herself.

❧

THE CLIMB to the cage was surprisingly easy, along what seemed to be a disused track that hugged the curves of the hill, carrying on further around the tarn than where they'd emerged the day before, then diving deeper into the hills. It was heavily grown over with grass, but where water softened the ground Miriam could see that someone had driven over it not long ago. With a trap on the back, no doubt.

"Do you think that's what happened to Gilbert?" she asked Mortimer. She was panting with the climb, but didn't slow. "He tried to free the goat and was trapped?"

"I imagine," Mortimer said. "He'd never have been able to leave it once he saw it."

"No," she said with a sigh. "But what about the pumpkins and the hut? We still don't know what happened there."

Mortimer just shook his head. "It's not far now."

It wasn't. They crested one more ridge, the land forming fingers of green that pinched at the tarn and made it hard to see what lay between the folds, and Mortimer said, "It's just—" He stopped, staring up the slope at a patch of grass like any other.

"Where?" Miriam asked, looking around.

"It was *here.*" Mortimer ran off the path, lunging through the tussocky grass as if he thought Beaufort might have merely sunk into the ground somewhere. "It was right here! I can still smell him!"

"What else can you smell?" Miriam demanded, hurrying up to him. Now she was standing close enough, she could see gouges in the earth where the dragons had braced themselves as they tried to tear the cage open, and her heart gave a horrible squeeze that stole her breath more than the climb had.

"I don't *know!*" Mortimer had gone a terrible, chalky grey, his voice rising to almost a howl. "Where's Beaufort? *Where's the High Lord?*" His cry echoed across the fells, setting some grouse fleeing out of the heather. *"Beaufort!"*

"Mortimer!" Miriam half-shouted, and he gave her a startled glance, already looking as if he were about to call for the High Lord again. "That's not helping! Now what can you *smell?*"

"How am I meant to—"

"If you don't figure out what you can smell, we've got nothing to go on. Nothing at all! Because Sykes hasn't been back via the tarn, has he?"

Mortimer shook his head, his snout trembling.

"Right. Then he must be working with someone else. And we need to find out who."

There was a long silence, and for one moment she thought Mortimer was going to start shouting again, then he took a shaky breath and said, "You're right. I'm sorry."

"Don't be," she said, and pointed at the ground. "Now, what can you smell?"

Mortimer closed his eyes, curling his tail around him and clutching it in both paws. She could see the scales flaking, and her heart gave another of those painful squeezes, but a hint of camouflaging green was coming back into the dragon's scales as he opened his eyes and looked at her. "Pumpkins," he said.

"What?"

"I can smell pumpkins. I can't smell Gilbert, but maybe whoever's been giving him pumpkins was here. I can smell …" He closed his eyes again. "Sykes is sort of opaque, like a wooden sign in the rain. But there's someone else, and I think it's really recent. They're kind of angry, and … they smell like lightning over the water. All sharp and bright and full of salt and edges."

Miriam frowned at him as he opened his eyes. "That doesn't sound very good."

"No," Mortimer agreed, and pointed with one paw. "But they came up here in some sort of truck or something. And I think I can follow that."

Miriam followed his pointing paw and found that she could see tracks that had been left by fat tyres. "Well, you could have said that first."

"I'm not sure I thought of it first," he admitted, and she patted his shoulder, then dug in her pockets to check her phone.

"Still no signal," she said, and found a handful of Werther's in her other pocket. "Caramel?"

"It might help," he said.

"It might," she agreed, and unwrapped one to hand to him as they started down the track of the dragon thief, the chicken trotting behind them.

17

DI ADAMS

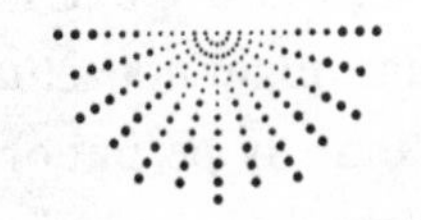

DI Adams stood on her back doorstep in the morning sun and shook a mug of coffee, the hot liquid spilling over her fingers and making her swear.

"*Ow.* Dandy? Here boy! Dandy!"

There was no sign of him, not at any size, but her neighbour popped his head up over the fence, making her jump.

"Do you have a dog?" he asked her.

"Morning, Finlay. Um ... not exactly."

"Well, you either do or you don't. Have you cleared that with Sarah? She's the owner of that house."

"Yes, I'm aware of who my landlady is, thanks. I'm just dog sitting."

"Are you trying to feed it *coffee?* No wonder it won't come."

DI Adams looked at the sky, already high and burnt at the edges, and swallowed a sigh. "This is my coffee. Obviously I'm not giving the dog coffee."

"Where is it?" Finlay asked, craning to try and peer over the fence.

"Inside. I was trying to get him to come out." She fixed him with a look that wasn't quite a scowl. "Anything else I can help you with, or can I have my coffee in peace now?"

"I'm just being neighbourly."

"No you're not," DI Adams said flatly, and they stared at each other. Finlay looked away first, and vanished back down his side of the fence, muttering something about stuck-up bloody southerners. DI Adams didn't feel particularly bad. She was quite certain he kept a bench on his side of the fence just so he could stand on it and spy on her garden. She supposed she'd have to think about moving to a more permanent place at some stage (this house was technically a short-term let she simply hadn't got around to moving out of), but some small part of her still harboured a tiny hope that she might not actually live in Skipton forever. She was fairly sure it was a futile hope, but one couldn't simply let go of it. That way lay flat caps and thinking "ay up" was an acceptable greeting.

She had a final look around the garden then went back inside, tipping the coffee into a stainless bowl and leaving it on the floor, just in case Dandy got back before she did. Then she grabbed her keys and left, feeling as though she'd suddenly looked down and found her shadow had vanished. She'd never thought that she'd miss having an invisible, red-eyed dog of variable size.

AT THE STATION car park she didn't even have time to get out of her car before Collins came charging out of the station, phone in one hand. Hers started ringing as she swung the car door open and called, "Collins?"

He looked up at her, hung up and said, "Drive," as he jogged to the passenger door.

She blinked, but decided that questions could wait, judging by the look on his face. She started the engine again and pulled out as he struggled with the seatbelt.

"What's happening?"

"Graham's just called to tell me that he's arrested Lloyd Cameron."

"Who?"

"Cryptid Kathy's sidekick," he said, managing to get clipped in.

"Right. What for?"

"Attacking the W.I."

"*What?*"

"Yep. Apparently he's accusing them of kidnapping Katherine herself. She went missing last night, and he's just tried to have it out with them."

"In Eldmere?'

"Obviously."

"Right." She pulled abruptly into a gap in the parked cars on the side of the road out of town.

"What're you doing?" Collins asked.

"I need decent coffee if we're tackling a W.I. kidnapping plot."

He started to say something, then stopped as DI Adams' phone rang. She checked the dashboard display and winced. *DCI Taylor,* it read. She hit answer on the handsfree. "Hello?"

"DI Adams, it's DCI Taylor."

"Um ... hello, Marm." Using titles seemed like a bad sign. The DCI usually insisted on being called Maud and had never called DI Adams anything but Adams.

"Are you in Eldmere?"

"Just on the way."

"Right. Well, DCI Sykes is saying that Mr Jake Cooper wants you to be removed from his case, and is considering filing a complaint against you."

"I'm sorry?"

"Yes, he's just here."

"Mr Cooper is there?"

"No, DCI Sykes."

That explained the titles then. "I see. Mr Cooper seemed perfectly happy with our handling of his case yesterday. And isn't his wife still missing?"

"There seems to be some question over whether she was ever missing at all, according to DCI Sykes. He appears to have the case in hand and feels that he can get the complaint dropped, but you obviously need to have no further contact with Cooper."

DI Adams looked at Collins, who shook his head, his mouth tight. "Understood," she said aloud.

"Good to hear, DI Adams. Carry on and all that." There was a click as the call ended, and DI Adams stared at the phone, then at Collins.

"*Carry on and all that?*" he said. "Since when did Maud – sorry, *DCI Taylor* start talking like some Oxbridge old boy?"

"About the same time she started insisting on using titles," DI Adams said, and looked longingly at the coffeeshop across the road. She could actually see the roaster beyond the display of mugs in the window. "So we've got the W.I. kidnapping a journalist—"

"They won't have done it."

"I mean, *probably* not," she said, and shrugged when he gave her a disapproving look. "It'd be one way to stop her chasing dragons. Maybe they're going to coerce a retraction of her story out of her."

"That's my aunt," he pointed out.

"I know." She rubbed a hand over her face and reached for the keys. "Right. We better move before Sykes gets wind of it and arrests the lot of them."

"Ah, yes," Collins said.

"Ah what? I don't like that."

"I've also been trying to call Cooper all morning, and there's no answer on his mobile or on the farm landline. So I don't know when Sykes has been in contact with him."

DI Adams turned the car off again. "No. I need coffee."

"Fair." Collins looked in the backseat. "Has Dandy reappeared?"

"No."

He regarded her for a moment, a frown tugging at the corners of his mouth, and for one horrible moment she thought he was going to say something sympathetic. Then he just said, "How many shots?"

"Three," she said, handing him her to-go mug.

"Bloody hell," he said. "Dandy better turn up soon."

He hurried across the road and DI Adams looked at her empty backseat. There was hair matted in the corners.

IT WAS a fast drive to Eldmere. She blipped her lights when she had to, and overtook on every straight stretch that appeared, earning them horns and shouts from anyone who hadn't spotted them approaching. Collins kept one hand on the dashboard and drank his mocha unsteadily with the other, grumbling when he spilt it on his shirt, and in less than an hour they were coasting past the cars lining the verge on the way into the village.

Collins looked up from his phone and said, "Graham's got Lloyd in the deli for now, but the W.I. are in an overflow car park just past town."

"The deli?"

"I asked him not to process him, just calm him down."

"Right. Let's see if we can find the W.I., then."

The streets were even more crowded than the day before, and the sense of being caught in some sort of very fringe festival was stronger than ever. DI Adams drove straight through the village and found a makeshift carpark set up in a field not far past the last of the buildings. The feel of a summer festival carried on over here, with campervans and food trucks and someone selling balloons – there was always someone selling balloons – and a lot of people wandering around barefoot. There was even a bouncy castle, and a makeshift band already starting up on one corner with a fiddle, a ukulele, and set of bongo drums. A bare-chested man and a handful of kids were dancing wildly in front of them, and DI Adams was fairly sure she could arrest a good portion of the field's population for possession, public intoxication, selling alcohol without a licence, and half a dozen other things besides. Which was always a good thing to have up her sleeve if everything went wrong later and she either needed a reason to be here or simply had a need to arrest someone.

They joined a queue of two other cars waiting to get into the field, DI Adams barely restraining herself from simply driving around them. Sometimes a gentler approach was needed.

There was a young woman in running shorts and bare feet standing at the gate, a large multicoloured umbrella over one shoulder to protect her from the sun, already strong before ten in the morning. She bent down to peer into the car as DI Adams drew up.

"Ay up," the young woman said, and grinned. She had a broad, infectious grin, and her shoulders were pink with sunburn despite the umbrella. "Just the one day, is it?"

"You do overnight stays?"

"'Course not. 'S'not allowed, is it? Multi-day pass, though, y'know?" Her grin broadened.

DI Adams looked past her at the caravans and campers with their awnings out and tables and chairs set up in the shade. "So I see," she said.

"Ten quid for the day," the young woman said, and peered past DI Adams at Collins. "If you lot are undercover you're right bad at it."

"We're just looking for someone," DI Adams said, and looked at Collins. "I don't have any cash."

"Bloody daylight robbery," he muttered, digging his wallet out.

"That's me," the young woman agreed as she took the money. She pocketed it and pointed to the corner of the field closest to the road. A white van, a small SUV, and a bright pink Honda were lined up neatly next to each other, an awning pulled out from the side of the van and some folding chairs leaning against it in the shade. "Your mate in uniform was sorting out that muppet who was hassling the ladies over there, if that's who you're after."

"Thanks." DI Adams inspected the field. "You having much bother otherwise?"

"Nothing I need the filth for," the woman said, and winked at DI Adams. "I'll let you know, though."

"Fair enough," DI Adams said, returning her grin, and drove across the crushed grass of the field as the next car pulled up behind them.

"Filth," Collins grumbled. "Bet she doesn't even have a permit for this."

"Better than cars parked all over the roads, causing accidents," DI Adams said as she pulled up behind the van. "Come on. Let's see what the W.I. are playing at."

❧

THE SUN WAS IMPOSSIBLY HOT. It had no right being this hot in the north of England, DI Adams thought as she regarded the W.I.'s little convoy. She grabbed the sunscreen from the glovebox and smeared some on her arms, then handed the bottle to Collins before she got out of the car and went to check the van. The doors were shut, and there was no sign of life. She knocked on the back, then tried the door.

"Locked," she said to Collins as he joined her, still rubbing sunblock into the top of his head.

"Bloody hell. All ten of them running riot about the place."

"I know." She peered in the passenger side window of the van, but there was nothing inside except a few bright yellow T-shirts with *I survived the Yorkshire Beast* printed on them. No bound and gagged journalists, which was something.

Collins checked the cars, and she turned to survey the field. People were relaxing in folding chairs, reading books and clutching cold drinks, and kids in swimsuits chased each other with water pistols, shrieking that they were hunting the beast. There was a greasy spoon type food truck doing a brisk trade in bacon butties and sausage baps, and an ice cream truck at the other end of the field had a queue five deep. But there was a distinct dearth of W.I. members, as far as she could see.

"Right, well. They're not here," she said.

"We'll need to take over from Graham," he said. "And do something with Lloyd."

DI Adams tapped her fingers against her lips. "We also need to get to Cooper and see what's going on before Sykes turns up again. Split up?"

"Sure." He looked across the field. "You drive up to the farm and see if you can talk to Cooper. I'll walk from here, see if I can spot any W.I., then meet up with Graham."

"Deal." She found herself scanning the field again. If Dandy were here he'd be trying to steal bacon butties from the truck, or sneaking drinks out of coolers, or just drifting through the shadows on his own quiet missions—

"He'll come back," Collins said. "There's a reason you can see him, you know. He's your weird magic dog."

"Sure," she said, and turned back to the car before the tightness in her voice gave her away, leaving him ambling across the field with his hands in his pockets on a trajectory that would take him straight to the ice cream truck.

The woman at the gate flagged DI Adams down as she went to drive out. She leaned down to peer in the window, her tanned hands on the door.

"What've these women done? The ones you're looking for? Half of them look like my gran, is all."

DI Adams smiled. "They've not done anything. They just keep meddling in stuff they shouldn't, and we mostly try to keep them out of it."

"Yeah? Two lots of police after them seems like a bit of overkill."

"Graham – the uniformed sergeant who came earlier – was dealing with someone who was hassling *them*, not the other way around. You said it yourself."

"Sure. But I don't mean him. *I* called him."

"You did?"

"Sure. Can't be messing with my clients, like."

DI Adams returned the woman's smile, then pointed at Collins, where he was accepting a 99 from the ice cream truck. "Collins, then? One of them's his aunt."

"Nah. Sykes. You know him?"

DI Adams looked at the woman closely. Her smile had died, and she was chewing the corner of her lip slightly. One of the cars waiting to get in parped at her, and she straightened up and yelled, "You want to wait longer? Go on, toot your bloody horn again and see how long it takes." The man behind the wheel held his hands up in defeat. "Should think so too," the woman said, and looked at DI Adams. "I didn't see what he might want with a bunch of women on a day out, you know?"

"Did you see him talk to them?"

"They were gone already," she said, and smiled slightly. "I might have texted one of them and told them he was snooping about, too."

DI Adams nodded slowly. Of course Alice had given the woman her phone number – and probably a little extra cash, too. It was a good way to know who was following them. "Do you know where the ladies went?"

"Yeah, they headed off into the village with a bunch of bags an hour or so ago. They were nice."

"Well, they *can* be," DI Adams said, and the woman laughed.

"Yeah, I got that idea too." She straightened up and patted the roof of the car. "Off you go then, before the punters riot. And tell your mate over there to bring me a 99 for my efforts."

DI Adams snorted, and as she slipped out of the gate she hit dial on the handsfree.

"Yeah?" Collins said, a moment later.

"Buy the woman on the gate a 99. And keep an eye out for DCI Sykes. Apparently he's looking for the W.I."

"Bloody hell. What's that all about, then?"

"Dragons, I should imagine," DI Adams said, and disconnected the call.

THE FARM BAKED in the unaccustomed heat as DI Adams crunched down the gravel drive, a faint shimmer rising in the air over the baked dirt of the yard. A quad bike was parked next to a four-wheeled trailer and a couple of bits of farm machinery DI Adams had a sneaking suspicion she should know the names of if she was going to be a country police officer. She resolved not to learn them.

She parked next to the quad bike and checked for lurking geese before she got out into a heat that seemed to be intensifying by the moment, the farmyard trapped in the windless hollow of the valley. A chicken *buk-buk*-ed dispiritedly toward her, and voices drifted on the still air from the campsite, words indistinguishable. She looked for Cooper's pickup, but it didn't seem to be there.

"Dammit," she muttered and knocked on the door to the house. There was no answer, but when she tried the handle it opened easily. She hesitated, then took her phone out and dialled the number on the door. It went straight to voicemail, so she tried the second one. It was no different, so she pushed the door wide, stepping into the cool interior of the house. "Mr Cooper? DI Adams, North Yorkshire Police. Is anyone home? Your door was open."

She waited, but there was no response.

"Mr Cooper, I'm coming in to check everything is okay." The house was stuffy and smelled of old woodsmoke and dogs and boiled potatoes. A short hall led her into a large, empty kitchen, a few plates and mugs stacked unwashed in the sink and the big table in the centre of the room cluttered with farming catalogues and half-used bottles of sheep drench and engine oil, as well as a fruit bowl with a couple of wizened apples languishing in the bottom.

"Mr Cooper?" she tried again, but the house gave her silence back. She found an empty dining room smelling of dust and neglect, and a lounge that was gloomily lit by light coming through red curtains. She took the stairs slowly, calling out again as she climbed.

The master bedroom was at the front of the house, furnished with a big bed and two huge wooden wardrobes that looked as old as the house. The doors of one were hanging open to show a mix of empty hangers and neatly hung shirts and jumpers. She checked the other, which was full of heavy tops and blouses and a handful of dresses pushed right to the back. There were two sets of drawers too, and she found the same there – one almost full of women's clothes, the other partly emptied but still offering thick woollen socks and men's T-shirts and some board shorts that looked like they'd never been worn.

"Interesting," she muttered, heading to the bathroom. No toothbrushes or shaving gear, but there was shampoo and conditioner in the shower, as well as the usual debris of half-used creams and gifted soaps that pile up in every bathroom everywhere.

She was about to step back into the hall when movement caught her eye through the net curtain on the window. It looked out onto the yard, and when she pulled it aside she spotted the teenager from the day before climbing onto the quad bike. She jerked the sash window up and yelled, "Hey! Ash!"

He jumped so violently he almost fell off the quad bike, and whipped around to stare at her, then started to fumble with the ignition.

"Stay!" she shouted, and ran for the stairs. She bolted down the short hall, hearing the engine roar into life outside, and sprinted straight out of the door and in front of the bike, raising both arms in an unmistakable *stop*. Ash hesitated, hunched over the handlebars, then melted into a slump.

"Engine off," DI Adams said, not moving, and he did, not looking at her. "Where are you off to in such a rush, then?"

"Nowhere," he mumbled to the bike.

"Where's Mr Cooper?"

A shrug.

"He know you're using his bike?"

This seemed to rouse him a bit. "He said it was alright."

"When?"

Shrug.

"When?"

"Always. It's like, part of my payment," Ash said.

DI Adams nodded. "When did you see him last?"

A shrug, and DI Adams wondered if shaking him would count as police brutality. Probably. She took a deep breath.

"Ash, I need you to answer me in complete sentences. We can't reach Mr Cooper on the phone, and we're worried about him. Now, it looks like he took a bag—"

"He didn't," he said, startling her.

"What?" she demanded.

Ash looked up at her warily. "He didn't," he repeated, fiddling with his bracelet.

"He didn't take a bag?"

Ash considered it. He seemed to have been having trouble looking at her, but now he examined her more carefully. "You're a cop."

"Yes. DI Adams, North Yorkshire Police."

"You work with Nate?"

"Who?"

"Nate Sykes."

"DCI Sykes?" She hesitated, aware of the teenager's evaluating look, then said, "Not directly. We're in different districts."

Ash didn't look away. "Do you like him?"

DI Adams tipped her head on one side. "Not particularly. You?"

"No," Ash said, and picked up a chicken that was pecking at his trainers. "He's always been weird."

DI Adams decided it would be unprofessional to agree, and said instead, "It looks like Mr Cooper took a bag."

"He didn't."

"Right. Got that. Who did, then?"

"Nate," Ash said, talking mostly to the chicken.

"DCI Sykes took a bag from Mr Cooper's house?"

"Yes."

She took a careful breath. "When did he do that?"

"About one a.m."

"You were still here at one a.m.?"

He petted the chicken, not looking at her. "I had some jobs to do. It's so hot, some of the animals are better with stuff doing at night."

"At one a.m."

Ash shrugged. "It's school holidays. I don't sleep well."

"Right. So you saw DCI Sykes take a bag from the house?"

"Yeah. I was there"—he pointed at the barn—"and he went straight inside. The lights were on upstairs, then he came out with a bag and left." Ash stopped, evidently exhausted by all the talking.

DI Adams examined him for a moment, then said, "How do you know DCI Sykes?"

"Everyone knows him."

"Just because he's from here, you mean?"

Ash made a funny, distasteful expression. "Because any time there's any *complaint* he gets called in."

DI Adams wondered what complaints Ash had suffered through, or if he was simply offended on behalf of Cooper and his animals. "Where do most of the complaints come from?"

"The W.I.," Ash said. "His aunty runs it."

DI Adams swallowed the sort of language one shouldn't use even in front of teenagers and said, "Of course she does."

18
ALICE

Gert and Murph had discovered the overflow carpark the day before, and had found it to be a welcoming market for monster T-shirts. Alice thought it would be a very good place to start from, and when she indicated to pull into the gate there was only one person ahead of her, although the field beyond was lined with cars and caravans and campers that had either started arriving very early indeed, or had, in fact, never left at all. Alice paid her money to the young woman at the gate to the field and looked up at her thoughtfully. She had smooth, strong arms with a hint of yesterday's sunburn on them, and sunglasses that kept sliding down her nose.

"What's your name?" she asked.

"Me?" The young woman tipped her head, then straightened and looked around at a shout from further in the field. "*Oi!* No fires, mate. You want to burn the whole damn dale down?"

A large bearded man yelled something back at her that Alice couldn't quite make out, and the woman's smile vanished. "I will *chuck you out,*" she bellowed.

The man's reply was indistinct, but Alice was fairly sure it involved disbelief.

The young woman looked around the field and shouted, "Big man here reckons rules don't apply to him. Everyone okay with us getting shut down?"

Roughly a dozen or so people emerged out of spray-painted vans and well-kept caravans and awnings tucked onto cars, and a shouting match started up. The young woman turned back to Alice.

"Sorry about that. Clueless, some people."

"I quite agree," Alice said, smiling. "I'm Alice."

The woman let her sunglasses slide down her nose again, peering at Alice over them with dark brown eyes, then said, "Vette. As in Corvette, not Yvette, 'cause my dad's got a real car thing."

"It could have been Lamborghini," Alice pointed out.

"Yeah, my brothers are Aston and Martin, poor sods," she said. "What's up, Alice?"

Alice took a fifty-pound note from her wallet. "I need someone to keep an eye out for a couple of people, is all."

"Always happy to help," Vette said, and took the money. "You got pics?"

"Jasmine?" Alice said, and the younger woman leaned over her to show Vette her phone. She flicked through a shot of DCI Sykes from a news conference, and two pictures of Katherine and Lloyd taken from their *Cryptids Today* bios. Vette looked at them, then nodded.

"You on the out with Sykes?"

"You know him?" Alice asked.

"Everyone knows him. Prowls about the place being disapproving at everything. Him and that bloody Dolphin."

"Dolphin?" Jasmine asked.

"The unlovely Delphine. Annoys the hell out of her when we call her Dolphin, but we're only peasants, so I think she actually reckons we're too slow to realise it's not her actual name." She grinned.

Alice smiled back at her. "Well, tell us if you see her, too."

"Shall do." Vette pointed across the field. "There's a stile onto the river track over that way, so if they're on foot they won't come through here, and I might not see them. Just so you know."

"Understood," Alice said. "Thank you."

"Sure. Fifty quid is fifty quid," the woman said, and winked at her.

❧

IT DIDN'T TAKE them too long to get set up. The women were already dressed for the day, Gert and Jasmine in bright yellow Yorkshire Beast T-shirts and everyone else except Alice in an astonishing array of creature-themed costumes. Alice was impressed by how quickly they'd pulled together so many things. They'd raided the hall's costume boxes and Pearl had been up most of the night stitching foam horns and gauzy wings and extra appendages to what had once been fairly standard clothing. Priya was swathed in a fetching red flamenco dress that had a towering structure over her shoulders and extra swirls of material hanging from her arms, and she looked like nothing so much as a rather lovely sea anemone. Rosemary and Carlotta had T-shirts printed with fake, muscular torsos, horns on their heads, and extra sets of legs trailing behind them that Pearl had somehow made out of two halves of a pantomime horse. Teresa had a bulbous purple dress gathered around her middle to make her look distinctly rotund, as well as four extra legs – or arms – and big shiny sunglasses she'd stuck extra googly eyes all over. Even Angelus and Pearl's Labrador, Martha, were dressed up, while Pearl herself was outfitted as a woodland fairy of some sort, and Rose had found an inflatable unicorn suit that she declared was her best disguise, as none of the cryptozoologists she knew could see it was her in it, and she was worried about ruining her reputation.

"Right," Alice said. "Does everyone know what they're doing?"

"We've got over five hundred entries on the Instagram page, and TikTok is going mad over it all," Jasmine said, not looking up from her phone.

Alice nodded, assuming that was a good thing, and Priya clapped. "That's *amazing!*"

"Absolutely," Alice said, as the others added murmurs of approval. "Shall we head off?"

"Let's go," Teresa said, bouncing from one foot to another. With her newly round torso, her legs looked even longer than usual. "This is going to be *wonderful!*"

Alice chuckled and turned to look for the stile. "We'll go along the river walk, shall we? We can hand out some fliers as we go."

"No need," Gert said. "I've got a few of my third cousins twice re —" she stopped, frowning. "Or is that second cousins three times removed? I've forgotten. Anyhow, they're on the fliers."

"Oh, good," Alice said, and shouldered her backpack as she headed for the stile, only to be brought up short by a man striding across the field toward her.

"*You!*" he shouted. "Where is she? What have you done with Katherine?"

"Excuse me?" Alice asked, shifting her grip on her walking stick. The man's face was red and distorted with heat and fury, but she could see it was Lloyd, the photographer.

"*Where's Katherine?*" He reached for her, as if he might try and shake the answer from her, and Angelus broke into a volley of barking, trying to hide behind Rose with his gauzy wings trembling. Lloyd hesitated, and Alice pointed her stick at him.

"What on earth are you talking about?"

"She's *gone!* She never came back to the camp last night! What did you do with her?" He wasn't a particularly imposing man, but he was shaking with fury, and Alice felt Gert step up next to her on one side, and Carlotta on the other.

"I assure you, we did nothing—"

"Don't lie, you—" He was cut off with a yelp as two rather large young men grabbed him, one on each arm. They weren't rough, but their grips looked exceptionally firm, and they lifted him onto his tiptoes effortlessly.

"Alright," one said to Alice. "Vette says get off, we'll deal with this."

"*Where is she?*" Lloyd shouted. "You can't get away with this, you—" One of the young men rapped him smartly on the head with his knuckles, and Lloyd yelped.

"And how exactly will you deal with it?" Alice asked. "He's very upset, not dangerous."

"There's a couple of coppers in the village," the second man said. He had the same haircut and build and features as the first, and they looked like bookends, holding Lloyd firmly in place. "Vette's got one on the way. We'll hand him over."

Alice looked past them at Vette, who gave her a thumbs up. "Right," she said, and looked at Lloyd. "I don't know where Katherine is. I haven't seen her."

"Liar," he hissed. "You've been trying to get her out of your bloody village for ages!"

"And she *is* out of our village, so I don't know why I'd still be bothered about her," she pointed out, and looked at the women gathered around her in their gauze and foam and extra limbs. "Let's get going, shall we?"

She led the way to the stile while Lloyd shouted after her that he was calling the police, and he'd see her arrested for this, see if he didn't!

"Good start," Rose said cheerfully, bobbing along the path with Angelus straining at his leash in front of her.

"Better now than later," Alice said, and wondered, with a twist of unease, where Katherine had got to. The same place as Cooper's missing wife, perhaps? Was it all a set-up?

If it was, they were just going to have to work even harder at proving it.

❧

GERT GRINNED. "Top job, Jaz. There's so many monsters in these woods that you wouldn't notice a bloody unicorn if it went prancing past in a top hat."

"It is quite remarkable," Alice said. They were sitting on the edge of the green, where the trees over the river offered some welcome shade, and from here they had a good view of the main street as well as the green itself. The village was heaving with monsters and aliens, crowds of them surging from one side of the street to the other, ranging from small children in dinosaur onesies with their parents trailing behind them to bearded men in mermaid tails and coconut shell bikinis racing (or hopping) along the river. She'd spotted a pantomime horse that someone had strapped some wings to, three people on stilts, and a contrite-looking clown who was currently wiping his makeup off while being harangued by a large man in a tutu, who was holding back a small girl in a matching skirt. She was waving what Alice sincerely hoped was a plastic axe threateningly. The more sedately dressed cryptozoologists scattered throughout the crowd were looking distinctly harried, and Alice actually saw one pull his hat off and fling it furiously into the river, only to have to go and pick it up, his face red with frustration.

And it had all been achieved through Jasmine's phone and Gert's contacts. There was some sort of costume competition on Instagram (Jasmine had explained it, but once she'd started talking about likes and hashtags, Alice had held a hand up and said, "I'll let you handle it, dear"), the first prize for which was a very nice yurt-style tent currently set up in the overflow car park. Gert had supplied all the prizes, and Alice had resolved not to ask where they came from. There was also a dragon egg hunt raging in the woods, with a large portion of the ladies of the Toot Hansell W.I. currently running through the trees in costumes hiding chocolate eggs, real eggs, and papier-mâché eggs with everything from slightly off-brand fitness trackers to toy cars inside them.

Alice checked her phone, but there was still nothing from Miriam, or Ervin for that matter. That side of things did not seem to be going so smoothly, and she was worried by the idea that Katherine was missing. It seemed awfully like a ploy to put them off their guard.

She put the phone in her backpack and got up. "Are you alright here?" she asked. "You know what to do next?"

"We've got it," Gert said, grinning, and offered her a T-shirt. "You want one? Murph's doing a roaring trade."

"I wouldn't deprive you of the sale," Alice said. Even through the throngs on the green she could hear Murph shouting, "*Get your Beast shirts here! Get them before they're gone! Only genuine Yorkshire Beast shirts in town!*" There were almost as many yellow shirts bobbing about the place as there were costumes.

"Where are you going?" Jasmine asked. "Do you want one of us to come with you?"

"No, you keep on. I'm going to nip back to the car and see what happened to Lloyd. It was very odd, that."

"Alright," Jasmine said, already looking back at her phone. "See you soon."

The question of the missing journalist niggled at Alice. Surely if it was part of the set-up, Lloyd would have known? She turned left off the green, skirting a troop of small children in multicoloured plumage with a variety of appendages. She wasn't quite sure what they were meant to be, but she smiled at them anyway.

Five minutes later she was hurrying up to the young woman at the gate to the field.

"Ay up," Vette said. "Back for more action?"

"There's been more?" Alice asked.

"Yeah. Some detective from down south was asking after you. Quite liked her, even if she is a copper."

"Definitely one of the better sorts," Alice said. "Anyone else?"

"Sykes was nosing around not long after you left. Think he'd heard about that journalist having a go, but we'd already handed him off to some uniform cop." The woman tipped her head to one side. "What *are* you lot up to? You bank robbers or some such?"

Alice chuckled and said, "Nothing so exciting."

"Honestly, you're *very* exciting. I want to be like you when I grow up."

"You have to go in the RAF for that."

"Ew. Pass." She broke off to take twenty pounds from a man in a flashy Mercedes convertible. He was wearing a shiny green bodysuit and his green face paint was already starting to run in the heat. "That missing journalist," the woman added, tucking the money into her bumbag. "Saw her last night."

"You didn't say," Alice said.

"Didn't know it mattered till her mate there started kicking off."

She took five pounds from a woman driving a battered people carrier with an astonishing amount of children crammed in the back.

"When did you see her last night?"

"I was heading for the pub for a pint just before closing, and she was talking to Dolphin on the green."

"Delphine?"

"That's her." The young woman peered into a car full of young men and said, "Ten quid each."

"*How much?*"

"Like it or lump it, mate," she said.

"Aw, come on—"

"Back it up, then," she said, twirling her hand lazily. "Don't waste my time."

The young men grumbled, but started digging out the money.

Alice watched them and said, "You may be wasted in the RAF, to be honest."

"Probably."

"Even so. How do I find Delphine?"

"You could try her place. Fancy pants B&B – you'll see the sign right enough. Just keep going out of town on this road and it's on your right in like a K."

"Thank you," Alice said.

"Yeah, mind her. My friends and I always thought she might turn us into toads when we were younger. Wouldn't put it past her."

"I'll bear that in mind."

ALICE STOOD OUTSIDE HER CAR, waiting for the air conditioning to fight back against the heat and considering what to do next. She'd tried calling both Ervin and Miriam, but there was no response from either of them, and she was painfully aware that securing the dragons was the priority right now. But Katherine being missing seemed quite important too. Eventually she pulled up DI Adams' number, but it went straight to messages.

"This is ridiculous," she muttered, and tried Colin instead, turning to survey the car park while she listened to it ring. There was a lot of noise going on everywhere, the screams of excited children and the shouts of adults who were only marginally less excited. And, in some cases, more so, judging by the two men standing at the edge of the field not far from Alice, where the small stile gave access to the riverside path.

"They've ruined it," one said, then turned and screamed at the woods, *"ruined it!"*

"Mac, calm down," his companion said. "It's kind of hilarious."

"Hilarious? *Hilarious?* There are *grown women* dressed as *octopi* running around in the woods, and if there's a beast in there it'll have been scared into hibernation for the next *hundred years!"*

"Octopuses," the second man said, then stepped back as his companion spun to face him, his hands clamped to his balding head. "Never mind. Let's get a pint, eh? Nice cold pint? Maybe some pork scratchings. You know pork scratchings always make you feel better."

There was a pause, during which Alice wondered if the first man was going to punch his friend or simply collapse on the ground, then he spun away and scrambled over the stile. The other man followed, his hands in his pockets, and from the river someone shrieked, *"Mum! Mum, I found an egg! Dragons have chocolate eggs!"*

"Bloody octopi!" the man screamed, out of sight among the trees, and Alice's phone gave a little bleep as it disconnected. She tried Colin again, but her phone just gave a dull beep and refused to connect. Ah well. She was just going to have to go and have a word with Delphine herself.

Shortly after, she waved to Vette and pulled onto the road heading out of town at a sedate pace. She wasn't sure what name she was looking for on the B&B, but she imagined there wouldn't be a lot to choose from.

It was more like a kilometre and a half, but just as she was wondering if she'd missed it she spotted a tasteful wooden sign, the lettering sunk into it and picked out in gold paint. *Eldmere Haven,* it read, with something else beneath it that was too small for her to read from here. She slowed, intending to pull in, but as she did so a silver Isuzu pickup appeared on the drive, and she kept going, checking her rear-view mirror. The pickup rumbled onto the road and headed for the village, and Alice swung her car into the first gate she saw, pulling into a tight U-turn to follow the pickup.

She wasn't *sure* – she'd only caught a glimpse as she drove past – but she could have sworn she saw Cooper driving, and Katherine in the passenger seat. Did that mean they were actually working together? If she could get a picture of them, it'd be much easier to sell the whole thing as a hoax. And if they'd set up Katherine's disappearance as part of the hoax, then that would be *perfect.*

She sped up, and by the time the pickup hit the village she was close enough to see it turn onto the bridge by the green. Maybe they were just going to the farm? It was possible. She'd need to be reasonably close to get a photo on her phone, though.

The pickup continued on past the farm, picking up speed a little as the road cleared. Alice frowned, and let the gap between them widen. She was unlikely to lose them out here. Was she wrong about the hoax? Were they holding Gilbert out here somewhere?

The curves and turns in the road meant that the pickup vanished and reappeared regularly, and suddenly she came around a bend and found a stretch of empty road in front of her.

"Dammit," she muttered, starting to accelerate, then glimpsed a single-lane track off to her right as she passed it. She checked the rear-view mirror then jammed the brakes on, slammed the car into reverse and revved the engine. The little SUV skittered back obediently, and she peered down the lane. A gate lay open onto it, a well-kept red and white sign fastened to the top bar. It said, *Private No Entry,* but beyond it she could see a soft haze of dust rising off the dirt track in the sun.

"There you are." She edged through the gate and picked up speed as much as she dared on the loose gravel of the track, wondering if it led to the tarn. It seemed likely. She checked the dashboard display, and her phone was showing no signal, which was hardly surprising. She shifted her grip on the wheel and kept going as bushes and trees crowded the old walls on either side, and here and there leaned through the gaps where the stones had tumbled away.

The track bounced her over a few more ruts and around a turn which gave her a view down to the tarn, the surface dark and still beneath the high green and grey hills. There was an old stone hut next to it, and parked near the stony bank were the silver pickup and a white van. Grass and tumbled rocks surrounded the tarn, and the pompom shapes of reed clusters dotted the shores. It looked old and cold and deep, and Alice stopped the car. The vehicles were both facing away from her, and it was impossible to see if anyone was inside them. As she watched, the van backed up, then started to bump its way around the tarn to her left, away from the track. The ground was firmer and rockier in that direction, and even if there was no path or roadway for it, the van made steady progress. She tried to see if there was another track it might be joining, but all she spotted was a small red car sitting near the water, and she stiffened. That had to be Ervin's car, although she couldn't see the make from here. But even if the van were going to investigate it, Ervin and Miriam should be off somewhere, looking for dragons. And there was nothing she could do even if they weren't. The van was going to reach them well before she could.

Alice sat where she was for a while, waiting to see if anything else happened below, but there was no movement from the pickup. She checked the phone again, but there was still no signal. Should she go back and find one? But this might be her best chance to expose Katherine and Cooper – or to find Gilbert, if they were holding him somewhere and the dragons hadn't already found him.

There was still no movement below, and she wondered if she'd been seen. There were some overhanging trees here, offering a little shelter, but probably not enough. She tapped her fingers on the wheel and looked around. She was going to have to reverse out if she left, anyway. She nodded slightly and checked her phone a final time, then rumbled gently down the lane until it disgorged her onto the flat land by the tarn. The track led her straight to the hut, and she stopped facing the pickup, turned the engine off, then climbed out of the van, taking her walking stick with her.

There was still no movement from the pickup, the air hot and sticky around her, and after a moment she said, "Katherine? I'd like a word."

19

MORTIMER

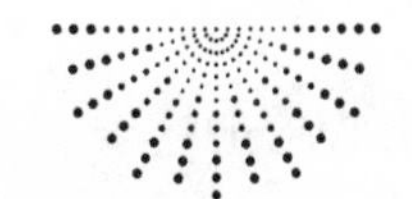

Every time Mortimer thought of panicking on the hilltop he could feel his scales flushing lilac with embarrassment. But it had been such a terribly long night, hunting over the fells for any sign of Gilbert and finding *nothing,* and such a terribly long day before that, hiding from monster hunters, and it had all just built up and up and up, until, when he found that Beaufort was just *gone,* it had felt as if the earth had given way beneath him. As if everything that he knew to be true was no longer to be trusted, and as if the sun might as well set in the east, because the whole world was spinning off its axis in all directions, rumpling the very fabric of reality while he sat here and screamed uselessly at his paws, like ... like a *hamster.*

"Hamster," he muttered.

"What?" Miriam panted next to him.

"I'm like a hamster," he said. "Just screaming at my paws and not managing to do *anything.*"

Miriam didn't answer for a moment. She probably agreed, he thought despairingly. *Of course* she agreed. Who would disagree? He was more a disgrace of a dragon than Gilbert. At least Gilbert went out and lived exactly as he wanted, and never minded if others thought it was strange. *He* wasn't shedding scales and almost permanently grey with stress. *Mortimer* should be the one running away from the mount in disgrace!

"I'm fairly sure hamsters don't scream," Miriam said finally. "And they must be desperately brave. Imagine being picked up and handled by giants all the time! And *children* – they always mean well, but you know they'll be loud and unexpected and sometimes clumsy. And little hamsters just put up with it all quite cheerfully, and run about their cages, and get on with their lives despite having giants poking them all the time."

Mortimer blinked at her. "What?"

"I'm just saying, I think hamsters are probably very brave. So it's a good comparison, other than the screaming. But I could be wrong on that. We can ask Rose." She stopped, pressing a hand into her side. "Ooh, these boots are killing me. But I don't want to take them off."

"No," Mortimer agreed. He was still trying to get his head around the hamster thing. He seemed to have lost control of his analogy entirely, and didn't know how to get it back. He gazed over the high, craggy moor and said, "It's very rough going."

The scent had led them cross-country, not following any track at all that Mortimer could see. It dipped and wound, avoiding the steepest rocky patches as well as the boggy areas, although here and there they found a tyre track torn into the soft ground where the driver hadn't quite skirted a wet patch widely enough. Miriam kept going determinedly, but Mortimer could hear her breathing getting more ragged with every uphill, and she paused at the top of every ridge to scan the landscape, holding her side as if expecting something to escape. He didn't think her heart was there, but he wasn't entirely clear on human anatomy.

"Are you alright?" he asked her.

"Yes, fine," she said. "It's these boots. I'm not made for boots."

Mortimer wisely refrained from pointing out that he didn't think the boots were the ones making her out of breath. Instead he just looked across the next fold of land and said, "Should I go on ahead? Maybe I can scout out where the tracks go and come back?"

"No," she said firmly. "We're not getting separated."

"I could give you a lift?"

"On your *back?* Absolutely not. You wouldn't even be able to take off!"

"I lifted Colin once. He's bigger than you."

"That was an emergency." She started down the next slope. The ground was wetter here and the tyre tracks had skidded in places. "I'm not having you sprain a wing and we both go crashing into the side of a fell or something."

"I don't think you can sprain a wing," Mortimer said dubiously, but he scampered alongside her as she kept going, hoping that the next ridge would show them *something*. Anything. Because at this rate they'd have walked all the way to the North York Moors, and wouldn't *that* be something.

The next ridge showed them nothing but more rough-edged land, getting steeper and harsher with every rise, the liquid cries of skylarks dropping down around them. Miriam didn't speak, just kept stolidly on, while the sun turned her bare arms pink.

The ridge after that, though, revealed a building.

"Mortimer!" Miriam exclaimed, coming to a stop at the top of the rise. "Is that it? Do you think that's where they took him?"

"Maybe? The trail's going that way." His throat was suddenly tight. What were they going to find? Who would trap a dragon and shove them in some old building all the way out here in the middle of the fells? *Why* would they?

Miriam was chewing her lip, but now she nodded, and said, "Right. Well, we'd best get on, then." And she marched toward the hut with her head up and one hand holding the bat firmly on her shoulder. Mortimer trotted alongside her, still catching the whiff of the trail under his paws, and the chicken clung to his back, wobbling with every step.

THE BUILDING WAS two storeys of old, solid stone, with glass persisting in the windows and peeling white paint still clinging to the front door. A small, lichen-encrusted slate plaque reading *Cutter Cottage* was attached to the wall next to the door, and Mortimer could see torn net curtains inside the small-paned windows to either side of it. A rudimentary garden had been staked out with pieces of slate as edging, but there was nothing in it except a tangle of nettles and wildflowers, and the lane they could see leading away from it in the opposite direction was deeply rutted and collapsing at the edges with erosion.

Next to the house was an outbuilding that consisted of a stone shed with double doors and a simple shelter built onto the side of it, with three walls and a patchy roof. A decrepit-looking tractor crouched in it wearily.

Mortimer and Miriam had paused in the cover of a large, friendly boulder, and now they looked at each other. "It looks abandoned," she said. "Or like it *should* be abandoned, anyway. One never knows."

"Do we knock?" Mortimer asked.

Miriam shifted her grip on the bat. "I don't know. Does the trail definitely go here?"

"Yes." There was no doubt. The sharp, salt scent of it was clearer here than earlier, as if its owner had spent enough time here to build up layers around themself. And not just from last night – they'd spent time here before. Mortimer snuffled carefully, sifting through the scents of the stranger and the half-wild land and the remnants of human life, and grinned. Deep, rich layers of smoke and the bright green twist of interest, like new shoots in the spring. "Beaufort's here."

Miriam looked at the house. "If he's in the cage, they wouldn't be able to get him through the door. Let's try the shed."

Mortimer looked at the chicken. It *buk-buk*-ed impatiently. "Let's go," he said, and crept forward on soft paws, his scales effortlessly taking on the colours of old stone and the brown-tipped summer grass. He didn't have time to be surprised that he wasn't a fretful grey, and he was just about to break into a run for the shed when he caught a *burr* of noise on the edge of hearing. He stopped so suddenly that Miriam tripped over his tail with a squeak and almost went spilling to the ground

"Mortimer! What is it?"

"Someone's coming. Quick, back to the rocks!"

They sprinted for cover as the sound of an engine grew louder, and ducked out of sight as a quad bike came bumping up the track on the far side of the house. Mortimer buried his talons in the grass. They'd been so close!

The quad bike grumbled all the way up to the shed, where the rider cut the engine and climbed off, pulling their helmet off as they did so.

"Who's that?" Miriam whispered. "I don't recognise them."

"I don't know," Mortimer whispered back. "A dragon-napper, I suppose."

The dragon-napper lifted two bags out of a crate strapped to the back of the bike, and turned to the shed before pausing.

"Oh no," Mortimer whispered.

"Oh *no,*" Miriam echoed.

The chicken strutted across the ground to the dragon-napper and *buk-buk*-ed up at him earnestly.

"Hello," he said, and crouched down to examine the chicken. "Where were you?" The chicken *buk*-ed and turned to trot back to Mortimer and Miriam. The dragon-napper watched her go with a frown, one hand already reaching into the bags, probably for some giant Taser.

Mortimer turned to say to Miriam that he wished he'd eaten the chicken, and she held out her hand in an unmistakable *stop* gesture. Then she stood up with her bat resting on her shoulder and stepped out from behind the rocks. "Excuse me," she called. "I think you have our dragon."

The dragon-napper gaped at her. *"What?"*

"You heard me. What's in the shed?"

"Miriam?" It was wonderfully familiar shout from inside the shed. "Miriam, is that you?"

"You *do* have him," Miriam said accusingly, striding across the yard with her muddied skirt swirling around her legs. "How *dare* you? Trapping a dragon? What's *wrong* with you?"

"I didn't—"

"I should lock you up in a cage! See how you like it!"

She stopped just short of him, pointing the bat accusingly at his face.

"I wasn't—"

"In fact, I'm going to do just that! And leave you in some horrible abandoned hut with no food and no—"

The dragon-napper snatched something out of one of the bags, and Mortimer came up and over the rocks in one fierce bound. In two more he had a paw on the dragon-napper's chest, and he *roared*, sending the chicken screeching for cover under the tractor and even Miriam stumbling back a step or two.

"This is what happens when you hunt dragons," he snarled at the man, realising his paw was a nasty puce colour and not even caring. "There are *consequences*."

The dragon-napper just pointed wildly at his bag, his eyes huge. "Not!" he managed. "Not dragon hunter!"

"Mortimer?" Beaufort called from inside the shed. "Mortimer, what on earth are you doing?"

"This man—" Mortimer stopped. The dragon-napper was more of a boy, really, even by human standards. "It's a dragon hunter," he said.

"Not," the boy said again. He was trembling, his chest desperately skinny and delicate under Mortimer's paw, and Mortimer was suddenly aware of how heavy he was. He eased the pressure as Miriam stepped past him and opened the bag.

"Ginger slice," she said. "Malt loaf. Fondant fancies. Apple pies. Flapjacks – what is this?"

"He said he liked cake," the boy whispered. "Gilbert does too."

"*Gilbert?*" Mortimer demanded, renewing his weight on the boy's chest and making him squeak. "Where is he? What have you done with him?"

"I don't know! I really don't! I was looking for him and I found Beaufort instead, and I couldn't open the cage so I moved the whole thing because I didn't want him caught and then I went and got some tools and cake because I thought he might be hungry and I'm going to have to break the cage open and *please can you not bite me?*"

"*Mortimer!*" Beaufort shouted from inside. "You're not biting the lad, are you?"

"*No,*" Mortimer said. "Of course not!" Although he had to admit that his teeth had been getting very close to the boy's face. But he'd never bitten anyone. Well, other than that time in Toot Hansell when someone had pushed Alice over. He took his foot off the boy's chest and sat back on his haunches. "Sorry."

"'S okay," the boy said, not moving from the ground. The chicken emerged from under the tractor and *buk*-ed crossly at Mortimer.

"Are you alright, Beaufort?" Miriam called.

"Other than the cage, fine. Ash's been doing his best to get me out, but it's a nasty piece of work, this. I think it's got charms on it, to be honest. There's a funny whiff to it. Nothing I recognise, though, so no dwarf work or anything."

Miriam offered the boy a hand and helped him to his feet. He darted a look at Mortimer and said, "I really was trying to help."

"Yes. Sorry again," Mortimer dusted his paws off. They'd shed the puce rather rapidly and were going a delicate lilac again. Wonderful. Who knew staging rescues could be so embarrassing?

"Ash," the boy said.

"Mortimer."

"Miriam," she said, and pointed at the shed. "Can we get in there now, please?"

"Oh, sure. It's not locked. No one comes up here but me." The doors were sliding ones, and they juddered unevenly apart as Ash and Miriam pushed them, light flooding the interior and revealing the High Lord sitting in a large cage of heavy iron bars, his tail wrapped neatly around his toes and a goat sitting on his back.

"Is that ..." Miriam trailed off, staring at the goat.

"Yes. He likes climbing, now he's got over his fright." Beaufort sounded as if he were trying very hard not to be irritated by it.

"I brought some metal files and stuff," Ash said, handing the High Lord the ginger cake.

"These bars are *very* thick," Miriam said. "I don't think a file is going to do it."

"I might be able to file the lock somehow?"

"How on earth did you get him here?" Mortimer asked. "I tried dragging the cage and it didn't move at all."

"With the tractor. I got it running over the summer just for the fun of it," Ash said with a shrug.

"And no, Ash does not know where Gilbert is," Beaufort said. "We think he was trapped as well."

"Sykes," Miriam said, folding her arms. "It was him, wasn't it?"

Ash shook his head. "I don't know. I just found the cage."

"And Gilbert?" Mortimer asked. "You were taking him pumpkins at that hut, weren't you?"

Ash nodded, picking up the chicken to pat it. His dark hair fell forward to hide his face. "Yeah."

"What happened?" Miriam asked. "Why was he there in the first place?"

For a moment Mortimer thought Ash wasn't going to answer, as he just stood there looking from Beaufort to himself and back again, but eventually he said, "I met him at the farm. Cooper's? He was trying to release the llamas—"

Mortimer groaned, and Ash stopped, giving him a wary look.

"It's alright, lad," Beaufort said. "Mortimer's not angry at Gilbert. Or you. Neither of us are. We were worried about him, is all."

Ash set the chicken down and rubbed one skinny arm. "Okay. Sure. Anyway, I said he couldn't, because Hetty and Jake are kind of cool, and they needed them for the treks and stuff. And I kind of joked and said, you know, unless he wanted to be the next attraction instead." He looked at each of them carefully as Mortimer swallowed another groan and Beaufort chuckled softly.

Miriam was just shaking her head gently. "Go on," she said. "What then?"

"Then we kind of hung out a bit, you know? And we came up with a plan to get Hetty and Jake money that didn't involve exploiting animals, using the paw prints and stuff. We thought Gilbert'd be safe if he just stayed up at the hut out of the way except when we needed to make some new prints or something."

"That was very silly," Miriam said. "The fuss! And there are actual cryptozoologists down there. What if one of them had seen him?"

Ash nodded, looking at the floor. "It got kind of bigger than we thought it would."

"Never mind," Beaufort said. "What happened, though? When did he disappear?"

"I'm not sure exactly. I just went back two days ago and he wasn't there anymore. I knew he wouldn't just *leave,* so I've been looking for him everywhere since." He hesitated. "I was looking for him when I saw the trap. I guess the same thing happened to him, but I can't believe he'd have just walked into one."

"No," Miriam said. "One would think dragons were more sensible." She raised her eyebrows at Beaufort.

"Never mind that," he said. "I need to get out of here so we can get after Gilbert."

"Let me try this," Ash said, going back to the quad bike to get a bag of tools. A moment later he was kneeling in front of the cage, filing away enthusiastically while Beaufort munched on some ginger cake and Mortimer helped himself to the fondant fancies. They were so sweet they made his teeth hurt.

Five minutes later Ash rocked back on his heels and said, "It's not working. Or it might be, but I'm going to wear the file out before I get through them."

Miriam had gone outside to try and find a phone signal, but now she came back in and said, "I've still got no signal."

"No, there's nothing out here," Ash said. "It's nice."

"Yes, until you're trying to warn people about a dragon-napper running about Eldmere," Miriam said. "We need to take the cage and find a way to get you out, Beaufort, then go after Gilbert."

"How can we do that?" Beaufort demanded.

There was silence for a moment, then Ash said, "Same way you came. Tractor."

❧

It wasn't one of the new sort of tractors Mortimer had seen in the fields before, all enclosed cabs for winter and glossy paintwork. This one had a single small seat high above its huge wheels, and Miriam had a set of ear protectors clamped over her increasingly unruly hair as she hunched over the wheel, following Ash as he bounced ahead on the quad bike. He'd offered her the bike, but when she'd gingerly revved it up it took off so fast that she almost fell off the back, and she'd declared herself much better suited to a tractor. It coughed and belched and left behind the sort of exhaust trail that put Mortimer in mind of forest fires, but it did have a pair of front arms that had probably once been used for hefting hay bales and other such stuff around. Currently it was carrying the cage with Beaufort and the increasingly hysterical goat in it, while Mortimer and the chicken tried to balance in the crate on the back of the quad bike.

Ash took a different route to the one that had led them up here, finding easier ground for the tractor. They crossed field after stone-walled field, Ash running to open and close gates as they went through each one, after it became rapidly clear that dragon paws are not suited for doing such things quickly. At one, Miriam took her ear protectors off and yelled, "How far to the tarn?"

"Ten minutes, maybe," Ash shouted back. "We're coming in from the other side."

Miriam nodded understanding, and Mortimer looked at Beaufort, curled in his cage. He was currently holding the unconscious goat so that its legs didn't slip through the gaps in the bottom. There was something horrifying about seeing the High Lord caged. It felt like it should be against the natural laws of the world or something.

Ash finally stopped on the crest of a hill, and Miriam pulled the tractor up behind him and turned the engine off. The tarn glittered below, the track leading down to the stone hut on their right. There were a couple of SUVs parked by the edge of the tarn, and a white van was working its way along the edge of the water in their direction.

"Busy," Ash said.

"It must be the W.I.," Miriam said. "That looks like Alice's SUV, and that might be Gert's white van."

"The W.I.?" the teenager asked, wrinkling his nose. "I hope not. Miserable lot. They think they're the keepers of the village or something."

"The Toot Hansell W.I.," Miriam said. "It's a very good W.I."

"If you say so."

They watched for a moment longer, Mortimer craning his head to follow the progress of the white van. It was taking its time, but now he spotted a small red car sitting right on the edge of the water. "Is that Ervin's?"

"Where?" Miriam asked.

"There. Where the van's going."

She shaded her eyes to look, then said, "Maybe. He was meant to go and tell the DIs about Sykes, though. And I don't know what he's doing all the way around there."

"And why would Gert be going around there?" Mortimer asked.

Ash was frowning at the water, and now he said, "Our W.I. has a white van, too."

The chicken gave a sudden *buk* and leaped off Mortimer's shoulder. She bolted straight down the side of the hill, heading for the white van. They watched her go, then Mortimer said, "Miriam, are you sure it was Sykes who set the traps?"

"Sykes basically *works* for the W.I.," Ash said. His face had gone pale. The white van drove around Ervin's car, stopping nose to nose with it.

"Oh no," Miriam whispered, then turned and ran for the tractor. "Beaufort, hang on!"

Mortimer barely heard her. He was already plunging off the hill, taking to the air in two great strokes of his wings, and who cared who saw him. He arrowed straight for the car, his shadow passing over the charging chicken like a vast bird of prey, his heart so loud in his ears he could barely hear the wind of his own passage above it.

Below him, the van's engine revved, and the little red car slid backward into the tarn, a wash of water rising up over its boot in the moment before the ground fell away beneath it. It bobbed as its wheels lost contact with the bottom, and rocked about for a moment, like a rubber duck trying to get its balance as it decided which way to roll, and Mortimer folded his wings and dropped out of the sky above, hoping he could reach it in time.

Hoping he could do anything even when he did.

20
DI ADAMS

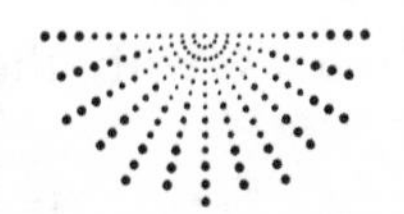

As DI Adams edged over the bridge, careful of the throng of pedestrians, she spotted families splashing in the river and picnicking on the green, and— she rolled to a stop. From here she had a view over the green and into the Main Street, and there were monsters *everywhere.*

She blinked, as if her eyes might be playing tricks on her, and took a sip of very cold coffee from her mug. It didn't help. In the short time she'd been at the farm, there had apparently been an invasion of cryptids. Nessie heads complete with tam o'shanters bobbed above the crowd, and gauzy wings flapped, and humps jiggled along the riverbank, and half a dozen inflatable T-Rexes were running at each other in the shallows, bouncing off, then jumping up to try again. There was also someone in a large chicken suit that had been spray painted with glittery purple paint handing out hats with cardboard monster heads on them, and next to it was a huge sign proclaiming numerous suspiciously good prizes to the winner of the best costume competition.

DI Adams pulled up next to the green, put her hazard lights on, and jogged up to the chicken. Gert's husband was standing next to it, bellowing cheerfully on his loud-hailer and promising a free hat with every T-shirt.

"Don't miss out! Beat the sun! Celebrate the Beast! One for twenty, two for thirty, three for fifty!"

DI Adams grabbed the chicken's shoulder and it swung to face her with a yelp. The unfamiliar face of a young man peered at her, smeared in glittery face paint.

"You have to buy a shirt to get a hat," he said.

"Right." She looked at Murph, who beamed at her.

"Buying a Beast T-shirt, Inspector?"

"Not right now, no. What's with the hats and the costume competition?"

Murph looked over the crowd thoughtfully. "It's a celebration of all that's unknown in the world. And also Gert told me to."

"Do you know why?"

He shrugged. "She has her reasons, Detective Inspector. And when it comes to the W.I., I tend to say yes first, ask questions later."

DI Adams looked at the sign, with its details of how to enter on an Instagram page – winner decided by likes, apparently – and said, "That's probably quite wise."

"I think so," Murph said, and lifted the loud-hailer again.

DI ADAMS DECIDED that she didn't have time to waste on costume parties. She wasn't sure how it was going to discredit the journalists, but it was keeping the W.I. occupied, if nothing else. What she needed to do was find out what had happened to Cooper, and that meant finding out if Sykes and Delphine were working together on something. Delphine had certainly been unhappy enough about Cooper's substandard campsite.

She hit dial on her phone as she edged out of the village. Collins answered almost immediately.

"Adams? All good?"

"Cooper's missing. Seems Sykes turned up at one in the morning and took a bag of his stuff."

"What?"

"And it also seems Sykes is Delphine's nephew. What is it with you lot all being related up here?"

"Hilarious and also inaccurate." There was a pause, then he added, "What do we do about that? Going to be touchy, approaching Sykes."

"*Way* too touchy, since my only witness is a kid who likes lurking in farmyards in the wee small hours."

"I'm sorry?"

"Me too. Look, I'm going to find Delphine and see if I can shake anything loose. Send me the address of her campsite, or glampsite, or whatever the hell it is?"

"It's straight out of town on the right, heading past the car park. You can pick me up on the way."

"No, you deal with the village. What was up with the Katherine thing?"

"Lloyd claims he hasn't seen her since last night at the pub. He confronted the W.I. about it, but I think your friend on the gate might've exaggerated somewhat to get Graham to remove him."

"The Toot Hansell W.I. Making friends and creating monsters everywhere."

There was a pause, then Collins said, "Sorry, what?"

"Have you seen the village? Looks like a bloody monster festival."

"Oh, yeah. I did notice that. Look, we're not charging Lloyd with anything, so why don't I come to see Delphine with you?"

"How about you find out where Sykes is now and keep tabs on him. I can handle Delphine."

"Are you sure? She's W.I."

"Fair point." She hesitated. But they really did need to know where Sykes was. He was claiming to have spoken to Cooper this morning. "No, I'll call you, okay?"

"Your call," Collins said. "Bloody mean leaving me to deal with Sykes, though."

"You'll survive." She hung up and pulled into the busy road, heading out of town.

DELPHINE'S PLACE was marked with an elegant, understated wooden sign, *Eldmere Haven* carved into the wood and highlighted in gold. Underneath it added, *Luxury self-contained accommodation.* Next to the sign was a set of open wooden gates, the property beyond hidden behind high hedges. DI Adams pulled in and headed up the gravel drive.

It was an impressive spot, she had to admit. The hedges concealed an undulating landscape of grassy lawn and mature trees that provided plenty of shade for those who wanted it, while riotous flowerbeds divided the property into bright pockets of colour. The upside-down boat hull shapes of the cabins each nestled in their own circle of flowers and grass, while the drive split off to allow guests to park right by their pod. There were two shepherd's huts, too, perched on high wheels and painted rather gaily in pastel blues, but there were no cars outside any of them. DI Adams kept the car to a crawl as she spotted a koi pond with a little bridge over it, and a vegetable garden with the sort of organisation Alice would have envied. A little wooden sign reading *Please help yourself!* was hung on a post next to it, and outside tables and chairs were positioned not just outside the pods and huts, but at strategic points throughout the garden.

"Where is everyone?" she said aloud as she drove up. Surely they hadn't *all* driven out for the day. Not with the monster hunt of the century happening a short walk away.

Another curve in the drive revealed the house, a line of trees screening it from the guests. It was a sprawling stone bungalow, the windows small and thick-paned, roses climbing up the walls and lavender sprouting from barrels by the door. DI Adams parked in a little turning circle and got out into the scent of lavender and the heavy drone of bees. She stood by the car for a moment, wishing in some unfocused way that Dandy was here. The heat made her arms itch and there was something tight and thick in her head, like the beginnings of a bad bout of hay fever.

She waited a moment longer, listening for kids or music or any sign of life at all, then went to knock on the door. There was a bell hanging next to it, white-painted and old-fashioned, and she jangled that for good measure, then waited, inspecting an old metal sign to the side of the door that read *ALARM*. It looked too old to actually be warning of an alarm system, but it was probably fake old. She'd never been good at telling the difference.

No one appeared, and she turned on her heel, examining the yard. There was nothing here, but she'd glimpsed a garage as she came in, so she followed the gravel path around the side of the house.

The garage was made of the same grey stone as the house, both the sliding door and the door to the side locked. DI Adams cupped both hands to her face and peered through the dusty window in the door, spotting a lawnmower and some outdoor furniture inside, the usual clutter that seems to collect in every garage. There were certainly no dragons or missing farmers – or journalists – so she continued around the house, where the gardens and lawn rolled up to a stone wall spanned by another wooden gate. A rough track led to the gate, not gravelled, and she examined it. There were the ruts of vehicles on it, but it was hard to say how recently they'd been through when the ground was so dry.

Still, there was nothing else to look at here, so she followed it, letting herself through the gate and finding a sloping field below, running to a cluster of stone buildings that looked like disused barns. She checked her phone, wondering whether to call Collins. But he knew where she was. She looked around once again, feeling the absence of Dandy in some strange sense of unsettledness she couldn't quite fathom, then headed down the field.

The buildings weren't ruins. Two of them were low things that must have been some sort of livestock shelter – she supposed she actually was going to have to learn the right terminology at some point after all – and the other was larger, a two-storey barn that she supposed would have had space for hay above and more livestock below. They were disused, no whiff of animal or sense of life about them, and although the smaller buildings had patchy roofs, the barn still looked solid. It was the sort of place that was described as *having potential* or being *a prime opportunity for renovation.* In other words, it had four walls and was bigger than a sheep pen. She stopped on the dusty track and stared at them, a certainty growing in her chest.

"Dandy?" she said quietly, and almost thought she heard something in her chest rather than her ears.

She pulled out her phone and scrolled through to Collins' number. *Checking out a building on Delphine's property,* she typed. She added a pin drop and hit send, then headed for the door to the barn, the skin on the back of her neck crawling with a strange uneasiness she recognised.

But this wasn't London.

❧

THE BARN'S few high windows were boarded up from the inside, and the two big wooden double doors were firmly shut. DI Adams didn't know if it was usual for abandoned farm buildings to be so carefully secured, but she was fairly sure that it *wasn't* usual for any unused place to have its doors reinforced with what looked like quite new plywood behind the age-darkened planks. There was also a heavy chain running right through both layers of the door and back out again, fastened with a very large, very shiny padlock. She crouched to peek through the gap the chains ran through, but with the sun behind her she couldn't see anything. She examined the lock, then called, "North Yorkshire Police. Anyone in there?"

The response was immediate – a scuffle as of someone scrabbling about on the floor, and some enthusiastic thumps that might have been an old wooden wall being kicked. No actual reply, though, and she frowned at the door. "Are you alright in there? Do you need assistance?"

More thumping, even more enthusiastic this time, and it sounded as though someone were maybe trying to shuffle toward the door. There was also a sense that she couldn't quite comprehend, something like heat in her chest, but a welcome one. *Dandy.*

"I'm coming in."

Or she was going to try, anyway. There was no give whatsoever to the padlock and chain set-up, and as old as the doors were, the hinges had no play either. She went around the side of the building, searching for a back door, but there was none. She shaded her eyes to peer toward the house, hidden behind the stone wall. There was still no one around that she could see, so she turned back to the building and eyed the high, small windows. One had a lean-to with a rickety roof underneath it, which was hardly ideal, but in a few moments she had scrabbled up on top of it, trying not to think about how ancient and rotten the wood supporting the slate tiles likely was.

There was more plywood barricading the window from the inside, but she could see where the old wooden frames had been split by the nails that secured it. She sat herself on the sloping roof, digging her fingers into the gaps in the tiles for grip, and gave the wood a good, solid kick. She was rewarded with a crack on the other side of the wall, and she kicked it again, trying for the edges rather than the centre. The window frame would give before the plywood did.

It wasn't easy, the nails in the old wood irritatingly stubborn, but it *was* working. She kept going, the shock of the impact jolting up her leg with every kick, the sheet of plywood giving more each time, until it flapped wide so abruptly that she almost lost her grip on the roof from the sudden lack of resistance. She swung around and pushed the wood clear of the frame, peering into shadowy dimness below. Other than the light washing around her and onto the floor, the rest of the barn was in darkness.

"Hello?"

"*Mmmph!*"

She leaned in the window, letting her eyes adjust to the dim light. Slowly the broken skeletons of old stalls and mysterious bits of rusty, dilapidated machinery surfaced out of the gloom. There were some pointless piles of dirt, too, and some spiny plants that had got lost along the way. More importantly, there were two sets of eyes staring back at her. One set was human and blinking a lot, the other prismed and wide. Jake Cooper and Gilbert, but no Katherine or Hetty Cooper. Still, it was a start.

"There you are," she said, and grinned. "I'll have you out in just a moment." She squinted around, checking for a way in, and spotted two metal crates. They looked like the type of things zoos might transport dangerous animals in, and she said, "Dandy?"

There was a thud from one of the crates, and a little of the tightness in her chest loosened. There was scuffling from the other crate too, and she wondered who was in that one. Not that it mattered – she just had to get them out. She could drop down from the window where she was, but there needed to be a way to climb back out. Maybe if they stacked the crates ...

She looked back at the captives. Cooper's hands and feet were cinched with cable ties, and he had gaffer tape over his mouth. It looked like he'd tried to rub it free, judging by the redness on his face. Gilbert's entire snout was taped shut with an excessive amount of tape, and there were what looked like quite serious shackles and chains securing his paws. There looked to be enough play for him to shuffle around, but not enough to run or climb.

"*Hmm.* Gilbert, have you tried pushing the door?"

He shook his head, and shuffled a little toward her. He was brought up short by a length of chain that secured him to a large ring in the floor. DI Adams frowned. It was all very well thought out.

"I'm going to need to get some help," she started, and Cooper promptly shrieked behind his gag, shaking his head desperately. "I'm going to call someone," she assured him. "I won't leave you."

That didn't seem to do much to reassure Cooper, but she ignored him and sat back on the roof. If she jumped down inside she and Cooper could likely get out by clambering over the crates, but that left Gilbert stuck. Plus she needed to be able to get the crates open, and all she had on her was her phone and her car keys. She had a small multitool on the keyring, but it wasn't going to get far on those chains. She supposed she could get Cooper out, then come back for the others, but something in her gave an ugly twist at the idea.

She pulled up Collins' number, and was about to hit dial when she caught the rumble of an engine coming from the house. She froze, staring toward the gate to the field, but the house was between her and whoever was coming. *Her car.* It was just sitting there, like a bloody calling card – well, too late to worry about it. She slipped off the roof to the ground and hesitated, hoping that it was just some guests going to one of the pods, someone who wouldn't even notice the car, then the sun bounced off a windscreen as someone pulled up to the gate.

"Bollocks," she hissed, and slipped behind the building, trying to keep an eye on the approaching vehicle. It bumped down the track, revealing itself as a windowless white van very similar to Gert's, and the driver killed the engine, parking in front of the double doors of the barn. DI Adams pressed herself to the stone wall, peering around the corner as carefully as she could to see Delphine climbing out of the driver's seat. She was wearing pink three-quarter trousers and a floral print blouse, and her blonde hair was held neatly back with a headband. She looked as if she'd just popped back from the village hall to pick up more clotted cream for the scones, other than the cattle prod in her hand. She stood there, looking back at the house, and DI Adams wondered what she was waiting for.

A moment later someone else appeared at the gate, on foot this time, and strode down to the barn with the sun glinting on his pale hair.

"I can't see her anywhere," DCI Sykes said. "That's her car, though."

"How inconvenient," Delphine said.

"Have you checked here?"

"If she's here, we shall deal with it."

"*No,* Aunt Delphine. She's a detective. This is already getting out of hand."

Getting? DI Adams wondered how many missing people would constitute actually *being* out of hand.

"She's interfering." Delphine was out of DI Adams' sight, and the inspector could hear the padlock clanking.

"You said that about the journalist, and now where is she? Someone's reported her missing."

"Don't fuss, Nathaniel. It doesn't suit you."

"Can't we just wait until we're sure the DI's not here at least? Then there's no need to do anything about her."

"We don't have time," Delphine said. "Let's just get this done."

DI Adams didn't like the sound of anyone *doing* anything about her, and she had no chance against both Sykes and a cattle prod. She retreated from the corner, stepping as carefully as she could, and looked at the wall behind the barn. If she got over that, she might be able to use it as cover to get back to the road, then run back into town. On the other hand, no one seemed to be rushing to find her. She peeked around the corner again, but all she could see was Sykes opening the back of the van and pulling a ramp down to allow easier access.

"Are you ready there, dear?" Delphine called from inside the barn.

"Yes," Sykes said with a sigh. There was silence for a moment, then DI Adams heard Gilbert give a muffled yelp, and she winced. The cattle prod was evidently being put to good use.

A moment later the dragon emerged, head down, and shuffled slowly to the back of the van and up the ramp. He didn't look around, just went docilely, and Sykes ignored him, ducking into the barn and emerging with the two crates. He pushed them into the van after Gilbert, then lifted the ramp back into place. He closed the back doors, and said, "Are you sure you don't know anything about Hetty, Aunt Delphine? Or the journalist?"

"Just run along, there's a good boy," Delphine said. "You know you're better not knowing everything."

"I'm already implicated. I had to lie to another DCI to make sure they dropped Cooper's case. This could come back to me so easily."

"You know it won't. I make your luck, Nathaniel. Now do get going."

Delphine sounded like she was still at the barn doors, so DI Adams crept forward a little as the van started up and backed its way through a three-point turn, then went bumping softly down the track. She tapped the licence plate number into her phone and sent it to Collins, then pocketed her phone again. Let him track the van down, and she'd deal with Delphine. She was quite looking forward to arresting a member of the W.I., and she certainly had plenty to go on.

DI Adams slipped to the front corner of the building and peered around, but she couldn't see Delphine. She took a quick breath, then came around the corner in two strides, her voice loud as she declared, "North Yorkshire Police. Put down …" The words died in her mouth as she stepped into the doorway of the barn and saw Delphine standing over Cooper. Her foot was on his hip and the cattle prod was pressed to his neck.

"Put down your phone," Delphine said.

DI Adams stared at her. "You don't want to do this."

"Not really, no," she agreed. "But you have put me in a most awkward situation. So I repeat – drop your phone."

DI Adams took her phone from her pocket and put it on the ground, then turned and looked down the track toward the retreating van. It didn't stop, and she had an idea Sykes was deliberately not looking in his rear-view mirror.

"Well done," Delphine said. "Now you're going to come along quietly, aren't you? Because if you don't, our Mr Cooper here is going to be the one who pays."

"Really? You're abducting a police officer?"

"No, Mr Cooper is. You rumbled his scheme of faking dragon sightings and threatened to expose him, and in a panic he attacked you." She considered it. "And killed himself in a fit of remorse, I suppose. Or his journalist sidekick did. Either way, it all ended in tragedy."

Cooper grunted against his gag, apparently in disagreement.

"Wonderful," DI Adams said. "And how's he going to do that?"

"You'll see." Delphine threw her a set of keys, and she grabbed them before they could hit her. "The pickup's in the outbuilding. You go first. And no silliness, Detective. I've been cleaning up messes for a very long time."

DI Adams turned and led the way slowly toward the outbuilding, glancing up at the house as she went. The gate was empty. Sykes had gone. She pushed the doors of the outbuilding open to reveal Cooper's silver Isuzu, with Katherine sitting in the front seat, her arms pulled back in a way that suggested to DI Adams there were some creative restraints going on. She saw DI Adams and rolled her eyes expressively.

Delphine looked at DI Adams and said, "You have cuffs on you?"

"Yes," she said with a sigh.

Delphine threw a handful of thick cable ties on the ground. "Get in the back. Use those to secure your legs, then cuff your hands to the grab handle."

DI Adams looked at the cable ties, wondering if she dared go for the cattle prod. Delphine gave it a sudden squeeze, the prongs hovering just over Cooper's neck, and he squawked as they buzzed, spitting sparks.

"This is a special edition, ordered from the States for my own personal needs," Delphine said. "It has a little more oomph than most."

"Well, we'll just add that to the list of charges, shall we?" DI Adams asked, and picked up the cable ties.

21
ALICE

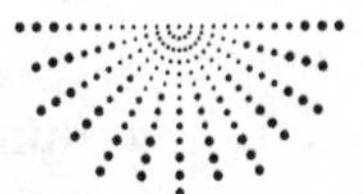

"Katherine? I'd like a word." Alice's words hung in the hot, still air by the tarn, and over it she could hear a tractor somewhere, labouring noisily in the hills. There was no movement from the pickup, and she couldn't see past the cage in the back to even know if anyone was in there.

"Hello?" she tried again, taking a few wary steps forward.

One of the back doors finally opened, and the trim form of Delphine climbed out, looking bright and unruffled despite the heat. She shut the door firmly behind her and walked toward Alice, her hands clasped behind her back. "Alice," she said. "Don't you know this is private property?"

Delphine. Of course it was. Aloud, Alice said, "Yes, I did see the sign. But I was hoping to speak to Mr Cooper and Ms Llewelyn."

"And you think they're here?"

"That is his car. And I saw them in it, which is why I followed." She raised her eyebrows at Delphine, but the other woman just chuckled.

"My. You are nosey, aren't you? Even more so than I thought."

Alice considered it, then said, "Where are the dragons, Delphine? You know, don't you?"

Delphine gave a delighted laugh and shook her head. "*Dragons!* How silly. I didn't realise you were one of those cryptid sorts."

"Are you protecting them? That's what we do, too. I can help. I have a plan to discredit Ms Llewelyn, and ... well, there's a cat who might be able to help with Mr Cooper."

Delphine tipped her head on one side. "Are you quite alright? The sun does get to one."

Alice clasped her hands behind her, matching Delphine's stance, and said, "Or is it the opposite?"

"I'm certainly the opposite to *you.* Running around talking about dragons." Delphine laughed softly. "A disgrace to the W.I., really. You should go, Alice. Before I get you arrested for trespassing."

"Which is also what you're doing."

"This is my land."

"I understand it's Hetty Cooper's land, actually."

Delphine's lips tightened over her teeth. "It was my family's land before. For *centuries.* And the Coopers don't deserve it. Eco camping and monsters? They're not protecting Eldmere. They're *ruining* it."

"Ah," Alice said. "Is that what you think you're doing? Protecting the village from magical creatures?"

"I don't know what you're on about with this magical creature rubbish—"

"ALARM," Alice said. "Alliance of Ladies Against Rogue Magic. Or whatever you call yourself now, since it's not just magic you're *protecting* against. It's anything you don't like, isn't it? Anything that *lowers the tone.*"

"That's just nonsense—"

"Is it? You have an awful lot of missing persons around here, Delphine. A lot of drownings in this tarn, and farming accidents. And it's always newcomers to the area."

"People are careless."

"Not that careless. So what are you doing with Mr Cooper and Ms Llewelyn?"

Delphine looked at her for a long moment, then said, "I'm dealing with the situation."

Alice looked at the tarn, its surface reflecting the sky, and said, "How? What do you think you're going to do?"

"What my family have always done. We don't tolerate nonsense in this valley."

"No. You don't, do you? No one with unauthorised businesses. No Folk. No dragons."

Delphine sighed. "You don't give up, do you?"

"Not often. I'm right, aren't I? About ALARM and the dragons? You have Gilbert."

"*Gilbert*. As if it has a name. And calling them dragons makes them sound so glamorous. Overgrown lizards, is all."

Alice's spine stiffened. "Have you not even spoken to him?"

"Why would I? It's just a beast. We've been dealing with them as long as my family have been here." She regarded Alice coolly. "And people like you, too. You used to be called witches."

"I'm sure I still am, by some people," Alice said, and Delphine almost smiled.

"Yes. But now I suppose you shall have to be dealt with too. Was it you that tried to bring that cat in? Poisonous little creature." She held a hand up, Band-Aids curling around the side of it. Her other was still behind her back, and it was making Alice vaguely uneasy. "The border trap snapped him right up. But he *bit* me."

"How terrible," Alice said mildly. "And Dandy?"

"Is that the mutt?"

"You can see him? Interesting."

"This is my valley. Everything's visible to me." She tucked a stray hair behind her ear, and glanced along the tarn. "He was almost as much trouble as the dragons."

"Oh?"

"The border traps are set for the usual nasty creatures that lurk about. Cats and sprites and so on. One doesn't expect *dragons* these days. I had to pull out some old charm cages and set physical traps for them. And whatever that mutt is, I had to actually *pick him up* at the farm and restrain him myself." She shuddered, wiping her hand on her trousers as if at the memory, then looked at Alice. "But I think this is quite enough chatting."

"So do I." Alice took a step back, and Delphine lunged.

Delphine brought a stick from behind her back as she charged, swinging it sharply toward Alice. Alice brought her walking stick up instinctively, the impact shaking her arms, and she heard the *bzzzt* of electricity whispering past her ears. She shoved hard, pushing Delphine back, and spun for her car. She had one hand on the door when the prod bit into her ankle, the shock juddering up through her bones, and she cried out, stumbling. Delphine grabbed Alice's walking stick and they had a moment's furious tussle, then the other woman tore the stick away and flung it over the car. They glared at each other, both breathing hard, and Alice could taste metal in her mouth.

"Car," Delphine said, pointing with the cattle prod.

Alice scowled, wondering if she could make a sprint for the track. But her hip wouldn't allow it, she knew that. She was better to follow orders for now. She pushed off the SUV and walked slowly toward the pickup, hearing birds calling across the water. She stopped by the back door Delphine had climbed out of.

"Now then," Delphine said, and smiled. Her hair was still carefully arranged, although a few wisps had made a break for it and were floating about her face. One corner of her mouth kept twitching.

"Are you alright?" Alice asked. "You look a little tired."

"I will be perfectly fine as soon as all this nonsense is dealt with."

"What's your plan for that, then? I'm assuming that as well as kidnapping Mr Cooper and Ms Llewelyn, you've also abducted *Mrs* Cooper. And then there's poor Gilbert. What on earth are you going to do with all of us?"

Delphine huffed. "I tried to explain. I *told* Hetty that any business coming her way due to this whole monster business wasn't the sort of custom our village needs. We're better than that. But she wouldn't listen." She sounded exasperated, as though they'd merely disagreed over the village fête. "How is one meant to protect one's way of life when people insist on being so *difficult?*"

"So you kidnapped her? That seems extreme." Alice kept her voice mild.

"Well, not immediately, of course. But I ran into her down here when I was hunting the monster, and she told me to keep my nose out of what didn't concern me." She gave Alice an outraged look. "It's *my* village!"

"Of course."

"So I thought I might be able to persuade her with a little one-on-one time." She shrugged. "She was very unwilling to cooperate, then Jake went to outside police instead of Nathaniel, so I had to take things into my own hands before it got out of control. That journalist seeing me was just pure bad luck."

"I suppose it was."

"It's really for the best," Delphine said firmly. "Some problems must be torn up by the roots. One can't have awful beasts crashing in here, threatening us all."

"Gilbert's a vegetarian," Alice said, and Delphine gave her an almost pitying look.

"The threat isn't necessarily in what they *do*, dear. It's simply that they *are*. It's against the natural order of the world. Humans aren't made to mix with such things. Certainly not in my valley." Delphine tapped her fingers against her leg. "I protect our borders. And you have *all* violated them, with your monsters and cats and horrid dogs. I won't stand for it."

"I see." There was one lingering moment, while Alice tried to think of some way to keep the other woman talking, because if she talked for long enough then maybe someone would turn up, DI Adams on their trail, or Colin, or even Miriam, then Delphine moved, too fast for Alice to evade her. Alice lurched toward the pickup, trying to jump out of reach, and her hip gave a squall of pain. She wasn't fast enough, and the cattle prod caught her across the side of the head, hard enough to turn her lurch into a fall. She hit the ground on all fours, biting down on a cry, and Delphine grabbed for her arms even as there was a sudden squall of metal further around the tarn, and a splash, and the rumble of the tractor became a roar.

Delphine looked up, startled, and the back door of the pickup flew open, driven by two booted, cable-tied feet, and caught her full in the face. She howled as she went down, and DI Adams yelled from inside, "Alice! Zap her!"

Alice didn't need telling. She threw herself on top of Delphine, trapping her right arm down before the other woman could bring the cattle prod up. She made liberal use of her knees as she scrambled over Delphine, and managed to get hold of the prod with both hands. She wrenched it away even as Delphine bucked her off.

"Stop!" Alice shouted, but Delphine was on her feet before Alice could gain hers, her hip throbbing. The other woman took off around the tarn at an impressive pace, presumably in pursuit of the white van.

"Damn," Alice muttered, using the door of the pickup to help herself up.

"Alice!" DI Adams shouted from inside. "Alice, are you alright?"

"I'm fine, I'm fine." She peered in the back at the inspector, who was cuffed to the door handle on the opposite side of the car. Alice could see blood on her wrists from where she'd been swinging on the cuffs to try and rip the handle off. "Where are your keys?"

"In my pocket. Hurry!"

Alice hauled herself into the back of the pickup and fished in DI Adams' pockets. Katherine and Cooper were both leaning in from the front, making a lot of desperate noise behind strips of gaffer tape. One of Cooper's hands was cable-tied to the wheel, and Katherine was firmly strapped to the seat with an astonishing amount of tape.

"Where's Gilbert?" Alice asked, as she fumbled the keys out. "Is he here?"

"In the van, with Dandy," DI Adams said. "He's chained."

Alice thought of the splash she'd heard earlier and bit her lip, jamming the key into the cuffs.

"Nice one," DI Adams said, shaking herself free, but the words were drowned by the revving of an engine behind them.

"Is that my *car?*" Alice demanded, and grabbed for the door as the revving became a roar. Someone drove into them hard enough to send her slamming into the back of the front seats and the pickup lurched forward. There was an eager splash as they hit the water and kept rolling.

"Dammit – Alice, go," DI Adams snapped, scrambling to get her car keys out of her pocket. "Go, now!"

"Your feet—"

"Get out!" DI Adams shoved her bodily across the seat, and Alice decided it wasn't time to argue with the inspector. She caught the edge of the door before she could fall out, and swung herself into water that was already knee-deep, hearing Cooper and Katherine's muffled screaming behind her. The pickup was still moving, her own SUV pushing it along with Delphine in the drivers' seat. She grabbed for the SUV door as it passed, trying to open it, but it was locked, and all she could do was watch helplessly as the silver pickup hit the drop-off and tilted forward, water surging up the windows. Delphine stopped and started to back up, and Alice ignored her, running forward as the water surged up to her thighs and the pickup started to sink. There were no heads appearing next to it, just swirling water. The bottom fell away under her and she felt the pull of the sinking vehicle, and she kicked her shoes off as she swam after it. She didn't have anything to cut them free with, but if she could get to the car, maybe there'd be something in there, something she could use—

The pickup wallowed and rolled, the tail appearing briefly, then vanished, and she felt the pull grow stronger. She let it take her, tipping into a dive and plunging into the belches of air coming from the sinking vehicle. It stayed ahead of her, the water pressing cold and tight around her, setting bands of chill about her head, and she still couldn't see anyone swimming free. She wasn't going to reach them, and they weren't going to make it out.

Then someone came paddling wildly past her, scrabbling for the surface, and she twisted to follow him, struggling for a moment against the pull of the car. She fought free of it, surging to the surface to find Cooper gasping and spluttering and doggy-paddling about the place wildly.

"DI Adams!" she shouted. "Is she coming?"

Cooper just splashed at her, his eyes wide as he gasped in as much water as air, arms flailing.

"Oh, for God's sake," she muttered, and ducked behind him, grabbing his chest and forcing him onto his back. "Float! Just float!" She started to drag him toward the shore, still scanning the water for heads. She wasn't sure they were coming.

Then something rose fast and furious out of the depths, and she had to swallow a scream. Cooper didn't bother, and he almost deafened her. Teeth and scales surged out of the water, and for one horrified moment she actually considered that some great water beast had been woken from its slumber and was coming to lay waste to the shore. Then she saw DI Adams clinging to its shoulders, and Katherine clutched to its belly, and she recognised the autumn orange scales.

"Gilbert! Is there anyone else?" Alice shouted. "Do you need me to take them?"

"That's it!" DI Adams shouted, before Gilbert could answer, then broke into a noisy coughing fit that sounded an awful lot like she was swearing at the same time.

Alice took a deep, shaky breath, then said, "Hello, Gilbert. Wonderful timing."

"Hi," he said, and gave her a toothy grin. "And everyone says there's no point in a swimming dragon."

"They really are quite wrong." Alice hit the shelf above the drop-off and pushed herself onto it, still towing Cooper.

"Hetty!" he shrieked. "Where's Hetty?"

"Please don't scream in my ear," Alice said. "And you can stand up now."

"Sorry," he muttered, fumbling to get his feet under him. He struggled to stand for a moment, then gave up and started to crawl toward the shore.

DI Adams had let go of Gilbert and was swimming for the rocky shoreline, but Katherine seemed quite content to cling to the dragon as he swam in, using his tail to propel them.

"Where's Delphine?" DI Adams asked, pulling herself to her feet in the shallows, and Alice turned to look. There was no sign of her car.

"Made a run for it, I imagine," she said.

"Dammit. I really wanted to arrest her," DI Adams said, and Alice nodded approvingly, then frowned as she looked around.

"Where are Miriam and Mortimer? And Ervin, for that matter?"

"And where's my Hetty?" Cooper yelled again, and there was the answering roar of a big engine from beyond the hut.

"What's that?" DI Adams asked.

"Can you let go?" Gilbert asked Katherine. They were both in the shallows, and she had one hand firmly hooked onto his wing where it joined his shoulder. He kept trying to push her away, but his paws were locked together with chains, making it difficult.

"No," she said. "You're proof."

"His name's Gilbert, and he just saved your life," Alice said, giving Katherine her best severe look. She had an idea she was a little too bedraggled for it to take. "Let him go right now if you know what's good for you."

"Or what? He doesn't look like he'll eat me." She examined Gilbert. "Can I see your teeth?"

"No," he said, covering his snout with one paw.

"I'll arrest you," DI Adams said. "If I can't arrest Delphine, you'll do."

"But you need to arrest Delphine!" Cooper insisted. "She's got Hetty still!"

"Have you seen Hetty, Gilbert?" Alice asked, and the engine revved around the corner again. "What *is* that?"

DI Adams was already wading out of the water, her boots sloshing as she hit the shore and broke into a jog. "Oh, bloody hell," she said, and the jog turned into a sprint.

Alice followed as fast as she could, as Gilbert shook Katherine off and lunged back into the tarn. Cooper overtook her as she rounded the hut in time to see a quad bike tearing up the hill, the sun shining off the driver's helmet. At the water's edge, where the red car had been, a white van was nose to nose with a tractor. Someone kept trying to get out of the driver's seat, but every time they did Mortimer spat a little flame at them, and they slammed the door hurriedly. Currently they were leaning out of the door waving at the driver of the tractor. They were probably saying something, but the engine was too loud to hear anything over it. Ervin was standing on the bank over a couple of crates, along with a woman Alice didn't recognise but who she guessed was likely Hetty Cooper, unless Delphine had been abducting more people she didn't know about. That was entirely possible, of course.

By the time Alice reached the tractor, DI Adams was bellowing, *"Turn the engine off, Miriam!"*

"What?" Miriam yelled back.

DI Adams repeated herself, and Miriam pointed to her ear protectors apologetically. DI Adams threw her hands up and scrambled onto the tractor, reaching over Miriam to switch the engine off.

"Ooh," Miriam said. "That really was loud."

"About bloody time!" Sykes shouted from the van. "This madwoman's been trying to drown me!"

"Really?" DI Adams said. "You're trying that?"

He stared at her. "I'm a DCI—"

"You bloody well abducted me and pushed my car into the lake!" Ervin shouted at him from the bank. "The only reason I didn't *drown* was that madwoman and her tractor!"

"I was trying to save you," Sykes snapped. "I didn't push *you* in. I told Aunt— Miss Harlow that I was going to do it, but I wasn't. Of course I bloody wasn't. That's why you were all in the van, not the car. But then *she*"—he pointed at Miriam—"hit me from behind and we just about all went in!"

The woman on the bank shook her head. "You had us trussed up like bloody Christmas turkeys!"

"So wrong," Gilbert muttered from the water. "Poor turkeys."

"Hetty!" Cooper yelled, and sprinted to the woman on the bank. She flung her arms around him.

"Jake! What're you *doing* here?"

"That bloody Delphine – she had the lot of us in the water!"

"Yes, explain that, DCI Sykes," DI Adams said. "She just about killed four of us over there. You telling me you knew nothing about that?"

"I would've stopped her if I'd been able to get away from Monster Madge over there," he said, pointing at Miriam. She was rubbing her ears and didn't even look offended. "I was *not* going to let anyone get hurt. But I didn't know where Hetty was being held, so I had to go along with it until I had an opportunity to act."

"You did not have to go along with it," DI Adams said. "There's this little organisation you might have heard of? North Yorkshire Police?"

He ran a hand back over his pale hair, his shoulders slumping as he said, "Yes, I know. But she's my aunt."

"Excuse me," someone said, and Alice peered around the tractor. She blinked at Beaufort. He was in a cage that was lodged onto the tractor's lifting arms, his talons hooked into the grille in the front of the van. "Can I let go? Only my paws are starting to cramp."

"Ooh, good job, Beaufort," Miriam said. "See?" she added to everyone else. "There was no risk of the van going in the tarn *at all.*" She waved DI Adams off and started the engine again. It roared, and smoke belched everywhere, then the tractor lurched forward, the van tilting over the drop-off with DCI Sykes shouting and waving frantically. Beaufort was evidently still holding on, though, and Miriam ignored the DCI, found reverse, and slowly backed away from the tarn, bringing the white van with her. DI Adams ran to the van door as soon as it was clear of the water and jerked it open, pointing at the ground like she was telling a cat to get down.

"Out," she snapped as Miriam pulled the tractor further back from the van and cut the engine, and there was the blip of a police siren behind them. Alice turned to see her SUV backing down the track with a police car following it, and the quad bike bounced out behind it, heading straight toward them.

"Gilbert!" the skinny young man driving it shouted. "Are you okay?" He stopped the bike and scrambled off. "You just vanished!"

"There was a goat," Gilbert said. "I had to save it."

"That makes sense," the young man said, and they grinned at each other while a chicken bounced happily between them. Alice presumed that meant Delphine had baited her trap with a goat, and Gilbert had gone to rescue it. She wasn't sure where the chicken came in, though.

"What a bloody circus," DCI Sykes said, shaking his head.

"Yes, yours," DI Adams said sharply. She pointed at the crates. "Is Dandy in there?"

"Is that the dog or the cat?"

"That's a yes, then. Open them."

"I don't have a key."

"*Seriously?* Who does?"

DCI Sykes nodded toward the police car, which had stopped in the mouth of the track, blocking it. Colin got out of the driver's seat and raised a hand to them.

"Miss Harlow has all the keys." Sykes said, and glanced at Gilbert, still bobbing in the tarn. "I don't know how that got out of the chains."

"I didn't," Gilbert said, grinning, and held his paws up to show them. "But I don't use my paws to swim, anyway." He glanced at Ervin. "I might've broken your car a bit getting out, though."

"That's fine," the journalist said with a sigh. "I think that's the least of its problems."

"Gilbert was in the car?" DI Adams asked.

Sykes didn't answer, but Mortimer did. "*Yes.* So were the crates." He looked accusingly as Sykes. "You might've been going to save the humans, but you didn't care about the rest of them!"

Sykes just looked at him blankly, as if he wasn't sure what he was hearing.

"Hey," Colin shouted. He was standing next to Alice's car. "I'm assuming I'm arresting this one?"

"Don't you dare," DI Adams yelled back. "You do *not* get to arrest a W.I. member before me!" She looked at Mortimer and pointed to the DCI. "Singe his toes if he's a problem."

"Um," Mortimer said, as the DI jogged toward Colin.

"It's alright," Alice said, and smiled at Sykes. "Miriam can just give him a little squish if needs be."

"Ooh, yes," Miriam said. "I think I rather like tractors."

DCI Sykes folded his arms and shook his head.

22

MIRIAM

DI Adams dealt with Delphine rather quickly but with every evidence of enjoyment, from what Miriam could see, and seated her in the back of the police car. She was still talking to her when Colin came jogging over to the tractor, a set of keys in his hands.

"Right," he said. "I need to get that car back to Graham quick-like, so let's get going. Who's first?"

"Beaufort," Miriam said immediately.

"I'd rather appreciate it," Beaufort agreed.

"*Hmm.* Let's see." Colin sorted through the keys, but they all looked a little on the small size. "Damn. I don't think it's on here."

"No," Alice said, and nodded at Sykes. "I believe he was his aunt's accomplice in all sorts of creature trapping. He'll have the key."

"Oh." Colin looked at the other man and cleared his throat. "Keys, DCI Sykes."

"Colin, come on. That's a monster in there. You can't let it out."

"Definitely can," Colin said, handing the keys he was holding to Ervin. "See if any of those fit the crates." He looked back at Sykes. "Keys, sir. I don't want to have to search you."

The moment stretched long and thin, before Sykes finally sighed and reached into the van, pulling a single heavy key from the glovebox. "You don't know what you're doing, Colin."

"Oh, I do, sir," he said.

There was a lot of muddling around after that. Ervin got the crates open, and jumped back from the first one, fending off something that Miriam assumed was a very small Dandy. Very small, but very wet, judging by the damp patches appearing on the journalist's jeans. She almost thought she'd seen him as the crate opened, a flash of deep grey, but that could've been a trick of the light. A moment later she saw DI Adams pick up something unseen and hug it to her chest, turning protectively away from Delphine as she did so.

Thompson came out of his crate very slowly and very silently, looked at them all and said, "Whose eyes do I take out first?"

"Behave," Alice said sternly, which sent the cat into such a diatribe that Colin ushered DCI Sykes away, since he seemed to be making such an effort not to hear that it was making his face twitch. The rest of them followed, Thompson padding behind and using the sort of language that made Ash repeat certain bits, presumably so he could remember it later.

DCI Sykes agreed, very stiffly, to get in the police car with his aunt, and Colin drove off with them after a muttered conversation with DI Adams. She turned back to the rest of them. "Right," she said. "Ash? Nice job on blocking Delphine from getting up the lane."

He mumbled something to his shoes, and Gilbert grinned at him.

"But now listen to me," DI Adams continued, and the teenager peeked at her without looking up properly. "In fact, *all of you* listen to me. No one's seen *any* dragons, have they?"

There was a silence, while everyone looked at each other, including the dragons.

She squeezed the bridge of her nose. "This is very easy. Repeat after me. *Dragons do not exist. There is no Yorkshire Beast.*"

"Of course," Alice said, and looked at Miriam and Ervin.

"*Obviously*," Miriam said.

"Didn't see a thing," Ervin said.

"Sodding dragons and bloody W.I. and—" Thompson broke off

when Ervin poked him with a very wet trainer. "*Sod off! I am not part of this!*"

"He means shut up," DI Adams said, and ignored the next thing the cat said, which Miriam felt was a rather heroic effort, as it was very detailed. "Ash?"

Gilbert nudged Ash and gave him a very obvious wink. "Oh. Sure," he said, and Beaufort patted his shoulder, almost buckling his knees.

"Good," DI Adams looked at Katherine and the Coopers with her eyebrows raised.

"Oh, come *on,*" Katherine started, and DI Adams pointed at her.

"I will do you on creating a public nuisance, or possibly inciting a bloody riot, given what the village looked like when I left."

"That might've been us," Miriam said, then winced as Alice shushed her. "Sorry."

"Of course it was." DI Adams looked at the Coopers, who had their arms around each other. "No such thing as dragons or beasts, yes?"

"But what …" Jake started, then trailed off as DI Adams shook her head at him.

"No such thing as dragons," she said again, enunciating clearly. "What a silly notion."

"You can't just expect us to ignore this," Katherine said. "These are *real dragons!*" She jabbed a finger at Beaufort.

"I might be an iguana," he said, and she scowled at him.

"No," she said. "No, we won't drop this. Or *I* won't."

"Causing a public disturbance," DI Adams said. "Here *and* Toot Hansell. There might have to be restraining orders put in place if *Cryptids Today* keep stirring things up like this."

"I can't wait to do my exposé," Ervin said, and grinned. "*The Truth Behind Cryptids Today*. I can see it already. Could even get picked up by Netflix or something. They love those documentaries."

"No," Katherine said. "You'll back me up, won't you?" She looked at the Coopers, who exchanged uncertain glances. "Come on! You know it's been great for business."

Jake looked at Gilbert, then at Katherine. "He *saved* you," the farmer said. "You'd be at the bottom of the tarn if not for him."

"That's true," Alice said. "Seems rather ungrateful after he went to all that trouble. After all, he did know who you were."

"I—" Gilbert started, and Ash trod on his paw. "Did," the young dragon finished. "I definitely did. And while I believe in all animals being treated equally, you're a journalist so it doesn't count."

There was a long silence, while Katherine tried not to look at the dragons. Then she threw her hands up. "Fine. *Fine!* But what the hell do I say about Eldmere? I can't just say, oh, I *lied*."

"Don't worry about that," Alice said. "We've got that in hand."

"Oh, God," DI Adams said, which Miriam thought was a bit rude.

IT WAS two weeks later before they gathered in Miriam's cosy, low-ceilinged front room. Summer had breathed its last, and rain was lashing the windows. The garden was still green, but the wind was stripping the last of the summer blooms away, and she had lit her first fire of the autumn. Not because it was really *that* cold yet, but it was lovely and cosy with the flames burbling away in her log burner, and it was the sort of day that invited it. She'd made four large batches of ginger cake, since Beaufort kept mentioning how the ginger cake Ash had given him *could* have been good, if only someone had made it at home rather than buying it off a shelf.

It was lovely having the dragons around again. It still made her a little nervous, but there had been no stories in *Cryptids Today*, or even on any of the forums that Rose frequented. Katherine had, so far at least, kept her word, and the Coopers had laughed off the whole Beast thing as a prank visited on them by a mischievous teenager. Miriam had trouble thinking of Ash as mischievous, but she supposed it didn't matter if no one knew him.

Now she poked the fire and gave it another piece of wood.

"Miriam, are you trying to *bake* us?" Priya asked, fanning herself with one hand. "I can't tell if it's a hot flush or heatstroke."

"But it's so nice," she protested.

"I don't think we're helping," Beaufort said. He and Mortimer were settled comfortably to either side of the fire, with Thompson lying directly in front of it, and Gilbert peering out the window.

"Open that a bit, would you, Gilbert?" Gert asked. "Can't have Priya fainting on us."

"I've never *fainted.* I'm not a Victorian maiden."

"I don't think anyone would mistake any of you for maidens," Thompson remarked, and Beaufort growled at him. "What? You're a dragon. You know all about maidens, right?"

"No," the High Lord said firmly.

"I've fainted," Carlotta said. "More than once."

"Is that due to the stench of garlic breath in the old country?" Rosemary asked.

"No, it's a way to escape your endless attempts at humour."

"Is it from lack of food?" Teresa asked.

"Rosemary's lack of humour?"

"No, the fainting. I used to have that problem, in my running days."

"I'm glad we've cured you of that," Pearl said, taking a piece of pear cake from one of the plates on the table. "Imagine not eating enough." She took a bite, then added, "Of course, I've never had that problem. Or fainted."

Miriam looked at Alice as she came in from the kitchen, bearing a plate of softly puffed sausage rolls. Jasmine followed her, carrying a very dissimilar tray.

"I don't understand it," Jasmine said. "I did *exactly* the same as you!"

"My old AGA's a bit temperamental," Miriam said, and Jasmine frowned at her.

"You're humouring me."

"No, I'm serious." She pointed at a tray of almond biscuits, half of which were a perfect golden brown, and half of which had singed edges. "It's very unpredictable."

"Oh," Jasmine said, and set the tray down on the overloaded table. "Well. Maybe."

"They're here!" Gilbert shouted, making Rose yelp.

"Gilbert! Not in my ear! I may be old, but I'm not deaf."

"You're not old," Gilbert said, taking his paws off the windowsill and looking up at her. "If you were a dragon, you'd barely be an adult."

"Maybe I am a dragon," Rose said. "That description fits."

Miriam went to the front door to let the inspectors in as they jogged up her little path, heads bent against the downpour. Something parted the rain at DI Adams' side, and Miriam felt the scatter of droplets as it swept past her into the house. She shivered. As happy as she was that Dandy was restored, it was still a very odd thing, having an invisible dog trotting past you.

"Hello Aunty Miriam," Colin said, and kissed her cheek as she ushered them into the hall.

"Hello, dear," she said, and took the container he handed her. "What's this?"

"Cinnamon muffins," he said. "I thought I should contribute."

"I brought coffee," DI Adams said, handing her a little stovetop percolator and a bag of coffee. "And bread." She looked at it. "It's from the bakery. Some of us don't have time to bake muffins."

"They would if they prioritised," Colin said, and DI Adams scowled at him.

"Come in," Miriam said. "We're all in the living room."

DI Adams squared her shoulders and led the way, Colin following after, and Miriam heard a chorus of welcome as she went to put the coffeepot on. If she could figure out how to work it, of course. She wondered if the water went in the top or the bottom.

She was still trying to figure out how it came apart, let alone where the water went, when there was a knock at the kitchen door and she yelped, almost dropping the pot. She peeked through the window over the sink and saw Ervin trying to shelter from the torrential rain in the little overhang of the door.

"What are you doing here?" she asked as she pulled it open.

"Collins said there was a thing here today. I'm part of the thing, aren't I?" He handed her a small potted violet and grinned.

"Can you make coffee in that?" she asked, pointing at the pot.

"I think so."

"Come in, then."

❧

THERE ALWAYS SEEMED to be a lot of fuss when it came to getting settled, but finally everyone was squeezed into the living room, in the old sofas and chairs or in Miriam's faded beanbags, and there was enough tea to go around, and Ervin had managed to make the coffeepot work, and Mortimer was eating Jasmine's sausage rolls with a slightly puzzled look on his face. Thompson was glaring at a damp spot next to DI Adams with his ears back, so at least Miriam could keep track of where Dandy was.

"So I suppose you all want to know what happened with Delphine and Sykes," DI Adams said, taking a sip of coffee. "Oh, good coffee, Miriam."

"I made it," Ervin said.

"It's a little bitter, actually," she said, and Colin snorted.

"And?" Beaufort said. "They were most unpleasant."

"Delphine is being charged with multiple counts of abduction, as well as assaulting a police officer." DI Adams wrinkled her nose slightly. "She initially mentioned nothing about dragons, but after a word with her lawyer is now claiming that the fuss over the Beast tipped her over the edge and she wasn't in her right mind. Not sure if that'll stick, plus there's a number of historical disappearances being looked into, and Sykes seems to be implicated in an awful lot of cover-ups."

"So he was always working with her?" Alice asked.

Colin seesawed his hand. "Apparently he believes that he owes her – that bit's not on record, it came out kind of by accident on the way back to the station. But he seems to have the idea that she can work a bit of magic herself, and that was the reason he reached DCI so quickly."

"But she hated magic," Miriam said. "How could she have done anything like that?"

"She might've hated *Folk* magic," Thompson said. "But there was plenty of nasty old human magic on those cages and in the hills."

"Oh dear," Beaufort said. "How unpleasant." He looked at

Mortimer. "That's why we missed it, lad. I've not come across that sort of thing since I was your age."

"Is it that awful?" Jasmine asked.

"Yes," the cat said. "You lot tend to force your charms with blood and sacrifice and any sort of pain, self-inflicted or otherwise, rather than just tuning in to the world like Folk and learning things."

"Sounds about right, really," DI Adams said, and Thompson gave her an approving nod.

Beaufort rumbled. "I'm not sure it is. And I wouldn't say *you lot,* really. Certain humans, is all. One mustn't paint everyone with the same brush, Thompson."

"Eh," the cat said, and swiped a piece of sausage roll off Mortimer's plate. "Suit yourselves. But Adams here seems to have a better handle on humans than you do."

"Different," Beaufort said, and Colin patted his shoulder.

"I'm with you," he said, and the old dragon grinned at him.

"So what are the historical cases?" Jasmine asked, leaning forward with both hands around her mug, and DI Adams smiled at her.

"Hetty's dad, for one. Some others too, but I don't have all the details. We're not actually on the case, what with me being abducted by her. Plus Sykes is kicking off about Collins having a grudge against him since some case back in Leeds, so as the cases are linked, he's off too."

"I do not have a grudge," Colin said. "He's just a truly awful person."

A murmur of agreement greeted that. "He *is,*" Miriam said. "He talked about you dragons like you're just animals."

"We're all animals, really," Gilbert said. "That's why it's so wrong to eat them." He looked pointedly at the sausage rolls.

"They're vegetarian, dear," Alice said.

"Oh!" Gilbert grinned at her. "I better have a few, then."

"*Vegetarianism,*" Thompson hissed. "Look where that got us."

"What about Sykes himself, then?" Rose asked, ignoring the cat.

"He's stepped down from duty," Colin said. "There's a good possibility he'll give evidence on his aunt and escape any sort of jail time, especially as he can argue that he did step in to save everyone at the tarn."

"Everyone *human,*" Miriam said.

"One has to expect it," Beaufort said. "If one is told often enough that anything different is monstrous, what else would one believe?"

"Rubbish," Teresa said. "He just had to talk to you to know that wasn't the case."

"Plenty like that out there," DI Adams said. "And people don't even have to be a different species to be monstrous to them. But Sykes won't be a cop again, that's for sure."

"That's something," Gert said. "Still seems to be getting away a bit lightly."

"I can send Walter over," Rose said, and cackled.

"That's our side of things," DI Adams said, and pointed at Alice. "What did you *do* to Eldmere?"

It had been most impressive when they'd driven through on the way back to Toot Hansell, Miriam thought. Music had boomed from a van on the green, shaking it on its suspension and blasted to distortion, and people danced with plastic cups raised above their heads, yellow shirts and dragon hats and inflatable dinosaur and unicorn costumes crowded among the bare chests and bare feet of the revellers. The river had been crowded with inner tubes, and children of varying ages (including those not technically children) raced through the woods and the town, sporting costumes that ran from the basic to the professional.

"Well," Alice said gravely, "it seems that the Yorkshire Beast was a publicity stunt for ... what was it again, Gert?"

"Monstrous Events," she said. "My niece's new venture." Everyone looked at her. "What?"

"Just your niece?" DI Adams asked.

"Yes. Why?"

"No reason. But how did you do it?"

"Lacey agreed she'd supply all the prizes – her sister-in-law's cousin's aunt's good for that sort of thing—"

"I don't want to know," DI Adams said.

Gert frowned at her. "They were legit! Or near enough."

"No," DI Adams said.

"Right. Anyway, Lacey and Jasmine just got it all out on the social medias, and everyone came. Easy."

"Easy," Colin echoed, and took a piece of ginger cake.

"Very good, that," Beaufort said, nodding at the cake. "Much better than Ash's, poor lad."

"Impressive work on the costume thing," DI Adams said to Jasmine, and she went pink.

"Yes," Colin said. "Please use your powers for good."

Ervin snorted around a bite of scone. "Remember who you're talking to, Colin."

"Remember whose house you're in," Miriam said. "And you *weren't* invited."

"Sorry, sorry." He held his hands up where he sat on the floor. "Look, I'm happy. It's a great story."

"Did you do the exposé on *Cryptids Today?*" Alice asked.

"No, I'm keeping it up my sleeve in case they misbehave. I think we have a sort of balance there. Cryptid Kathy likes her weird job, and Lloyd is still half-convinced you're all iguanas. So between Adams threatening to charge her with harassment and her already looking silly over Eldmere, *and* me promising to expose her as a fraud if she hassles anyone here ... last article of hers I saw they were hunting selkies in Ireland."

"Oh, that's not good," Beaufort said. "Very tricky creatures, selkies. She'll offend them without even trying, and end up having to live in a sea cave for a century."

There was a thoughtful pause, then Priya said, "It couldn't happen to a nicer person."

There was a ripple of laughter, and Ervin said, "I still don't know how it started. *Were* those your paw prints, Gilbert?"

"Yes," he admitted, shooting a sideways glance at Mortimer.

"Don't look at me. It's your sister you have to answer to."

"Yes, only you haven't told her."

"We're holding that over you," Beaufort said, and grinned at him.

Gilbert went a lighter shade of orange. "There being no Folk in the valley, because Delphine and her family had locked them out, and dispatched of anyone who got in, no one knows about it except us and Thompson."

"Who is never helping you with anything ever again," the cat said. "I was in *water*. In a *cage*. I almost lost my fifth life!"

Colin blinked at him. "You actually have nine lives? That's a real thing?"

"Of course. Doesn't mean I want to waste any."

"Right." He thought about it. "Couldn't you do your teleportation thing?"

"*Shifting*. It's magic, not science fiction. And no, we can't shift out of cages, or you'd never get any of us to the vet."

There was a moment's thoughtful silence, then Ervin said, "The paw prints?"

"Oh, right," Gilbert said. "So there's a *petting zoo* at that farm. A petting zoo! And they have llamas. It's a disgrace."

"I quite like llamas," Colin said.

Gilbert sniffed. "I do too. And Ash and I had this whole plan where the Coopers could cash in on the monster craze, and make enough money that they wouldn't need a petting zoo, and we could release all the animals." He hesitated. "It *almost* worked."

"I still can't believe you just stayed up there in that hut the whole time," Miriam said. "It must've been so lonely!" She hadn't had a chance to talk to Gilbert since they'd got back. Amelia was apparently very reluctant to spend any time apart from him.

"It was really nice, actually. Just up in the hills, and Ash brought pumpkins, and we'd roast them and look at the stars and talk about how animals should all be equal."

"Oh," DI Adams said, and took a sip of coffee.

"Wow," Ervin said.

No one else seemed to know what to say, and finally Gilbert said, "He's going to come to Toot Hansell for a visit."

Beaufort sighed slightly, but neither he nor Mortimer said

anything. Miriam supposed they couldn't, given that they were currently drinking tea in their human friend's living room.

"I think that's very nice," she said. "He seemed like a nice boy."

"He was a bit weird," DI Adams said.

"Says the woman with the magic dog," Colin said.

DI Adams looked down at her side and rested a hand on something invisible. "Fair," she said.

Miriam looked around the room, at Pearl and Teresa sharing the little sofa, and Priya in the beanbag and Alice in one of the kitchen chairs, and Rosemary and Carlotta and Gert all crushed into the bigger sofa together, and Rose with her feet swinging from the armchair, and Jasmine perched on the arm, and Gilbert sitting next to them, and the DIs and Ervin sitting on the floor, the windows steamed with the heat of them and the fire crackling behind the dragons, and she understood, in some little way, how Delphine had wanted to protect Eldmere. She thought she'd do almost anything to protect the people in this room, all these glorious and different people of all species. Even Thompson, preening in front of the fire. She'd face goblins, or Christmas faeries, or drive an ancient tractor over half the Yorkshire Dales if she needed to. And she'd do that not because she wanted to shut them away from the strangeness in the world, from the uncertainty and *otherness* of it. She'd do it to protect that wonderful strangeness, because it lived in every one of them. Because everyone is a little strange, in their own beautiful and complicated way, and that should be celebrated, not hidden. Perhaps that strangeness *was* magic. And it should be shared, and more of the same welcomed, where *the same* meant that the heart understood it, not that it matched what one expected.

She would never fight to stop the magic of the world coming in. She'd only fight to protect that magic from those who couldn't see it existed in the strange, and the different, and the unknown. That the real magic was in embracing the world, not inflicting pain on it to shape it to one's own preconceptions.

Mortimer looked at her and said quietly over the babble of conversation in the room, "It's wonderful to be back."

"Oh, Mortimer," she said, and put her hand on his shoulder. "You have no idea just how wonderful it is."

And she took another sip of tea and felt the wonderful, human magic of friendship and tea and all shapes of love fill the room and flood the world, just as it always should.

❧

A BEAUFORT SCALES MYSTERY

THANK YOU

Lovely reader, thank you once again for joining me in roaming the hills of Yorkshire in the company of dragons, dandies, ladies of a certain age, and other magical creatures. Of course, you're keeping good company, as you are just as magical as any of them.

Trust me on this. I'm a writer. We deal in magic.

And while I may write the books, the actual magic is in someone – in *you* - picking one up and reading it. And sometimes reading the next one too, and the one after that, and chatting about them, and recommending them, and reviewing them, and just generally embracing the idea of tea-drinking, crime-solving dragons. In embracing the magic in our world.

And I can't thank you enough for sharing your magic with me.

But we must spread the magic, too! So I'd appreciate it immensely if you could take the time to pop a quick review up at your favourite retailer. More readers means more dragons!

And if you'd like to send me a copy of your review, chat about dragons and baked goods, or anything else, drop me a message at kim@kmwatt.com. I'd love to hear from you!

Until next time,

Read on!

BEWARE THE SNAP-SNAP-SNAP ...

Baton. Light. Chocolate. Duck.

This is not DS Adams' usual kit. This is not DS Adams' usual case. She doesn't think it's *anyone's* usual case, not with the vanishing children and the looming bridge and the hungry river. Not with the *snap-snap-snap*.

But six kids are missing, and she's not going to let there be a seventh. Not on her watch. And she knows how to handle human monsters, after all. How different can this really be?

So: Baton. Light. Chocolate. And the bloody duck.

Let's be having you, then.

ARM YOURSELF WITH LEMON SLICES!

Your free recipe collection awaits!

… and remember that homemade ginger cake is better for soothing trapped dragons than store-bought.

Grab your free collection of (almost) W.I.-approved recipes today, and be prepared for beast hunts, monster festivals, and dragon rescues!

Plus, if this is your first visit to Toot Hansell and my newsletter, I'm also going to send you some story collections – including one about how that whole barbecue thing started …

Happy baking!

Scan above to claim your free recipes collection, or use the link: https://readerlinks.com/l/2706435/blpbm

ABOUT THE AUTHOR

Hello lovely person. I'm Kim, and in addition to the Beaufort Scales stories I write other funny, magical books that offer a little escape from the serious stuff in the world and hopefully leave you a wee bit happier than you were when you started. Because happiness, like friendship, matters.

I write about baking-obsessed reapers setting up baby ghoul petting cafes, and ladies of a certain age joining the Apocalypse on their Vespas. I write about friendship, and loyalty, and lifting each other up, and the importance of tea and cake.

But mostly I write about how wonderful people (of all species) can really be.

If you'd like to find out the latest on new books in *The Beaufort Scales* series, as well as discover other books and series, giveaways, extra reading, and more, jump on over to www.kmwatt.com and check everything out there.

Read on!

amazon.com/Kim-M-Watt/e/B07JMHRBMC
bookbub.com/authors/kim-m-watt
facebook.com/KimMWatt
instagram.com/kimmwatt
twitter.com/kimmwatt

ACKNOWLEDGEMENTS

To you, magical reader. For believing in dragons, ladies of a certain age, the formidable power of friendship, and the healing qualities of a good cuppa. Thank you for sticking with me. There is more to come!

To my wonderful beta readers, who rose valiantly to the challenge of my erratic writing schedule over the last couple of years (well, life, actually, but *writing schedule* sounds all sorts of professional), and somehow made room in busy lives to point out that I'd dropped the chicken in the tarn, hedgehogs shouldn't drink milk, and black is a terrible colour for barn-wear. Thank you for your endless patience, your time, and your completely wonderful friendship.

And to Lynda at Easy Reader Editing, as always. For your friendship, support, and relentless commitment to breaking me of my en-dash habit. My books would be poorer without you, but my life would be even more so.

Finally, to Dad. He didn't get to see this book published, but he will always be the Beaufort Scales origin story. He never did get tired of saying, "My daughter's a writer, you know." Or suggesting Walter do unspeakable things over the heads of crowds ...

ALSO BY KIM M. WATT

The Gobbelino London, PI series

"This series is a wonderful combination of humor and suspense that won't let you stop until you've finished the book. Fair warning, don't plan on doing anything else until you're done ..."

- Goodreads reviewer

The Beaufort Scales Series (cozy mysteries with dragons)

"The addition of covert dragons to a cozy mystery is perfect...and the dragons are as quirky and entertaining as the rest of the slightly eccentric residents of Toot Hansell."

– Goodreads reviewer

Short Story Collections

Oddly Enough: Tales of the Unordinary, Volume One

"The stories are quirky, charming, hilarious, and some are all of the above without a dud amongst the bunch ..."

- Goodreads reviewer

The Cat Did It

Of course the cat did it. Sneaky, snarky, and up to no good - that's the cats in this feline collection which will automatically arrive on soft little cat feet in your inbox as a thank you for joining the newsletter (either via *You Better*

Watch Out or any other link). Just remember - if the cat winks, always wink back …

The Tales of Beaufort Scales

A collection of dragonish tales from the world of Toot Hansell, as a welcome gift for joining the newsletter! Just mind the abominable snow porcupine … (this one will follow *The Cat Did It* in the newsletter emails, because one lot of stories is not enough!)

A BEAUFORT SCALES MYSTERY

Printed in the USA
CPSIA information can be obtained
at www.ICGtesting.com
LVHW091454100923
757501LV00002B/194